STORM GOLD

STORM GOLD

LEE NELSON

COUNCIL
PRESS

Council Press
P.O. Box 531
Springville, Utah 84663

ISBN 0-936860-32-4

Printed in the United States of America
First Printing, December, 1994

Readers respond
to Lee Nelson books

One night at the dinner table I was telling my mother about Lee Nelson's books. I picked up one of the books to show her some of the pictures. I thumbed through the pages a full five minutes before I realized there were no "real pictures," only the word pictures created in my mind.

David Noyes
Preston, Idaho

Lee Nelson and Louis L'Amour are the most popular authors in the Utah prison system.

Dennis Christensen
Librarian, Utah State Prison

Walkara, by Lee Nelson, is truly one of the most interesting, educational, and fascinating books I have read. Once I got into it, I simply didn't want to put it down until I had reached the final page at 3:30 a.m. this morning.

Judge Donald Nicholson
Corsicana, Texas

I am a teacher of 8th grade reading. Mr. Nelson's Storm Testament books are the most widely circulated books in our school library.

Janet Carroll
Hyde Park, Utah

Lee Nelson's books captivate me to the point where I do not want to put them down. It gives me much pleasure to sit down and get lost in one of these stories. My favorite authors are Shakespeare, Dumas, L'Amour, Twain, and now Lee Nelson.

Janet Howard
Hampstead, Maryland

My favorite Lee Nelson book is Storm Testament V. I have read this book at least a dozen times, and love it every time.

Ryan Stout
Colorado Springs, Colorado

Lee Nelson is the best western writer of them all. When I read one of his books, it puts me in the saddle right next to the main character all the way through the book. One of the marks of a good writer is the pain and suffering the reader goes through when the book is finished and there is nothing more to read. Lee Nelson does this.

Scott Morrison
Provo, Utah

Oh how much I enjoyed a borrowed copy of Walkara. I hate to give it back. I keep thumbing through it. I bought the rest of the Storm Testament series, thinking they would provide an entire winter of reading, but I found I could not leave them alone, and was finished long before the snow melted.

Elaine Freestone
Bountiful, Utah

To Mother and Dad

Introduction

During the winter of 1991 while I was writing about Butch Cassidy, I received a call late one night from Nick Stevenson of Altamont, Utah, about a hundred miles east of Salt Lake City. He had just finished my book on Ute chief Walkara, the greatest horse thief in the history of the American West. Nick asked if I knew anything about Walkara's involvement in the massacre of hundreds of Spaniards and Mexicans in eastern Utah before the arrival of the Mormons. I said I had not, but if a massacre of white men by Indians, larger than the one at Little Big Horn had taken place, it would have been widely studied and written about by historians--and everybody, even me, would know about it.

Nick didn't argue, but instead invited me to go with him on a helicopter ride, promising some dramatic changes in my views of western history if I went with him.

Soon after my Cassidy book was released, I called Nick, and accepted his challenge. It was a sunny but cool September afternoon when Nick's private helicopter lifted off the cement pad. We headed west towards the boundaries of the Ute Indian reservation, where Rock Creek enters the Duschesne River.

1

Storm Gold

Slowing down, Nick inched the chopper close to a sheer rock face, several hundred feet above the valley floor. I saw a perfect Catholic cross carved in the stone face, maybe four feet high and about three feet wide--perfect enough to have been carved by a stone mason with a tape measure and T-square. Not very far away, on another rock face, we saw a panel of Indian drawings. One figure looked like a man wearing a helmet, hanging upside down with arrows in him.

We continued up Rock Creek until we came to an open area called Daniels Flat. Nick pointed to a place near the stream where he said Spanish miners had built a water-powered mill for crushing ore, which was packed on mules to the area from numerous mines further up in the mountains. He pointed out other locations, the probable site of the Spanish mission, the barracks, where early settlers had found the remains of two-wheeled *carretas* or donkey carts. We could see circles of rocks which he said were fox hole pits where Spanish miners defended themselves during the Indian assault.

Nick showed me a nearby canyon where his father had found human skulls, two of which he said were taken to the University of Utah where archaeologists determined they were of European origin, not Native American. His father found no other human bones in the area. Nick explained that after the great battle the victorious Indians had removed the heads from the bodies, then taken the bodies to one side of the valley, and the heads in the opposite direction, believing the bodies could not be resurrected if the heads could not be found.

Nick told me about a cave where a friend of his father's had found a pile of dried mules' hooves. Apparently, the victors had removed the hooves from the dead pack animals, believing that by so doing the animals would be ineffective beasts of burden for their greedy masters in the world of spirits.

Nick landed the chopper and showed me a hollow rock where he believed the only Spaniard to survive the battle, a nine-year-old boy, had hidden, before escaping to Fort Robidoux near what later became the town of Vernal. We

2

Introduction

continued our journey northward to what the Utes call Big Boom Hill, where until recent years many people claimed to have seen a 12-foot brass cannon.

From the helicopter we could clearly see what Nick said was the old San Pedro trail, leading to Spanish mines, and eventually the north slope of the Uinta Mountains, which the Spanish called the Sierra Madre de Oro.

Nick had captured my curiosity, but I was still cautious in believing all he said. Upon returning home I rushed to the library, and to my astonishment, discovered much had already been written and published on the early Spanish history of Utah and the Great Basin. I became familiar with the research and writings of George Thompson, Dr. Donald Moorman of Weber State University, Herbert Auerbach, Charles Kelly, Frank Silvey, Edgar Wolverton and Burt Silliman.

Patsy Christensen of Talmadge, Utah showed me dozens of photos she had taken in the Rock Creek area, depicting Spanish and native American symbols carved on trees and rock faces. Steve "Doc" Schaffer, who has spent many years exploring the south slopes of the Uinta Mountains, showed me hundreds of photos depicting everything from Spanish diggings and smelters to writings on trees and rock faces. He marked my maps so I could see for myself many ancient Spanish smelters, arrastras and diggings. Steve is part Navajo, and was raised with the Utes. He introduced me to Lloyd Arrowchs, a Whiterocks Ute, who shared with me what his father had told him about the Rock Creek massacre of the Spanish, and other great battles involving raiding Indian tribes from the north. While Lloyd's stories about his ancestors contained much interesting detail, he could not give me specific dates. "My father said only that it was a long time ago," he said.

As my research continued, the evidence continued to build. There had been significant Spanish activity in the rocky Mountain region before the arrival of the Americans. Some of the evidence is circumstantial in nature, but some is rock

3

solid, like the following. In 1858, when General Albert Sidney Johnston's army was marching on Salt Lake City to unseat Brigham Young as territorial governor, soldiers found a brass cannon in Kamas Valley about 40 miles east of Salt Lake City. Stamped lettering on the cannon revealed it had been cast in Seville, Spain, in 1776. The cannon is on display at Fort Douglas in Salt Lake City, for anyone to see.

In 1961 a Spanish sword, the kind used in the early 1700s, in remarkably good condition, was found near Dayton, Wyoming. It can be seen in the museum there.

A friend returning from vacation showed me a recent Wyoming highway map, with the inscription "Spanish Diggings" south of Casper. Another friend, who works for the Forest Service, showed me a map of Loafer Mountain above Salem, Utah with a spot high on the mountain marked "Old Spanish Mine."

A rancher living at the southern end of the Deep Creek Mountains on the Neveda-Utah border offered to introduce me to a friend who found what he thought were Spanish tools in a cave near Montezuma Peak in those mountains. There's another report of ancient tools being found in a cave in North Canyon in the nearby, but equally remote, House Mountains.

When the first Mormon pioneers arrived to establish a settlement at Parowan, Utah, Mormon apostle Parley P. Pratt grabbed a shovel and started digging a hole to plant a flag pole. Pratt and those around him were amazed when he dug up two Spanish doubloons. In 1852 Ute chief Walkara rode into Parowan and purchased food from James Martineau, using gold coins, later thought to have been minted in the British East Indies. The Ute chief said he had found the coins on the floor of a cave in the Escalante River Gorge.

In 1858 Bishop James Rollins of Beaver was riding his horse near the southwest end of the Mineral Range, west of Beaver, Utah where he found a mine tunnel containing rusty tools and rotting wooden neck yokes. At the back of the tunnel he found what he thought was a thick vein of lead. Since the Mormons were at war with the United States,

4

Introduction

Rollins obtained permission from Brigham Young to start mining the lead and pouring bullets for the Mormon forces. When Rollins had trouble making bullets, Young sent down a mining engineer who quickly pointed out that the rich vein at the back of the tunnel was not lead, but pure horn silver which later assayed at 3,000 ounces per ton of ore. This abandoned Spanish tunnel became the Lincoln mine which produced large quanties of silver for many years.

A neighbor whom I have known at least ten years told me about a stone tablet he discovered while hunting deer on Boulder Mountain in south central Utah. A Maltese crose was chipped on one side. Nearby he found a cave. Inside he discovered another stone tablet, also with a Maltese cross carved on one side. He offered to take me to the cave.

Another neighbor said he was the grandson of Mormon V. Selman, one of the first settlers in Utah Valley. Selman recorded in his personal journal that Spanish pack trains came out of Provo Canyon, in the fall of the year, and camped in his meadow before heading up Spanish Fork Canyon. He said the packs the mules carried were small, but heavy, and were carefully guarded by the Spaniards.

All Utah school children learn about the well documented Dominguez-Escalante expedition into northern Utah in 1776. But there were others. Probably the first was Francisco de Ibarro in 1565. Fray Estevan de Peria entered Ute country in 1604, Vincent de Salvidar in 1618, Fray Geronimo Zarate Salmeron in 1621 and 1624, describing the Ute people, and naming the Wasatch Mountains. In 1669 Alonzo de Leon carved his name and the date on a cliff up Dry Fork near what later became Vernal, Utah. In 1712, the Spanish governor in Mexico City, Ignacio Mogollon, forbade unlicensed trading with the Utes. Why would he forbid trading if no one was venturing into Ute country?

In 1705 Juan de Urbarri followed escaped slaves to the San Pete Valley of central Utah. Fray Juan de Rivera traveled into the Utah area in 1761 and 1765. The journal of the

Escalante expedition mentions finding Rivera's name carved on a tree near Moab. In 1852 Brigham Young arrested Mexican slave trader, Pedro Leon, in the San Pete Valley of Central Utah.

The launching point for all these expeditions was Santa Fe, New Mexico, established by Juan de Onate in 1598. The government building there, still standing on one side of the town square, was completed in 1610, less than a hundred years after Cortez and Pizarro plundered the Aztec and Inca empires. Before Americans had their first Thanksgiving on the rocky New England coast, Spanish caravans, led by adventurers, Jesuit priests, and miners were outfitting at Santa Fe and heading north into the Rocky Mountain west in search of gold and baptisms--and some of these expeditions ended up at Rock Creek on the Duschesne River.

I am not aware of any formal archeological studies on the Spanish history of Rock Creek, but the oral history of the Utes, passed down from parent to child, combined with the many artifacts that have been found there--cannons, cannon balls, bronze church bells, Catholic crosses, remains of two-wheeled ore carts, rubble stone ruins, Spanish spurs, a sword, breast plate, piles of mules feet, and human skulls--convince me that something significant happened there, something involving Spanish miners and priests, and Indians, mostly Utes, but not all.

Since the Utes did not keep written records, and because none of the Spanish survived to tell their side of the story, and since no band of competent archaeologists have set up camp at Rock Creek, I suppose it is up to me, a historical novelist, after three years of book and field research, to attempt to recreate what happened, or might have happened there, in the following pages.

Foreword

In 1912, there had been considerable discussion among the Mormons in Mexico about abandoning their colony and returning to the United States. The civil war that had begun far away in Mexico City had now spread to the northern provinces. No one was safe. Wandering bands of bandit insurgents took supplies and prisoners at gunpoint. It was difficult to distinguish between political activists and common thieves using the political unrest as a license to plunder.

Above all, the several hundred Mormon families in Colonial Juarez, Colonial Pachecho, Colonial Diaz and Colonial Dublan, feared for the safety of their families. United States President, William Howard Taft, was urging the Mormons in Mexico to move their families temporarily across the border to Hatcheta, New Mexico. The president promised to send troops south of the border to establish order so the Saints could return.

The most notorious of the outlaw bandits was Pauncho Villa. Much of the supplies for his gang, which sometimes numbered in the hundreds, came from the Mormon colonies. When the bandit leader had money, he purchased supplies.

When he didn't have money he used his gunpoint line of credit.

What gave the Mormons a glimmer of hope, that perhaps they wouldn't have to abandon their homes and farms, was an unexpected spark of decency on the part of Pauncho Villa. He ordered his men to leave Mormon women alone. The penalty for ignoring this order, was a bullet from Villa's pistol. Nowhere across northern Mexico were women safe, except at the Mormon colonies.

The Mormons told themselves a man who would give an order like this couldn't be all bad. So they hung on, hoping things would get better.

Then the thing they thought would never happen, did happen. A Mormon woman was abducted by one of Pauncho Villa's lieutenants.

Ben Storm was in the fields at the time, tending his bean crop. Of the ten or more years he had been farming at Colonial Juarez, this was his best crop. He hadn't fertilized the land, nor had there been more water in the canal, nor had the weather been any different. In northern Mexico the weather was always the same. The difference was that Ben Storm spent more time tending his bean crop than any man in Colonial Juarez.

His first few years as a bean farmer were different. It seemed he and his bride, Nellie, found too many excuses to go on picnics, or all-day horseback rides to explore some remote mountain top, or just check the cattle. They had been married upon her arrival at the colonies, and the honeymoon had been a long one.

Then Ben became a serious farmer, and began producing decent crops. At least they were as good as anyone else's.

But something went wrong in the marriage. Nellie began talking more and more about her career as a reporter for the Salt Lake Tribune. She missed the excitement. If she told him once, she told him a hundred times, how she had been offered a job with the Chicago Tribune. Now, she thought she had made a mistake in not taking it. When Ben reminded her that she would not have met and married him if she had been working for the Chicago Tribune, she became mysteriously silent. Or jabbered aimlessly about writing opportunities in San Francisco and New York.

Nellie became increasingly critical of life in the Mormon colonies, where the most exciting social event was weekly sacrament meetings. She said she was tired of the same church leaders giving the same sermons week after week, interrupted only by semi-annual stake conferences where the same leaders gave the same sermons again. She said the only thing that could make matters worse, would be for Ben to take a plural wife, and it was just a matter of time until that would happen, she believed.

Sometimes in the night, Ben could hear Nellie crying-- softly, so as not to disturb him. But Ben was a bean farmer, with no money. He could do nothing for her, and she had no children to keep her occupied, so he spent more time in the fields. He was in the fields every minute he was not required to be somewhere else. That's why he had the best crop in Colonial Juarez.

It was during the early part of another unhappy year, that he and the blacksmith, George Hardy, took a day off to look for some stray cattle. George and Ben ran livestock together, and a neighbor reported some of the cows were missing, not an unlikely occurrence with so many rebel bandits in the area.

While checking out a brushy draw in hopes of finding some of the strays, George saw what he thought was a dead man, a Mexican bandit shot full of holes. The man was covered with dust and flies. His bullet wounds were clogged with black scabs. There was no fresh blood. The body looked like it had been there several days, but there was no bloating.

When Ben grabbed the man by the shoulder to pull him over, a feeble groan forced its way between the dusty lips. The man was alive, but just barely.

"Wouldn't hurt a thing if there was one less bandit,"

Ben said, wondering if they should leave the man to die.

"On the other hand," George added, "if we saved his life, maybe his friends would show more kindness to the Mormons. His clothes are torn and dirty from his rough treatment, but he is not wearing rags. The buckle on his belt is made of silver. Perhaps he is one of Pauncho Villa's men, perhaps one of the top lieutenants. If we saved him, Villa would be in our debt."

Carefully, they lifted the man onto Ben's horse, and started back to Colonial Juarez. George was one of the bishops, and knew several homes where the injured man would receive good care, but Ben insisted they take him to his home. He told George that Nellie had excellent nursing skills, but he didn't tell George that Nellie needed something besides her unhappy thoughts to occupy her time. Ben thought a bandit full of bullet holes would be a splendid distraction for her. It would give her something to think about besides writing careers in New York, Chicago or San Francisco.

He was right. By the time the doctor had removed four lead slugs from the man's shoulder, back and hip, Nellie had a bed prepared for the patient in the front room of Ben's house. When the doctor finished his work, Nellie and her friends stripped off the man's clothes, washed away all the filth, cut his hair, dressed him in white bed clothes, and settled him comfortably in his new bed. While all this was going on the doctor just shook his head, commenting that if bullets couldn't kill the man, all the scrubbing and womanly handling probably wouldn't either.

And it didn't. The man lived. Within two days he was drinking soup and chattering cheerfully with the friendly ladies who cared for him, in Spanish and English. His name was Francisco Balboa.

As it turned out, George Hardy's comments when he found Francisco were prophetic. Francisco was indeed one of Pauncho Villa's top lieutenants. He had been a magazine publisher in Monterey before joining the rebel band. He had a degree in literature from Dartmouth College. Francisco was an idealist, determined to see sweeping changes in the country he loved.

As Francisco recuperated, Ben's house became the busiest place in Colonial Juarez. Nellie became Francisco's full-time nurse. She didn't have to cook anymore, thanks to the Relief Society sisters and the regular meals they brought in. It made Ben happy to see Nellie happy. But there was no room for Ben in his own home. After a few days he found himself back in the bean fields, from sun up to sun down.

After a week, Francisco was walking about, with the help of a cane. After two weeks he was going on morning walks with Nellie, and trying to get on the horse Ben said he could use when he was ready to go. In the middle of the third week, Francisco disappeared, and he took Nellie with him.

News of the kidnapping spread like gossip of an excommunication. Ben was in the middle of a bean field when a boy ran from town to give him the news. He raced to the end of the field where his horse was tied, and galloped to George Hardy's blacksmith shop, the central gathering place whenever there was an emergency of this sort.

By the time Ben arrived, men were scattering in every direction to get horses, guns and supplies. The posse was supposed to depart in an hour, and every man was supposed to bring provisions for four or five days. Hopefully the chase wouldn't last that long, but one never knew. In his wounded condition, and dragging along a female hostage, Balboa would have a hard time outrunning a posse. The men had been told to assemble at Ben's house, and begin the chase there, where the trail was still fresh.

Ben hurried home, rolled up some supplies in a slicker, tied it behind the saddle, cleaned and loaded his rifle and pistol, and replaced a loose shoe on his horse, all within an hour's time.

When the posse finally headed out, following Balboa's trail, Ben was in the lead with 23 of his friends and neighbors close behind. Except for the concern he felt for Nellie's safety, it felt good to be on the trail again, to have something

11

besides beans to worry about, to be involved in another great adventure (Ben Storm's earlier adventures leading to his exile in Mexico are chronicled in *Storm Testament V*, by Lee Nelson).

Ben realized he had been too involved in growing beans. His mind and heart had become dull and lazy. Maybe that was why his marriage was going sour. Finally, he had an excuse to shed himself of the bean field. From now on things would be different.

Balboa's tracks were easy to follow, and while some in the posse guessed it would be only a few hours until they caught up with the wounded outlaw and woman, Ben guessed it would be a lot longer. He was only a bean farmer, but he had cattle too, which was justification for keeping a string of fine horses. The two sorrel geldings Balboa and Nellie were riding were Ben's two best horses, both seasoned and hardened desert horses. Ben knew there weren't two or three horses in the entire posse that could keep up with his two sorrels. The success of the chase was dependent on the wounded Balboa and Nellie needing rest, being too soft to endure the rigors of the trail for long periods of time. Ben knew if Balboa and Nellie could stay in the saddle, the posse would never catch them. When evening arrived, and no one in the posse had caught a glimpse of Balboa and Nellie, Ben was not surprised.

The next day, about noon, seven of the men turned back, for various reasons--lame horses, sore backs, sick families, even the need to get ready for irrigation turns.

As the day progressed, Ben hoped they were getting closer. Balboa's tracks seemed to be getting fresher. But the men in the posse were getting tired, along with their horses. Everyone worried about the families they had left behind, mostly undefended in an area of extreme political unrest.

The tracks they were following remained on a true and direct course along the foothills at the edge of the Senora Desert. Balboa, it became obvious, knew exactly where he was going, and was not wasting an ounce of energy deviating to the right or left. But the Mormons could only guess where Balboa was going, and how far his destination might be. By morning of the second day, the Mormons found themselves in unfamiliar territory. The worst part was not knowing how far between water holes. But Balboa knew where the water was, and as long as the posse stayed on his trail, the Mormons had water too. At the end of the second day, there was still no sight of the bandit and his hostage.

By the middle of the third day, everyone in the posse was grumbling. Some were already out of food. Others were willing to share what they had, but in another day everyone would be without food. And it was a three-day ride back to the colonies. Some of the horses wouldn't be able to make it back, meaning some of the men would have to ride double or walk.

A vote was taken, whether to continue, or to turn back. Fifteen voted to turn back. Ben was the only one who voted to continue. His friends tried to convince him it would be suicide to go on without supplies. He agreed, and was about to turn back with the rest of the men, when someone suggested that perhaps Nellie had been a willing hostage. Perhaps she had decided on her own to run off with the bean-eater, in which case she wasn't worth saving.

Ben thought about what had been said. He was not angry with the man for verbalizing what had worried Ben off and on during the chase. Was Nellie capable of running off with another man? He didn't think so. She had been frustrated with the simple life in the colonies, but she was a religious woman. She had made sacred marriage covenants. She was not the kind of woman who would run off with a wounded bandit. And she was not the kind of woman who should be abandoned by her husband.

Ben announced he would continue by himself. When the others tried to talk him out of it, instead of wasting precious energy arguing, he merely guided his horse back onto the trail made by Balboa and Nellie. The others did not follow. Soon he was too far away to hear their words. The posse returned

13

to Colonial Juarez without Nellie, and without Ben.

It was two days later that Ben spotted the outlaw camp. He was on a rocky ridge, looking down into a lush valley. A clear stream ran through one of the prettiest places Ben had seen in this part of Mexico. A hundred horses were grazing in several meadows. There were 15 or 16 white wall tents. Many men, and a few women, were engaged in numerous tasks--shoeing horses, repairing tack, cleaning guns, cooking, gambling, training and racing horses. There was no sign of a woman hostage. Perhaps Nellie was inside. Ben watched the traffic coming to and from the tents, looking for any kind of evidence that might indicate where she was being held. No clues were forthcoming.

Ben decided the only reasonable course of action was to sneak into camp under cover of darkness, try to peak inside the tents, and steal some food. He hadn't eaten in nearly 24 hours. He needed strength.

Ben was caught while trying to sneak past the line of sentries. Realizing beforehand there was a strong likelihood this might happen, Ben had already decided how he would react, if caught.

"I have come to see Pauncho Villa," he said, in Spanish. "I demand you take me to him."

Apparently, the guards had been instructed to do that anyway in situations like this. Demands on the part of the prisoner were not necessary.

Villa was seated behind a table in one of the larger tents. He was a somewhat paunchy man, older and balder than Ben had supposed. Cleaner too. Dusty, sweaty, and smelly were the adjectives Ben had always heard when people described Pauncho Villa. But these descriptions came from Mormons who had seen the rebel leader on the trail, many days from his home camp. Apparently, in camp, near a bath, he was a man of cleanliness.

In front of Villa, on a silver platter on the table, was the roasted hindquarter of a goat that had just been brought in. It was still steaming, filling the tent with the aroma of roasting flesh. Villa had not yet begun to eat. A bottle of red wine and a loaf of freshly baked bread were on the table too, but there were no eating utensils or cups. Apparently the rebel general was going to eat the flesh and bread with his hands, and drink the wine from the bottle. Ben found the food more than a little distracting. His mouth was watering so much he found it difficult to talk.

"Who are you?" Villa demanded.

"Ben Storm, sir, a Mormon from Colonial Juarez. Came to get my wife."

"How do I know you are not an American soldier scouting our camp?" Villa asked.

Ben unbuttoned his wool shirt and slipped it off, showing Villa his Mormon underwear with the special markings, evidence he was a Mormon and not a spy.

"A clever scout might steal some Mormon underwear and use it as his disguise," Villa said. "Even if you are a Mormon, maybe I will kill you anyway, now you know where my camp is."

"Francisco Balboa knows who I am," Ben said. "I saved his life before he kidnapped my wife."

Villa told one of the guards to get Francisco.

"If you will excuse me, I will eat my supper while we wait for Francisco," Villa said as he reached out and tore off a fist-sized chunk of goat meat.

"Why is it you believe Francisco kidnapped your wife?" Villa asked, his mouth full of meat. "I told my men not to bother the Mormon women, that I would shoot anyone who did."

"He was a guest in my home, recovering from his wounds. When he left he took my wife with him. I hope you will shoot him."

"There is a much better chance I will shoot you," Villa responded.

"Do you mind if I sit down and have something to eat before I die," Ben said, his boldness surprising both himself and the rebel general. Ben couldn't stand looking at and smelling that goat meat any longer without having some of it. If he was going to die, he might as well do it with a happy stomach.

"Of course," Villa laughed. He reached out and tore off a big chunk of dripping meat and slid it across the table to Ben who wolfed it down in less than a minute. While he was doing this, Villa sent another guard to fetch the Mormon woman.

"Maybe we'll let the woman decide who dies tonight," Villa said, suddenly looking forward to what he thought might turn out to be a very exciting evening.

A minute later, Ben, his mouth covered with melted goat fat, turned to watch Francisco and Nellie enter the tent. She had lost weight in the four days since leaving home. Her face was sunburned. She looked tired, but there was a glow about her Ben had not noticed in a long time. She did not say anything to her husband. Francisco and Nellie seated themselves on chairs along the side of the table between Ben and the rebel general, waiting for Villa to tell them what to do.

"This man says he is the husband of your new woman," Villa said to Francisco.

"He speaks the truth," Francisco said, his tone submissive.

"I have ordered my men not to bother the Mormon women," Villa said.

"I have not bothered this woman," Francisco responded. "She wanted to come with me. I did not make her come. She wants to stay with me."

"That's a lie," Ben shouted, standing up, clenching his fists, suddenly finding himself looking down the barrel of Pauncho Villa's cocked revolver, a colt .44.

"Sit down," Villa growled. "Everyone be quiet. This problem is easily solved. Everyone listen." He kept the cocked revolver in his hand, pointing it first at Ben, then at Francisco. Ben returned to his chair.

"The woman will decide," Villa said. "But before she

16

does, let me explain what is going to happen." Villa picked up the bottle of wine and drank deeply. After placing the bottle down on the table, he wiped his mouth with the back of his hand.

"If the woman says Francisco took her by force, I will shoot Francisco because he disobeyed my order," Villa explained. "If she says she wanted to come with Francisco, I will shoot her greasy-mouthed husband because he lied to me, telling me Francisco had forced his wife, hoping I would kill Francisco, one of my best men." Villa paused, waiting for the full meaning of his words to be digested. Ben wiped the grease from his mouth. Francisco looked at Nellie, who looked like she was about to be sick. Villa was the only happy one in the tent, besides some of the guards.

"Tell us what really happened," Villa said to Nellie. "Then I will shoot the one who lied to me." Nellie began to cry. Villa began to laugh.

"Just tell the truth," Villa said, when they had waited a full minute or two, and Nellie still hadn't said anything. "God will not punish you for telling the truth. If you lie, the man you want to be with will die. You must tell the truth. I am the killer here, not you."

"I love Francisco, I begged him to take me away from the bean fields," Nellie cried, looking down at her hands. Suddenly, she looked up at Ben. "I love you too, Ben, but I don't want to be your wife anymore." Then she looked at Pauncho Villa. "Please don't shoot him. He doesn't deserve to die. If anyone deserves to die, it is me. Shoot me, if you must shoot someone." Now, Francisco was the only one smiling.

Villa raised the cocked pistol, pointing it at Ben's forehead. Ben didn't flinch or cringe. It wasn't that he was particularly brave, or ready to die. He just didn't care anymore.

Slowly, Villa's thumb allowed the hammer to move forward to its resting place against the back of the revolver. He returned the pistol to its holster.

"I think I understand men, horses, revolution and death," Villa said. "But I do not understand women. I will not kill a man because he does not understand them either. I have changed my mind about killing you, Senior Storm. You may return to your home, without the woman."

"Thank you," Ben said, standing up. And he was sincere. Villa had killed many men, and one more would not have made any difference to the rebel leader. Ben looked at Nellie, and she at him. She was the love of his youth. What had gone wrong? It didn't matter now. He turned to leave.

"Wait," Villa said. "If you die of starvation on the way home, the Mormons will think I killed you, and they will write letters to President Taft. Take some meat."

Ben reached back across the table and grabbed the entire shank of goat. Without looking at Nellie, he then turned and disappeared into the night.

It was evening two days later. Ben was working his way back along the same foothills where he had trailed Francisco a few days earlier. Ben was in no hurry to get home, but this is the way his horse wanted to go, so he let it have its head.

His food was gone. His canteen was empty. He seemed to remember a spring up ahead. Maybe he would reach it before dark. Maybe he wouldn't. He didn't care.

Then in the distance he saw a tiny column of smoke, white smoke, probably willow. His first thought was to make a wide circle around what was probably a bandit camp. That was the safe and smart thing to do. But he didn't care about being safe and smart, not tonight. He reined his horse towards the smoke.

The smoke did not come from a campfire, but from the chimney of a small cabin. It was nestled behind some juniper trees, against a rocky ledge. Without the smoke he would never have seen it.

There was no sign of a horse outside the cabin. That was strange in this country. Everybody needed a horse to get around. There was no stream nearby, and no sign of a well, but for a cabin to be here, there had to be water near, and since his canteen was empty and his horse was thirsty, he decided to ask for water.

He dismounted, removed his canteen from the saddle horn, and walked to the cabin door. It opened before he could knock.

Ben was surprised. The person who greeted him was a woman. She was not young, but old, very old. She was an Indian. She wore a clean, white deerskin dress. Her gray-black hair fell neatly about her shoulders. Her large brown eyes were bright and alert. When she smiled he could see two of her teeth were missing.

"My canteen is empty, and so is my heart," he said, without thinking. At least he had the presence of mind to speak in Spanish instead of English. It had been a tough couple of days. "May I have some water."

"I can fill your canteen," she said, "but I think I am too old to fill your heart." Ben laughed, something he hadn't done in a long time. She invited him in, and offered him a chair beside a clean, plank table.

A skillet full of peppers, onions, tomatoes and spicy venison was simmering on her little wood stove, filling the cabin with a wonderful aroma. On a tin plate beside the skillet was a pile of freshly cooked tortillas. Ben was sure he hadn't seen so many good things to eat since leaving the United States.

"Who are you expecting for dinner?" Ben asked, there being more food on the stove than an old woman could possibly eat at one sitting.

"When I cook I prepare enough for a couple of days. Sometimes Indians help me eat it. Sometimes I eat it all myself. If you want to help me eat it, I can cook again tomorrow."

While she was talking, Ben was looking in astonishment around the cabin. He saw stone jars containing sugar and flour, a big jar of dill pickles, eggs, butter, a side of bacon, even cans of peaches and pears, and the kind of stone jug that usually contained the best Missouri corn whiskey. The only place he had ever been where there was a larger assortment of food was a grocery store in Salt Lake City.

"If Pauncho Villa knew all this food was here, you would not be safe," Ben warned.

"Pauncho knows I am here. He does not bother me."

"Why not?" Ben asked, suddenly very curious.

"The Indians protect me."

"Which Indians?"

"All Indians."

For the first time Ben noticed the rawhide disc or wafer that hung from a leather thong around her neck. On the clean white surface of the disc was burned the image of a large bird, perhaps an eagle. It had one eye, and three feathers extending from the top of its head.

"Are you some kind of medicine woman?" he asked.

"No, but I am a good cook. Let me fix you something to eat." She placed a flour tortilla on a tin plate, and piled the spicy venison with peppers, onions and tomatoes on top of it. She handed him the plate, then fixed one for herself. She poured each of them a cup of coffee.

Earlier, Ben didn't think he was hungry, but with the savory food in front of him, he suddenly found an appetite.

"Have you lived here long?" he asked, as he finished the first helping.

"I do not live here," she said. "I am like you. I came here with an empty heart. This is a good place to heal a wounded heart. But that was a long time ago, when I was young like you. Now I come back every few years. I stay for a month or two. I remember when my heart was empty. But the memories do not make me sad, not anymore. Then I go home to Santa Fe."

"What is your tribe?" he asked.

"Ute. My name is Nanshinob. That means she-wolf. The Spanish called me Isabella. This is a long way from home. But this is my healing place. Maybe it will be my dying place."

20

"Why do the Indians protect an old woman, and bring her so much good food?" he asked.

"That is a long story," she said.

"I have time. Please tell me."

"I do not tell my story to every stranger who comes to my door," she said. "If your heart is truly empty, as you said it was, then maybe I will tell you what happened to me. But first tell me the circumstances that brought you to my door. Then I will decide if you get to hear how my happiness was swallowed up by a very unusual chain of events."

"All right," Ben said, leaning back in his chair, kicking his boot out and placing it on a third chair. He popped the last pepper from his plate into his mouth.

He told the old woman everything, how he had met Nellie during the anti-polygamy persecutions in Utah, how he had persuaded her to join him in Mexico to become his wife, the wonderful first years of marriage, and how things had gone stale.

Ben described finding Francisco Balboa, and bringing him home for Nellie to take care of, thinking she needed something like that to take her mind off her problems. Then, to Ben's amazement, she ran off with Francisco.

Ben described in detail the meeting in Pauncho Villa's tent. When he finished, the old woman remained silent for a long time. It was dark outside. She lit a coal oil lantern and placed it in the center of the table.

"Your story is a sad one. Mine is tragic. Do you want to hear it?"

Ben felt a chill run up and down his spine. He felt like he had been guided to this hidden cabin and strange old woman. But why? What had happened to her that could make his loss more bearable? Was this cabin and this night a healing place for him as it had been for her? He would find out. "Go ahead," he said. "Nan-shin-ob, or Isabella, tell me what happened to you. And don't leave anything out."

She reached over to the stove, picked up the pan of simmering food and placed it on the table in front of Ben.

Then she leaned back in her chair, folded her arms, looked Ben square in the eye, and began telling him the following story.

Chapter 1

The Ute woman leaned forward, carefully stirring the steaming contents of the clay pot. Her stirring tool was a freshly peeled cottonwood stick, about the same thickness and length as her thin arm. It was a cool April afternoon. Her thick, black hair, streaked with silver, hung loosly about her shoulders. In addition to her deerskin dress and moccasins, a shawl of sewn-together rabbit furs was pulled tightly about her shoulders.

The clay pot was resting on a mound of gray-white coals, the remains of what had been a blazing pile of limbs and branches less than an hour earlier. The pot contained chunks of slowly melting wild honeycomb, brought in by some of the boys that same afternoon.

Other women, in similar animal skin dresses, were standing in a group a short distance from the fire, making idle conversation with each other while the first woman continued to stir the steaming contents of the pot. The men belonging to this small Ute clan had left on a hunting expedition several days earlier. A gentle, but chilly, breeze from the northwest was pushing the smoke away from the women.

In the meadow, beyond the half circle of brush wickiups, nearly 20 children, of all ages, seemed busily engaged in some kind of game, the older ones thrashing at the ground with sticks, while the younger ones scampered about in the tall grass, some on their hands and knees. The children were not engaged in idle child's play, but were catching field mice, placing the stunned or dead rodents in leather pouches.

When the honey in the pot began to boil, the woman who had been stirring called to the children. The older ones dropped their sticks, and all began running towards the fire. Several men, too old to go with the hunters, emerged from the wickiups.

Upon reaching the adults, the children opened their pouches, dumping the dead and stunned mice on a flat rock. Everyone helped with the cleaning. A mouse was held between thumb and forefinger and squeezed until the entrails squirted out the back end. Next the head was bitten off and thrown away, then the skin peeled away, care taken not to remove the tail. In a few minutes all the mice were cleaned, and lying in formation on the flat rock, a total of four or five dozen.

Yobe, an over-fed, bear cub of a boy, perhaps 11 years old, was invited forward to cook the first mouse. Yobe was the one who had found the bee tree and collected most of the honey. There were several welts on his arms and legs where bees had attempted to drive him away from their golden treasure.

Yobe didn't waste any time selecting the largest mouse, picking it up by the end of its tail, and hurrying over to the pot of boiling honey. All of the children gathered around to watch as Yobe carefully dipped his mouse into the bubbling sweetness. The boy continued to hold onto the tail as the pink carcass turned gray, then gold in the simmering syrup. Everyone watched in silence.

After about a minute, Yobe lifted his partially cooked rodent out of the honey and held it high for all to see, and to wait for it to cool in the spring breeze. Then he popped the

Chapter 1

entire mouse in his chubby mouth, biting off the tail which he threw on the ground. As he began to chew, the sound of crunching bones was drowned out by grunts of congratulation and approval from those around him, who began turning towards the flat rock to grab a mouse of their own. Soon a dozen mice were simmering in the boiling honey.

Nobody seemed to notice when a little girl began to cry. Maybe those around her thought the girl was unhappy because she couldn't have a second or third mouse. In truth, the girl had forgotten all about the mice and honey, and was looking towards the nearest hilltop. What she saw frightened her to tears.

Chapter 2

Fray Cigarro de Sinbad was disgusted by what he saw. It was bad enough the savages had to eat mice, but even worse was the fact that they actually seemed to enjoy eating the tiny rodents. The priest was sure that if he presented these heathens with a roast piglet on a silver platter, they would prefer the honey-roasted mice.

Like all other savages Sinbad had observed in New Spain, these too were in desperate need of the Holy Catholic Church, and the civilized ways of living that accompanied conversion to Christianity. And he was the instrument in God's hand who was going to save them.

Sinbad was a Jesuit Priest, on special assignment from Rome. It was the Jesuits who had started the work of Christianizing the heathens in the New World, but the work had ended abruptly in 1767 when King Carlos III of Spain ordered the arrest of every Jesuit in New Spain. Hundreds of surprised priests were shipped back to Spain in chains. Not only was there an immediate drop in heathen conversions, but the flow of gold and silver to Rome, maintained by the Jesuits over a 200-year period, suddenly ended, too.

27

Storm Gold

In the early 1800s the king of Spain succumbed to pressure from Rome to begin letting a few Jesuits return to the New World, Sinbad included. But any hope Rome had of a rebirth of Jesuit influence, ended abruptly in 1821 when Mexico declared its independence from Spain.

Most subjects loyal to the crown returned to their mother country, but a few stubborn loyalists remained, especially those in the remote hinterlands north and west of Santa Fe, the northernmost outpost of Spanish civilization. These remote outposts were out of reach of Mexican soldiers.

Fray Sinbad belonged to such an outpost, a remote place called Rock Creek on the north fork of the Rio des Damian, or the Duschesne River.

Fray Sinbad was dressed in the standard flowing black robes of the Jesuit order. He wore a black cap and was mounted on a black mule. A large golden cross hung from a chain around his neck. Sinbad was a thin man--too thin, with sunken eyes, and hollow cheeks, too pale for a man who spent a lot of time outside.

Sinbad was riding with nine soldiers and prospectors, licensed by the crown. The leader of the small expedition, the *maestre de campo*, was a middle-aged, battle-hardened soldier named Islero Ramos. Like the soldiers he led, Ramos wore a metal helmet and breastplate. His sword, made of the finest Seville steel, hung at his side.

Ramos had been leading his men on a prospecting expedition, ordered by his commander, Victorio Del Negro. Regulations required that a priest accompany the troop. They had come upon the tiny band of Ute women and children quite by accident.

Normally, Ramos avoided conflicts with the Utes. First, they were fierce fighters, even against Spaniards with swords and armor. Second, the Utes were the largest supplier of slave labor for the Spanish mines, bringing in a fairly steady supply of Goshute, Shivwit and Piede men, women and children. But this village didn't have any warriors to fight back, and the priest insisted he needed more baptisms before sending his

Chapter 2

next report to Rome. Reluctantly, Islero agreed to invade the camp of mouse-eaters.

After dividing his men into two groups, Islero led the attack at a gallop down the hill and into the Ute camp, surrounding the surprised Indians before any had a chance to escape.

Some of the women and children began to cry, fearing their lives were in danger. The old men stared helplessly at the armed Spaniards. The only Ute to do something was the fat boy, Yobe, who grabbed a piece of deerskin and covered up the last of the uncooked rodents, fearing the Spanish had come to finish off his mice and honey. It didn't occur to the boy that the Spanish might have different food preferences.

Islero nodded to the priest to read the *requerimiento*, a document required by order of the king to be read to heathens before engaging them in battle or enslaving them. In a loud voice, the priest began reading, in Spanish, a language none of the Utes understood.

"I certify that with the help of God we shall make war against you in all ways and manners that we can, and shall take your wives and children and shall make slaves of them, and we shall take away your goods and shall do you all the harm and damage that we can, as vassals who do not obey their lord, and that the death and losses which shall accrue from this are your fault and not that of his highness."

The requirements of the law satisfied, three soldiers, swords drawn, dismounted and began walking among the frightened Utes, separating four of the women and nine of the older children from the others. These were lined up in front of the priest for the customary approval.

Sinbad dismounted and began his systematic inspection of the heathens. Carefully, he checked the teeth, feet, bodies and breasts of each of the four women. The inspection of the children went faster, until he came to the last, a girl about 16 or 17 years old. She allowed the priest to look at her teeth, but when he attempted to pull up her deerskin dress, she jerked away, drawing blood as she clawed at the black-robed

29

arm. The white hand finally lost its grip on her dress. The girl fell backwards to the ground.

When the priest stepped forward to grab the girl again, he found the cold steel of Islero's sword pressed against his chest. Sinbad was furious, but held his tongue. During the days of the inquisition, such interference in the business of a priest would have meant certain death, or at least years of imprisonment. But the days of the inquisition were gone. Islero's punishment for interfering with God's business would have to be more subtle.

Islero knew what the priest was thinking, but didn't care. In Santa Fe, where his Hopi wife lived, Islero had an adopted daughter of his own, about the same age as the Ute girl. There wouldn't be any more lifting of dresses this day.

Gathering his composure, the priest announced that the nine children and four women were worthy candidates for baptism. The announcement brought no joy to the candidates, however, as the soldiers herded them like sheep up the valley, away from the wickiup village. In fact, most of them were crying, especially the boy, Yobe, until one of the women handed him the last honey-coated mouse.

Sinbad was pleased. He was in the process of saving 13 more souls. There would be 13 more baptisms in his report to Rome. It didn't occur to him that one of these heathens would refuse baptism.

Chapter 3

Much to the frustration of Cigarro de Sinbad, Islero was in no hurry to return to Rock Creek. Though he was headed in the right direction, Islero was still focused on the original purpose of the expedition, to seek out new ore deposits. The party stopped at every spring, where several of the men removed wooden *bateas,* or gold pans from the mules' packs and panned gravel and mud removed from the bottom of the spring. Sometimes in mountainous areas, springs were plentiful, and every one had to be checked out.

Veins of metal sometimes caused fissures in surrounding bedrock, allowing spring water and sometimes gasses to escape from the earth beneath. When placer gold was found, the smoothness of the specks and nuggets was noted. The further the gold had moved from the vein, the smoother it became.

Islero and his prospector soldiers also kept close watch on the groves of trees as they rode along. The men looked for discoloration of leaves on the upper branches, perhaps a bluish or leaden tint. They watched for stunted growth, split trunks, or an unusual number of fallen trees, indicating weakness, particularly when such aberrations occurred in a line--evidence gasses might be escaping along the seam of a vein, gasses which sickened and weakened plants. Such places, although infrequent, had to be prospected very carefully.

Early every morning, when there was frost on the ground, some of the men would climb to the top of nearby hills, scanning grassy areas of valleys and hillsides for streaks or lines where no frost had formed on the ground, where foliage was wet instead of frozen, an indication that heat from inside the earth was being conducted to the surface by a vein of metal, or by warm air escaping along the edge of a vein.

When afternoon thundershowers rolled in from the west, men would climb to the tops of hills to watch the storm, looking for places where lightening struck with abnormal frequency, believing metal deposits near the surface attracted lightening.

When such places were identified, the men prospected with forked sticks, or dowsing rods. Holding the forks of the stick, one in each hand, the front of the stick pointing straight forward, the prospector walked across the ground. When he crossed a vein, the end of the stick pulled towards the ground, indicating the spot where the prospector should start digging. A man who was good at dousing usually had an assortment of dousing rods, made from different materials. Hazel was the favorite for finding silver deposits, ash for copper, pitch pine for tin and lead, and iron for gold.

Noticing discoloration on tree leaves and studying frost patterns on ground plants was most effective in the spring of the year when plants were growing and had a higher moisture content. Studying lightening patterns was most effective in late summer and early fall when electrical storms were frequent.

Sometimes in the late summer and early fall of particularly dry years, the prospectors would start forest fires in hilly areas. The intense temperatures, sometimes exceeding 1,000 degrees, could melt metals in veins near the surface. The molten metal would flow out of the vein onto the ground where prospectors could find it, if not immediately, perhaps after the first rain had washed away the ashes. If a thousand acres of virgin forest were destroyed to find a single vein of tin, the prospector congratulated himself on a job well done.

While some of Islero's men were occupied with the prospecting, the others scouted for hostile natives, hunted and fished to maintain the party's food supply, kept a watchful eye on the slaves and horses, repaired clothing and equipment, sharpened swords, polished breastplates and helmets, and nailed new shoes on the horses and mules, though most of the time the mules didn't need shoes because their feet were harder and more compact than those of the horses.

While the soldier-prospectors were thus occupied, Fray Sinbad was busily engaged in teaching prayers and catechisms to the Ute women and children in preparation for baptism. He was frustrated, not only at what he thought was their inability to learn, but their lack of desire to memorize rote phrases in Spanish. But the priest persisted, sometimes holding back food until the desired phrases could be recited. He planned to baptize these new additions to his flock as soon as they reached Rock Creek.

While the priest was occupied in the work of God, Islero was occupied with the horses, particularly the young, green ones. Those who knew Islero considered him to be one of the finest, if not the finest, horseman in all New Mexico-- but a soldier horseman, not a cowboy horseman. He taught his mounts to start and stop on voice commands, to turn and change leads with foot commands. He taught his horses to rare and paw the air in front of them, and kick back with both hind feet on command--techniques proven to be useful in close-quarter combat against an enemy on foot.

While working with the horses one afternoon, Islero noticed he had a spectator, the girl who had defied the priest. The first time he noticed her, she was standing back in the juniper trees, trying not to be noticed. By the next day she was at the edge of the trees. When he asked her to hold one of the horses, reaching out to hand her the reins, she eagerly complied.

By the third day, Islero persuaded the girl to get on one

of the green colts and ride with him into the hills. To his surprise, she was already an excellent rider, but her style was not Spanish in that she used leg pressure instead of stirrups for balance.

In what little he knew of the Ute language, Islero tried to converse with the girl as they rode through the forest. He learned her name was Nanshinob, meaning young she-wolf. She was an orphan. Her father had failed to return from a horse-stealing raid against the Comanches, and her mother had been carried off by Blackfoot raiders, nearly two summers ago. Nanshinob had been living with her mother's sister, the woman of the village chief.

It didn't bother Islero that he was taking the girl from her native home to make her a Spanish slave. She probably wouldn't have to work in the mines, but would be a domestic servant. She would marry one of the Spanish soldiers or miners--certainly a better life than being a savage, wandering from hunting ground to hunting ground, living outside, even in winter.

On the morning of the seventh day, after the prospectors had left with their dowsing rods to check out a place where some unusual frost patterns had been observed that morning, Islero removed a short-handled branding iron from one of the pigskin mule packs and placed it on the hot coals of the morning cook fire. The brand was a backwards Arabic numeral 2, about two inches high. Spanish and Mexican law required slaves be branded. Islero had purposely waited a week, knowing that by now the Indians would be less likely to think they could escape and find their way back home.

The fat boy, Yobe, was the first victim. He struggled valiantly to avoid the branding, but he was no match for the four soldiers who pinned him face down on the ground. Yobe screamed loud and long as Islero slapped the smoking steel against the back of the boy's right shoulder. Islero held the brand firmly in place as the boy struggled against the firm grip of the soldiers. The unpleasant smell of burning flesh filled the air.

Chapter 3

The rest of the slaves received their brands standing up, a soldier holding each arm. All of the children cried, but only one of the women.

Nanshinob's turn came last. Not wanting the soldiers to grab her, she walked voluntarily up to Islero and turned her bare shoulder towards him, indicating she was ready to be branded, without the soldiers help.

Gently, Islero took her by the arm, and applied the brand. She neither flinched, nor cried out, but looked straight ahead, her eyes calm. When Islero was finished, she walked over to the horse she had been riding and started petting its neck, paying no attention to the burn mark on her shoulder.

After placing the brand on the ground to cool before putting it away, Islero looked at Nanshinob. She was not an ordinary slave girl. There was something in the way she handled her horse, in the way she accepted the brand, that was not the way of a slave. She had an inner calmness, and a sense of self far beyond her years. Even with a rope on her neck and a brand on her shoulder, she was not a slave. Maybe she never would be.

And she was beautiful, more so, Islero thought, than any Indian or Spanish girl he had ever seen.

Still, she reminded him of his stepdaughter. His interest in Nanshinob was not sexual. She was a gift from God, something to revere, to protect, to watch over. And that wouldn't be easy in a community of soldiers and miners. And priests.

Islero didn't like her name. Nanshinob was too Indian, too savage. As he watched her pet the horse, he tried to think of a better name. Maria was a good name, but too common. Half the women at Rock Creek were named Maria.

He thought of Queen Isabella who had married Ferdinand in the fifteenth century, a union which finally united Spain. She was responsible for recapturing the last of the Moor strongholds on Spanish land. She had financed the expedition of Christobal Colon in 1492 resulting in the discovery of New Spain. It was Isabella, more than anyone

35

else, who was responsible for launching Spain's golden age, lasting nearly a hundred years before grinding to a halt under the heavy hand of the inquisition. Isabella was prudent and beautiful. She inspired awe, reverence, and loyalty from her subjects.

Islero wondered if it would be acceptable to name a slave girl after Isabella. Finally, he walked over to Nanshinob. When she turned to him, he said.

"You no longer Nanshinob, but Isabella. You Isabella."

The girl said nothing.

Chapter 4

One afternoon, after the new slaves had been on the trail with Islero and his company about 10 days, the prospectors returned to camp very excited. They had not found a gold or silver deposit, but a huge tomb containing the bodies of dozens of dead Indians, a mass burial site.

The next morning Islero went to investigate. He invited Isabella to ride with him. Sinbad decided to go too. Two prospectors from the previous day's discovery party led the way. The camp was about 80 miles south of the Rock Creek settlement, in the high foothills near the headwaters of a long canyon that ran almost straight east towards the Buenaventura River, later named the Green River.

It was late morning when the party halted in a grove of juniper trees at the edge of a high mountain meadow, an ideal campsite with plenty of water and grass. The large number of lodge poles leaning against juniper trees indicated frequent use of the meadow by wandering bands of Indians, probably Utes. Poles left on the ground soaked up water and rotted much faster than those leaning against trees. Sometimes pieces of thick bark were placed under the butts of the poles to keep them off the ground and retard the rotting process even more.

After securing their horses and mules to juniper limbs, one of the prospectors led the party towards what looked like a sheer, smooth cliff on the far side of the meadow. As they drew near, they could see a few cracks or breaks in the smooth surface. The prospector explained that what they were looking at was not a sheer cliff, but what had once been a rock overhang sheltering a number of ancient Indian rock dwellings so common in this area of New Spain.

The prospector explained that apparently a band of Indians, who were camping in the meadow, had gotten sick with the dreaded smallpox. As people died, their bodies were placed under the overhang in the ancient ruins. Once the bodies were in place, the opening was sealed up with rocks and clay plaster. By the time people finished dying, the entire opening had been rocked and sealed off, creating a huge tomb.

The prospector pointed to a crack in the rock work and plaster. Islero climbed up and looked into the dark cavity. Through the stale, dusty air he could see the remains of several Indians. The closest was a woman, partially wrapped in furs. The skin had dried on her skeleton, leaving the bones covered. There was a gold bracelet on her left wrist.

Isabella climbed up beside Islero and looked in. Then came the priest. The prospector pointed out other cracks where more bodies could be seen. Islero and Isabella went from crack to crack, looking inside, feeling the sadness of the place, trying to comprehend the pain and suffering that had been endured there. The priest, on the other hand, hurried back to his horse to fetch his bag of church vestments which included candles and a small, leather-bound logbook. While doing so, he ordered several of the prospectors to build a fire near the tomb.

When Sinbad returned to the tomb, he announced he was going inside. Islero objected, sensing a sanctity about the place, that going inside would desecrate that holiness, and show disrespect for those who had died there. The place had not been consecrated by Christian prayers and ritual, but by the human agony and suffering that had been endured by the Indians. Even though the sufferers had been ignorant savages, they were still human beings and children of God. He told Sinbad it was time to leave.

Isabella wanted to leave too. She had been taught burial grounds were sacred places. She did not belong here, but even more so, the Spaniards should not be here.

But the priest wasn't about to be denied, and expressed this sentiment to Islero.

"Why must you go in?" Islero asked.

"Save these poor heathen souls from purgatory," Sinbad responded, coolly.

"But they're dead, it's too late," Islero said.

The priest cited a verse in the New Testament, part of a letter from Paul to the Corinthians, in which he mentioned baptisms for the dead (I Cor. 15:29). When Islero said he had never heard of such a thing, Sinbad said something about there being many holy things not commonly discussed outside the circles of the priesthood.

Using a burning stick from the fire, Sinbad lit one of his candles, then motioned for Isabella to follow him into the tomb. She didn't want to go, and looked to Islero for help. None was forthcoming. The captain nodded for her to go with the priest. Islero respected the power of Rome, and figured he was in enough trouble with this priest already. He would indulge the foolish man in this harmless fussing over the dead.

Reluctantly, Isabella followed Sinbad into the tomb. When both had crawled inside, and were kneeling next to the first woman, the one wrapped in furs, Sinbad handed the candle and vestment bag to Isabella, then promptly named the woman Maria, and proceeded to baptize her in the name of the Father, the Son and the Holy Ghost.

When he was finished, he removed the logbook from the vestment bag. He wrote the date, the woman's new name,

Maria, and the approximate location--five leagues west of the Rio Buenaventura. When he was finished, he handed the log-book back to Isabella so she could return it to the vestment bag.

Sinbad was about to crawl to the next body when he noticed something he hadn't seen earlier, the gold bracelet on the woman's wrist.

"Gold makes entry into the kingdom of heaven more difficult," he explained to Isabella as he removed the bracelet and placed it in the vestment bag. Isabella didn't understand what he was saying. But she understood clearly what he was doing--robbing the dead. As Sinbad crawled ahead of her to the next body, Isabella quickly removed the bracelet from the bag and returned it to the woman's wrist. The priest was so busy naming and baptizing the next Indian that he didn't notice what she had done.

Slowly, they worked their way through the tomb. Sinbad was careful to name and baptize each body, and make a careful entry in his book for each one. Isabella thought he baptized some of them twice, but in the dark, dusty confines of the tomb she couldn't be sure. She returned several more gold bracelets to their rightful owners without the priest noticing.

She observed that the priest used a large number of names for the men--Pedro, Jesus, Jose, etc.--but all the women, before he baptized them, he named Maria. Isabella didn't know enough Spanish to ask him why he did this.

When they were finished, and crawled outside into the fresh air and sunshine, Islero and the prospectors placed rocks in the openings to seal the tomb. It wasn't until they arrived back at camp that Sinbad looked in the vestment bag and discovered the missing bracelets. When he confronted Isabella, she had an idea what he was talking about, but merely shrugged her shoulders, as if she didn't understand a word he said.

Chapter 5

Three days later, the Islero Ramos prospecting party was following the Rio des Damian upstream in a northeasterly direction. Islero was leading the way on a good trail. Isabella, as usual, was riding at his side. Upon reaching a place where a smaller stream came in from the right, Islero pointed towards a rock face high above the trail. With her keen eyes, Isabella didn't have any trouble seeing the huge cross carved into solid rock. She didn't understand the religious significance of the cross, only that this symbol was important to these strange white men. Most of the soldier-prospectors had small silver crosses hanging around their necks. The priest had a big gold one.

Islero led his men and slaves onto another well-used trail leading up the east fork of the Rio des Damian. An hour later they reached the Rock Creek settlement.

Isabella was overwhelmed with the new and strange things to be seen. It had never occurred to her that a village could be so large, containing perhaps a hundred huts, some of stone, some of brush. There were bigger buildings, too; a church which also served as a school, a barracks for soldiers and miners, and a huge mill for processing ore. The mill had a waterwheel on one side which turned as the water flowed onto it.

A string of about 30 mules, each carrying a heavy pack of ore, was lined up at the mill. There were numerous two-wheeled carts, most pulled by donkeys, but some by oxen, moving here and there. The oxen, donkeys and mules all were branded, with the reverse 2, the mark Islero had burned on Isabella's shoulder.

Isabella had seen small patches of corn and tobacco in her Ute village, but here there were huge patches of corn, squash, beans and a vine-like bush with broad leaves which she later learned were grape vines. Some of the fields were several acres in size.

There were small corrals made from stones and sticks containing short, thick, hairless creatures with flat noses. They squealed, grunted and had a strong, sour smell.

In the grassy areas around the village, cattle, sheep and horses were grazing. Dogs and turkeys wandered among the dwellings looking for things to eat.

As the caravan neared the church, a boy ran outside and started pulling on a rope. Isabella heard the most beautiful sound she had ever heard. Each time he pulled on the rope, Isabella heard the beautiful sound. She guessed it was coming from a large metallic object, similar in shape to half an egg shell. Every time the boy pulled the rope, the object moved, making the beautiful noise once again.

Islero's first order of business was to distribute the newly-acquired slaves to the places and assignments where they were most needed. Except for Isabella and Yobe, the children were sent to the various mines. The three women had already been spoken for by three of the soldiers, and would move into stone or brush huts the men had already built. Their duties included working in the fields and caring for livestock.

Yobe was assigned to two boys who had the unusual task of collecting urine from the pregnant mares, both donkeys and horses. With wooden buckets in hand, the boys would watch the grazing mares, ready to catch the urine whenever a mare let it out. The urine was dumped on a huge mound of crushed ore by the mill. The urine helped prepare the ore for processing, making it easier to separate the metal from the crushed stone. Pregnant women in the community were required to urinate on the ore pile too.

The mound was larger than normal due to the lack of mercury. A shipment from Santa Fe had been due for some time, but had not yet arrived. Islero guessed that if it didn't come by the time he was through with the spring prospecting, he would be making a trip to Santa Fe to find out what had happened. Mercury was essential for getting the gold and silver from the crushed ore.

While waiting for the mares to urinate, the boys were kept busy with stone mallets, pounding animal fat or tallow into wads of cactus fiber. The finished product was lashed to the ends of sticks to become torches to be used in the mines.

Islero introduced Isabella to two Shoshone women, Maria and Juanita. The two understood very little Spanish, or Ute. But using sign language, Islero made it clear to them that they were to take Isabella, watch over her and take her with them to work in the fields.

Once he knew his instructions concerning the girl were understood, Islero rode off to attend other duties. It being planting time, there was much to do, and within half an hour, Isabella found herself in the fields, placing beans in long, straight furrows in the soft black soil.

Normally, an attractive young slave girl would get a lot of immediate attention from the soldiers and miners, but Islero gave strict orders for the men to leave Isabella alone, at least for the present. He knew that sooner or later she would become the woman or wife of one of the men, but he didn't want to deal with that now. He was under pressure from Del Negro to find new ore deposits, and the spring of the year was the best time to do it.

In fact, Del Negro was out prospecting himself, to the southwest, looking for the lost Josephine de Martinique mine in the mountains the American trappers called the Henry Mountains.

Islero had no intention of waiting for Del Negro to return. He would handle the pressing problems which couldn't wait, then in a day or two, he would head out on the prospecting trail once more--believing Isabella would be content, working in the fields with Juanita and Maria. But Fray Sinbad had other plans.

Chapter 6

Isabella didn't plant enough beans to become bored with the task. Islero and his prospecting party hadn't been gone more than a few hours when Fray Sinbad strolled into the bean field and ordered the two Shoshone women to move Isabella and her things to one of the stone huts behind the church. The two old women never questioned orders from a Spaniard, especially not from a priest.

They marched Isabella back to their brush hut, gathered up her blanket and the few items of clothing she had brought with her from the Indian village, and hurried her over to the church.

At first Isabella didn't resist, not understanding what was happening, but when they threw her things into the stone hut behind the church, and started to leave, she tried to leave with them.

Juanita and Maria couldn't understand her reluctance. Duty at the church was much more desirable than field work. Isabella would probably get to polish the wonderfully mysterious church ornaments and decorations, in addition to cooking, cleaning and working in the priest's private garden.

When Isabella tried to follow Juanita and Maria back to the fields, they grabbed her by the shoulders, turned her around, and pushed her towards the church.

Reluctantly, she returned. It wasn't that she wanted to be with Juanita and Maria, or that she liked working in the bean field. She knew nothing of the church, either. She knew only that somewhere deep inside her a warning sounded whenever Fray Sinbad came near. It was not a feeling she could verbalize, even in her native language. But when the priest was near, she had a strong urge to turn and flee, probably a feeling similar to what wild animals felt when hunters came near.

When she returned, she was greeted by Juan, a *genizaro*, or trusted Ute servant. Juan was the first adult male Indian Isabella had seen since coming to Rock Creek. She knew there were many more, all working in the mines, some near and some many days away.

Juan was friendly, and kind to her. He did not trigger her escape mechanism the way Fray Sinbad did. Juan was a young Indian, possibly in his early 20s. He had worked in the mines when he first came to Rock Creek, but soon after his conversion to Catholicism, the priests brought him to the mission. They thought the ease with which he was converted, and his eagerness to accept both Catholic and Spanish beliefs and customs, would make him a good example to new Indians coming to Rock Creek. And he spoke a dialect of her native Ute language.

In addition to working in the priest's vegetable garden, Juan assigned Isabella the responsibility of changing the tallow candles in the church. Isabella had never seen candles before meeting the Spanish, and was intrigued by the little lights that never seemed to go out. Juan showed her how to break the old wax free of the tin candleholders, light the new candle, and how to use hot wax to seat it in the holder. There were hundreds of candleholders in the church, in rows along shelves, and just as many in the front of the church next to the golden cross and the wooden statue of the Spaniard called

Chapter 6

Jesus.

In addition to the many candles along the walls and across the alter, there were two circular wheels hanging from the middle of the ceiling, both with 20 or 30 candles mounted along the outer edge of the wooden circle. Juan showed Isabella how to lower the big wheels of light. They were hanging from long ropes which passed over a beam in the center of the ceiling and tied to pegs in the walls. Juan showed Isabella how to untie the ropes and lower the wheels to the floor so the candles could be changed. Isabella soon fell into a daily routine of checking and changing candles, a routine that consumed hours of her time, every day.

Isabella became familiar with the many decorations in the church. Especially she liked the many-colored drawings on smooth slabs of wood. Most of these depicted the Jesus nailed to a wooden cross, or laying wounded and dead in a woman's lap. There was always a wreath of thorns around his head, and big drops of red blood running down his face. She thought it strange that the Spanish god could be so vulnerable, so easily injured by enemies. The Ute god, Towatts, was much stronger.

Isabella wasn't always alone while changing the candles. Every day, groups of Indian slaves were herded into the church for religious instruction consisting of listening to the priest and trying to repeat what he said--learning catechisms and prayers in a language few of them understood.

Sometimes Sinbad would invite Isabella to join the Indians in memorizing what he called the words of God. But she always refused. It didn't occur to her that she was probably the only Indian in Rock Creek who dared refuse a request from a Spaniard and get away with it. It wasn't so much a matter of refusing the Catholic religion, as refusing Sinbad and anything he offered. Had he been teaching Ute history, she would have refused to take part in that too.

Sometimes when she was alone in the church, doing the candles, she thought she could feel someone watching her from behind, but when she turned, no one was there.

47

Then one night she was awakened from a deep sleep by a voice calling her name, her Spanish name, Isabella. Rubbing her eyes and rolling onto her knees she looked out the open doorway of her little hut. In the partial moonlight she had no trouble identifying Fray Sinbad standing directly in front of her doorway, feet apart, hands on hips, his long black robes hanging silently at his sides.

She had never before seen him without his little black skull cap before. In the pale moonlight his partially balding head had the same white, lifeless look as a buffalo pelvis bone left to bleach in the sun and wind.

He called her name again. Still, she didn't answer. But when his knees started to bend, an indication he intended to crouch low enough to enter her hut, she could no longer resist the urge to flee.

In an explosion of energy she lunged from her hut, quickly turning to the right to avoid a collision with the surprised priest, who made a feeble attempt to hold onto her shirt, but turning and jerking with all her might she pulled herself free and began running up the trail leading away from Rock Creek towards the distant mountains.

She thought she heard footsteps behind her and ran faster. Reaching the top of the first hill, she stopped for breath and looked back. The man in black robes was approaching the bottom of the hill. He wasn't running, but walking swiftly, his long skinny legs taking huge confident strides, a pace he could probably maintain all night.

She felt helpless. Feelings of panic and fear swelled in her heart. Nausea filled her throat. Again, she was overwhelmed by the urge to flee. She turned and ran, staying on the main trail where the footing was better in the partial moonlight.

At first, she felt tireless in her flight, but soon her lungs were burning, demanding more oxygen. Her legs were refusing to cooperate, the muscles screaming for air. She began looking for hiding places where the priest couldn't find her, but could find nothing.

Chapter 6

Seeing a less-used trail branch off to the left, she turned onto it, hoping the priest wouldn't do the same. A minute later she looked back, and saw the priest follow her footsteps onto the new trail. She realized she could not outrun him. She would have to find a hiding place, or give herself up to him.

As she turned to run again she suddenly discovered the reason for the new trail breaking off from the main trail. Before her was the opening to a cave or tunnel, an excellent hiding place, she thought, providing the priest didn't have a torch or candle. Holding one hand ahead of her and touching the side wall for guidance with the other, she hurried forward into the mine.

After turning the first corner, Isabella found herself in total blackness. But keeping her hand on the side of the tunnel she pushed forward. Had she been aware of Spanish mining techniques and the frequent use of vertical shafts, she probably would have stopped, but since she knew nothing of Spanish mining she hurried forward through the darkness.

She came to a place where the tunnel divided into two new tunnels. She went left, keeping her hand on the sidewall for balance and direction. Cautiously she pushed ahead.

She heard the priest calling her name. She guessed he had entered the tunnel, too. She did not answer, but stopped in an effort to be completely silent. She waited, listened. She could not hear the priest's footsteps.

Gradually she became aware that the damp, musty smell of the tunnel had changed. There were new smells. Human smells. Sweat. The smell of unwashed bodies.

Then she heard a rustling sound, coming not from the mouth of the tunnel where the priest might be, but close, too close. She heard it again, perhaps in front of her, perhaps to one side, but not very far away. She thought she heard the soft clanking of metal against metal, like the sound a chain would make moving snake-like along the ground.

Someone or something was very near. Her vision was useless in the impenetrable blackness. Her fear, which she had been holding down like a wad of undigested raw flesh in the

49

bottom of her belly, was churning and pushing. She thought she might throw up.

She heard the chain sound again. The fear turned to panic. She bolted. Not back the way she had come, still fearing the black-robed priest, but straight ahead into the unknown darkness.

She hadn't gone more than a few steps when she suddenly found herself in the grasp of powerful arms--too powerful to be those of a woman or child. A man had grabbed her, or perhaps a beast. The stench of dirt and sweat was overwhelming. She did not scream as she struggled to get out of the powerful grasp. Only a whimper of despair escaped her lips as the powerful arms wrestled her to the ground.

She waited for sharp teeth to penetrate her flesh, or a blow to knock her senseless, or eager hands to start probing her soft, young body.

No sound came from her attacker to indicate who he was or why he had grabbed her. But no matter how hard she struggled, he would not let go.

Finally, her struggles ceased. She was exhausted, but more than that, she was beginning to realize the powerful arms that held her were probably not going to harm her. Still they would not let go. When she attempted to speak, a dirty finger pressed against her lips, a sign she should remain silent.

In the distance she heard the priest call her name one more time. His voice sounded further away. She, and the man who held her, remained silent.

Again she tried to push free of the powerful arms. Again they refused to let her go. A big hand took a firm but gentle hold on her hand and attempted to pull it above her head. When she resisted, the hand jerked at her fist, but would not let go. Finally, she relented and let her attacker pull her hand above her head, along the tunnel floor.

When her hand would reach no further, she felt an edge, a sharp downward incline in the tunnel floor. The hold on her hand was released. She pulled her hand back to her body.

A moment later a stone was placed in her hand. Her first reaction was to use it as a weapon and strike the man who held her. Instead she let the man guide her fist to the edge of the incline, and pull her fingers apart so the rock could roll out.

There was silence for several seconds. Then she could hear the rock striking other rocks, far below.

The message her captor had been trying to convey to her was clear. Ahead of them in the tunnel was a deep vertical shaft. In grabbing Isabella, and wrestling her to the ground, her captor had saved her from certain death.

Isabella reached forward and touched the face of the man who held her. It was not the bearded face of a Spaniard she touched, but the smooth face of an Indian. Slowly, she pulled her hand away. Suddenly, the powerful arms that had held her so long, released their grasp. Carefully, she sat up, still unable to see anything.

When her new friend moved, she could again hear the rustle of a chain. When she tried to ask him about the chain, he answered in a language she could not understand. He wasn't speaking Spanish, but a native language. It sounded to her like the language she had heard Goshute slaves speak. Maybe he was Goshute. Had there been light she could have used sign language to communicate.

Leaning forward onto her hands and knees she groped about until she found the chain. She followed it to one end which was secured to an iron ring attached to the wall of the tunnel. Following it back the other way, she discovered it was attached to the ankle of her new friend. The poor fellow could not leave the dark tunnel.

She wondered how he lived. Surely, someone from the village must bring him food and water. She wondered what his crime might have been to receive such a horrible punishment.

As she moved her hand away from the chain, her fingers touched the end of his foot. Something was wrong.

51

Something was missing. She touched again. The toes were gone, all of them.

Now she knew what his crime had been. She had seen other Indians with missing toes, the punishment for those who tried to escape. Isabella wondered if her toes would be cut off for running from the priest.

Isabella's first impression of the Rock Creek village was that it was a peaceful, desirable place to live. Everyone seemed to be happily at work, and there was plenty to eat. The shelters were comfortable, and with the Spanish soldiers around, there was no fear of attack by enemies, at least none that she was aware of.

But somewhere behind all that peaceful living, there was someone with a sharp knife cutting off the toes of people who tried to leave. Again, she wondered if someone might be getting ready to cut her toes off. She decided she wouldn't stay around to find out. She would try to find her way back to her home village, if she could find her way out of the cave. She decided to wait until morning when the sun was shining on the cave entrance. Then, perhaps there would be light at the end of the tunnel to guide her to the outside.

Chapter 7

When Isabella emerged from the mine tunnel the next morning, into bright sunshine that temporarily blinded her, two Indians and the priest were waiting for her. Her first thought was to try to run past them. But in the bright sunlight the priest didn't seem nearly as threatening as he had the night before. She consented to go with them back to the village.

As they marched down the trail, the priest leading the way, Isabella and the two Indians close behind, she couldn't help but wonder about the man she had found in the mine. Who was he? Who brought him food and water and took care of him? She didn't know enough Spanish to ask the priest, and the two Indians accompanying her were not Ute, perhaps Navajo or Apache. Nevertheless, they didn't speak her language. She decided she would ask Juan about the strange Indian in the long tunnel.

It didn't occur to Isabella that anything would be any different when they reached the church. She assumed she would do her usual chores, including changing the candles, then return to her hut. She decided she would take several of the candles, hide them under her dress and take them to her hut. When no one was looking, she would return to the mine and take food and water to her new friend. The candles would give her light in the dark tunnel, and would allow her to see the man who had saved her life.

She wondered when night came, if the priest would come to her again. If he did, where would she run this time? She wished Islero had not gone away. She wondered when he and his men would return. She thought Islero would protect her from the priest, and anyone else who might want to harm her. Upon reaching the church, Isabella was totally surprised and off guard, when the two Indians who had accompanied her, grabbed her by the arms. She tried to pull away, but the strong hands maintained a firm hold on her.

Fray Sinbad disappeared inside the church. When he returned, he was carrying a long chain, a heavy iron bracelet attached to one end. He used a big key to open the bracelet, then clamped it shut on her right wrist. It was quickly apparent the bracelet had been designed for the bigger bones and hands of men. The fit was too loose. Isabella pulled her hand out of the shackle, giving the priest a defiant glance as she did so.

Ordering the two Indians to hold her tighter, the priest quickly unlocked the bracelet. Roughly, he pushed the cold iron against her throat. The crude hinge at the back of the bracelet pinched her skin as the priest tried to close it. While it had been too large to restrain her hand, it was too small to close around her neck.

Rather than withdraw the iron shackle, the priest continued to hold it on her neck, slowly letting his hungry fingers extend beyond the iron, touching the soft skin. While the cold iron had been uncomfortable against neck, the eager touch of the priest's fingers was totally revolting. First, she felt an overwhelming helplessness to do anything about it. Then she felt like she was going to faint. Her eyes began to close.

The priest misunderstood what was happening. He

thought the half-closed eyes, and the apparent relaxing of her muscles was a warming, welcoming response to his touch. He allowed his fingers to probe further.

Suddenly, Isabella's senses returned. Once again she was in control. Like a trapped animal she struck out with the only weapon available to her, her sharp white teeth. She grabbed the side of the priest's right hand, at the base of the thumb, biting down as hard as she could. She could hear and feel the crunching of flesh and bone. Salty blood spread over the end of her tongue. The priest screamed and tried to pull his hand away. Fiercely, she held on, trying to sink her teeth even deeper.

Finally, a blow from the priest's free hand knocked her senseless. When the two Indians let go of her, she fell to the ground. When she awakened, the iron bracelet was locked tightly around her ankle. The far end of the chain was secured to a juniper stump behind the church. Her head throbbed, and she was thirsty.

She looked at her feet to see if her toes had been chopped off for trying to run away. They were still there.

Juan was the first person to come close enough to talk to her. He brought her some water and corn cakes. She wasn't hungry, but she gulped down all but the last few swallows of water, which she splashed on her bruised face.

She asked Juan what was going to happen to her. He said she had broken Fray Sinbad's thumb. Juan was surprised the priest had not killed her. Attacking a Spaniard, especially a priest, was a crime usually punishable by death. But just because she had not been killed yet, didn't mean it wasn't going to happen.

Isabella changed the subject. She asked Juan about the Indian she had discovered in darkness at the end of the abandoned tunnel, the one who had saved her life, the one in chains.

Juan said the man was Raphael, a Goshute slave who refused to work in the mines, or anywhere else. Whenever Raphael's chains were removed, he tried to leave. Even after all his toes had been cut off, he would still attempt to leave whenever his chains were removed.

"He refuses to be their slave," Juan explained, in the native Ute language they both understood. "They can't make him dig their gold. He will not obey their orders, even when they whip him, even when they drag him by his feet behind running horses, not even when they cut off pieces of skin or an ear. Both his ears are gone. Raphael is not afraid of the Spanish. He is not afraid to die. And he will not dig their gold. They can't make Rafael their slave."

"Then why don't they kill him?" Isabella asked.

"Del Negro," Juan said, a tone of awe and reverence in his voice. "Del Negro will not let them kill Raphael."

"But why?"

"I can only guess," Juan said, thoughtfully. "Del Negro controls everything. Because of him this settlement is here. Because of him hundreds of men go into the mines every day to dig the gold and silver. Del Negro controls everybody, even the priests, but he does not control Raphael."

"In death, Raphael is the victor," Isabella said, answering her own question.

"I think so," Juan said. "As long as he is alive the battle will continue. Del Negro is determined to make Raphael his slave. Raphael is determined to be no man's slave."

"What will Del Negro do next, to Raphael?" she asked.

"I don't know, but when he returns from the Henry Mountains he will think of something."

"Who will win?" she asked.

"If death is victory, then I think Raphael will win. They have cut off his toes, his ears, some skin and some fingers. What will Del Negro cut off next? How much can be cut off a man before he dies? I think Raphael will die, but he will not die a slave."

"I do not like this Del Negro," Isabella said.

"You have never seen him."

"That does not matter."

Chapter 7

Juan had to leave. He had work to do. Slave work which he did willingly and cheerfully. Isabella decided she liked Raphael better than she did Juan.

Chained to the juniper stump with nothing to do, Isabella had plenty of time to think. She wondered about herself and how she should behave towards the Spanish. If she tried to be like Juan, agreeable and submissive, they would undoubtedly treat her kindly. If she remained defiant, like Raphael, they might kill her, or be cruel to her in ways worse than death. Who should she follow, Juan, or Raphael?

Perhaps it didn't matter. Perhaps they had already decided to kill her because of her defiance towards the priest.

Several hours later, Juan returned. He was bearing grim news. For trying to escape, Fray Sinbad had ruled that two of her toes be removed. For infidelity, spending the night in the tunnel with Rafael, her nose was to be cut off.

It took a minute for Juan to explain the meaning of infidelity. When she finally understood what he was saying, she insisted that no such thing had happened in the cave. Juan said he believed her, but it did not matter what he thought. The ruling had been made.

"There is only one way to avoid these horrible punishments," Juan said.

"What is that?" she asked.

"Repent."

She didn't know what he was talking about. He tried to explain the meaning of the word.

"I repent," she said, when she thought she understood his meaning. "Now take off the chain."

"It is not that simple," he said. "True repenting requires baptism into the holy church, and..." He hesitated.

"You can baptize me," she said. She had seen others baptized, the sprinkling of water, the mumbling of meaningless words. She could put up with that, if it got her out of chains, and saved her nose and toes.

"There is one additional requirement," he said.

"What?"

"You have to become the personal servant of Fray Sinbad."

"What does that mean?"

"You wash his clothes, help cook his meals. You move into the room next to his. You become his woman."

Isabella understood what Juan was saying, but still, she was confused. The Spanish were going to cut off her nose for what they called infidelity, but she could save her nose by agreeing to be involved in more infidelity.

"It is a religious thing," Juan tried to explain. "With a Spaniard, especially with a man of God, it is somehow different. I do not understand, only that it is so. What is your answer? Will you consent to baptism and becoming Fray Sinbad's woman?"

Isabella's head was spinning. She loathed the priest so much. Perhaps death would be preferable to sharing his bed. But she did not want to lose her nose. Though she had never seen herself in a mirror, she knew she was beautiful and desirable. People liked to look at her, especially men. Without a nose, all that would change. She would become ugly and despised, for the rest of her life.

She believed Islero was the only one who could save her from this tragic decision, and he was gone. But he would return. She must stall.

"Tell the priest I need time to think," she said. "I will try to have an answer tomorrow."

"Fray Sinbad will return to Spain in a few years," Juan explained. "Then you can do as you wish. If they cut off your nose it will be gone the rest of your life. Let me tell Fray Sinbad you have agreed to the most holy Catholic repentance."

"Tell the priest I will give my answer tomorrow," she insisted.

When Juan returned the next day, Isabella said she needed more time, that she would have an answer the following day. After Juan departed, she spent the remainder of the day watching the main trail, hoping desperately that

58

Chapter 7

Islero would return. He did not.

After the fourth day of stalling, Juan said she could have no more time for thinking. She must consent to baptism and becoming Sinbad's servant, or soldiers would be sent to cut off two of her toes, and her nose, and that the punishment would be carried out that same day.

Isabella had had plenty of time to think about her decision. Without taking her eyes off the main trail, she said, "I will not consent to your holy, most Catholic repentance."

Chapter 8

As soon as Juan turned to take Isabella's answer to Fray Sinbad, she began to cry. The tears flowed, more from frustration than fear. She didn't understand why she was doing this to herself. As she looked around at the other Indians, they seemed more or less content to be slaves, especially Juan. Everyone had food to eat, in a land where people often went hungry. Why did she insist on being like Raphael?

But she wasn't like Raphael, she decided. He was refusing to be a slave. She was refusing to be the woman, or mistress of a man she despised. If slavery were the only issue, she might consider this thing Juan called repentance. But whenever she thought of giving herself to the priest, voices deep inside began screaming, "No, no, no!" She didn't understand what caused the voices, and why, only that they were loud and clear, and she found herself unable to ignore them.

Wiping the tears from her eyes with the back of her hand, she noticed that the bell was ringing, the signal for everyone to gather at the church. She decided the priest had not been bluffing. Juan had told her whenever a slave was

61

punished, the rest of the slaves were required to watch, so the lesson being taught to one, would be a lesson to all.

She could see people coming to the church--from the fields, from the stone and brush huts, from the barracks, from the mill where the ore was crushed, from the furnaces where the ore was melted. A lot of people were coming, more it seemed than came to the mass and vesper services at the church.

She wished she looked better. She had not been able to bathe or wash since they chained her to the post. Her long hair was matted and greasy. Her face was tear stained. Her deerskin dress was the dirtiest it had ever been.

Isabella couldn't help but smile at her vanity. After her nose was removed it wouldn't matter how dirty she was. People wouldn't want to look at her, except curious children.

Two soldiers walked around the corner of the church. They seemed to have little enthusiasm for the task at hand, as they slowly removed the bracelet from her ankle and led her to the front of the church. They escorted her beyond the church to a little hill.

At the top of the hill, a stout juniper post was planted upright in the ground. The soldiers guided her to the post, then turned her around so she was standing with her back against it. They tied her hands together with a strip of rawhide, then raised her bound hands high above her head and lashed them to the post. The soldiers left, leaving her unattended as the people gathered in front of her.

She looked at the faces, recognizing many of them. Expressions were grim. Like at Sunday mass, few seemed glad to be there. Then she noticed Juanita and Maria. Both were crying. Isabella was surprised, but moved. She had known them only a short time, yet they seemed to have genuine concern for her.

After what seemed a long time, Juan walked to the top of the hill and stood beside Isabella. He held up a wooden plaque, with something written on it, and cleared his throat, the signal for everyone to be quiet and listen to what he was

Chapter 8

about to read.

As Juan began, it was obvious from the smug look on his face, and his slow, deliberate manner, that he was very proud of his ability to read Spanish, a language few of the Indian slaves understood.

Isabella understood some of the words, and caught some of the meaning, particularly the part about her not being an obedient subject to the Holy Catholic majesty, the king of Spain, and the penalty for such disobedience to be the immediate removal of two of her toes.

When Juan was finished, the same two soldiers who had escorted her to the hill, walked up to her. One was carrying a block of wood which he placed on the ground in front of her. The soldier dropped to one knee, taking Isabella's bare foot in his hands and placing it on top of the wooden stump, holding the foot firmly in place.

When the second soldier drew a long knife from his belt and dropped to his knees in front of her, Isabella tried to pull her foot away, but could not.

The knife must have been very sharp. There was no chopping or hacking, just a quick slice and two of the middle toes on her left foot were gone, almost before she realized what had happened. She looked in disbelief as two tiny streams of red blood spurted from the stubs that had once been toes. Quickly, the soldiers moved away so they would not be squirted.

What surprised Isabella even more than the quickness of the knife, was the almost complete absence of pain. Her foot did not hurt.

She was so engrossed in watching the blood squirt from her wound, forming a red-black pool around both of her feet, that she did not notice the approach of Juan and Fray Sinbad until they were standing directly in front of her. She looked up, first at Juan, then at Sinbad, who had replaced his usual black robe with a white one. She didn't know why.

She hated both of the men in front of her. What she felt was not just anger, but a deep, simmering, revengeful rage.

63

Someday they would pay.

Juan was the first to speak. He told Isabella that if she would consent to repentance before the second verdict was read, there was still time to save her nose. The conditions of repentance had not changed.

Isabella knew it would be wise to accept the conditions and save her nose. She also believed it would be wise to suppress the feelings of rage and anger welling up in her throat. But she could not.

Without warning, she lifted her left foot, the one with the bleeding stubs, high in the air and pushed it against the priest's chest, smearing his golden cross and clean white robe with her blood. As Sinbad looked down in surprise, one of the stubs that was still squirting, sprayed his face with her sweet, warm blood. Quickly, the priest pulled back, ordering Juan to read the second verdict.

This time she paid little attention to what was being read. It didn't matter. She tried to tell herself she didn't care about the thing that was about to happen.

The hairy arm of a soldier, who had come up behind her without being noticed, reached around her neck. Another hand grabbed a handful of her black hair and guided her chin into a comfortable position over the first arm. Isabella could not move her head. With a little additional pressure the soldier could cut off her air. With a little more, he could break her neck. Isabella knew she was totally helpless to prevent what was about to happen. Still, she did not cry.

The second soldier, the same one who had sliced off her toes, stepped in front of her and drew the long knife from his belt. Isabella looked into the bearded face. There was no expression, at least none that she could detect. She wondered if the soldier enjoyed his work. She could not tell by looking at his face.

The soldier raised the knife. With her hands tied to the post above her head, and the hairy arm tight around her neck, Isabella could not move. She did not cry, or scream, just watched the knife as it drew closer to her nose.

Chapter 8

"Para te!" shouted a strong male voice, a voice Isabella did not recognize. In amazement she watched the knife return to its home in the soldier's belt. She felt the hairy arm withdraw from her neck. Both soldiers disappeared into the crowd.

At first she thought Islero had returned, but the sound of the voice was strange. It did not belong to Islero. She turned her head to see who dared interrupt the priest's dirty business.

The rider, who was pushing towards her through the parting crowd, was the most magnificent man she had ever seen. And he was riding the most beautiful horse she had ever seen.

"Victorio Del Negro," someone whispered, in awe. Everyone else was silent.

Victorio's breastplate, shield and helmet glistened like polished silver in the afternoon sun. His powerful arms were bare. The sweaty coat of his black stallion glistened like satin.

Pulling the horse to a halt, Del Negro reached up with a muscular right arm and removed his helmet. His black hair was curled, damp with sweat and matted against his head. He had a strong nose and a square jaw. His piercing eyes were blue like the sky. The corners of his firm mouth were twisted into a teasing grin--the grin of a man who viewed his existence not as an unhappy struggle, but as a grand game, and an exciting one at that.

"Anyone who would decrease the number of beautiful women in New Mexico, even by one, ought to be whipped," Del Negro roared. "Who is the *cabron* who ordered this girl's nose removed?"

"I did," Fray Sinbad said, stepping forward, his face flushed over Del Negro's insult. The priest had never been called a male goat before. But he knew Victorio del Negro was in control at Rock Creek. Sinbad would remember the insult. There would be opportunities for revenge later, perhaps after he and Del Negro returned to Spain. The priest would not forget. Sinbad was still dressed in the blood-stained white

65

robe.

"My deepest apology for comparing the most holy, reverent, immaculate, full of grace servant of God to a creature with *cajones*," Del Negro said. There was contempt in his voice. Some of the soldiers were snickering. Del Negro was close enough now to notice Isabella's bleeding foot.

"Why are we slicing up an Indian princess?" he demanded.

"The toes for trying to run away," the priest answered, cautiously. "The nose for infidelity."

"Infidelity. Who is the lucky devil?"

"She spent a night in the mine, with the slave, Raphael."

Del Negro dismounted, handing his horse's reins to a soldier. He walked up to Isabella, looking her over, carefully.

"So you are Raphael's woman?" he asked.

She thought she understood what he was saying, but made no attempt to answer. She looked into his strong face, wondering what he was thinking. Was there compassion in those intense blue eyes? Or only curiosity. Would he save her from the priest's bloody sentence? Or would he allow the priest to continue? There was nothing in his look that answered any of her questions. She watched and waited, like everyone else.

"Raphael's woman," Del Negro said to himself, thoughtfully, rubbing his bearded chin with the thumb and forefinger of his left hand. He looked down at her bloody foot. Some blood was still oozing out of the stubs, but the squirting had stopped.

Del Negro drew a knife from his belt, then looked at her face.

"If I cut your nose off, you would look more like Rafael," he said, gently. She did not respond, nor did she look away.

Suddenly the knife shot forward. Isabella closed her eyes. She did not scream, or try to turn away. Instead of cutting her nose, the knife cut the rawhide lashings holding

Chapter 8

her wrists to the pole. Not anticipating the sudden release in tension, she crumbled to the ground.

"How can we expect Indian slaves to be loyal and obedient if we're always cutting off something to teach them a lesson?" Del Negro asked, turning to the priest.

Then he turned to a second priest, a Franciscan padre named Carlos de Castilla, who had been traveling with Del Negro on his recent journey. The priest was a younger man, a little plump, with pink cheeks. He was dressed in brown robes.

"Take her," Del Negro said. "Have the women dress her wound and clean her up.

Chapter 9

Carlos Castilla and several Indian servants helped Isabella onto a horse. As the servants led the animal up a small canyon in an easterly direction, she began to feel a throbbing sensation in her foot, gradually increasing in intensity. The pain that had been absent when the toes were removed had finally made its onslaught. She began to feel dizzy, light-headed. She had trouble keeping her balance, and would have fallen from the horse, had the Indian at her side not grabbed her leg. Slumping forward on the horse's neck, she lost consciousness.

When Isabella came to, she found herself in a stone building. It was more than a stone hut, but smaller than the church. She was on her back on a corn husk mat, looking up at a ceiling of lodge pole rafters covered with lashed bundles of buffalo grass. She was alone, and from the sunlight coming in through the open door, she guessed it was the middle part of the day.

She moved her hands and feet to see if chains were restraining her. They were not. She was free to get up, and move about as she pleased. But she had no desire to get up. Her foot throbbed with pain. She looked at it, but could not see the wound. It was wrapped in a mat of clean, yellow grass, and bound with rawhide strings.

She noticed her dress had been changed. The soiled deerskin had been replaced with a thick smock made from the wool of sheep. The wool dress was rougher than the smoke-tanned deer skin, and made her skin itch.

Her hair was no longer matted, but clean and combed. Her skin felt clean, too. She wondered who had been caring for her. Even with the pain in her foot, she felt good.

But there was another pain, in her stomach. She was very hungry, and thirsty. Beside her mat was a clay jar with fresh water. She quenched her thirst, but could find nothing to eat. Rather than try to walk on her injured foot, she decided to be patient.

She didn't have to wait long. The priest in the brown robe, the one they called Fray Castilla, entered the room. Upon discovering she was awake, he gasped with delight. His smile was warm and genuine. She didn't feel threatened as she had with Fray Sinbad.

When he noticed she had been drinking the water, he turned and disappeared through the doorway. A minute later he returned with a tray containing flattened corncakes, smeared with mashed beans, boiled meat, and flavored with chopped onions, peppers and salt. She began wolfing down the food while the priest watched, the smile never leaving his face.

When she finished, Fray Castilla opened a large black book. He looked at the marks on the white pages and began saying things she didn't understand. At first, she thought he might be reading another punishment order, like Juan had done when she had been tied to the post at the top of the hill. But such was not the case.

Carefully, she watched the priest, soon figuring out that marks on the pages prompted the words coming from his mouth. Later, she learned this was called reading. Few at the

Chapter 9

Spanish settlement could do it--the two priests, the slave Juan, and Del Negro.

When the priest was finished, he taught her some words, mostly nouns. She was a willing student. He explained that Del Negro wanted her to learn Spanish.

When the language lesson was finished, he gently changed the dressing on her foot, humming to himself as he did so. Isabella felt safe.

Life fell into a simple routine for the Ute girl. Her days were spent eating, sleeping, learning Spanish, being read to, and caring for her wound. Within a few days she was moving about, with a wooden crutch.

When she went outside she could not see the church, mill, and the huts where she had stayed before. She guessed these were just over the hill to the west.

After several weeks, without warning, Del Negro entered her room. She felt frightened, uncertain. She knew he was the one who had ordered the fine treatment she was receiving, but she didn't know why. Del Negro had saved her from Sinbad's wrath. Still, he was a stranger, and a foreigner, and obviously different than the kind priest who had been taking care of her.

"Raphael's woman," he said. "how's the foot?"

"I'm not Raphael's woman," she said, surprising him with her Spanish. He looked at her, not sure whether or not to believe her.

"Why you bring me here?" she asked.

"To frustrate that damned Jesuit," he said, a hint of anger in his voice.

"Why you not like Sinbad?" she asked, seeing a chance to learn more about this strange place she had been brought to.

Del Negro looked intently at the Indian girl. She was as beautiful now as he first remembered her--tied to the post, blood squirting from her foot, defying the priest who was about to cut off her nose. Del Negro was glad he had saved her from the priest. He wondered how much she would

71

understand if he attempted to answer her questions. It did not matter. He found a stool beside her sleeping mat, and seated himself beside her. She did not withdraw as she would have done had Sinbad attempted to sit by her.

"My grandfather was Diego Penalosa," he began. "Have you heard of him? Of course not." He looked towards the window, wondering what his grandfather would have looked like as a young man. Isabella remained silent, intent on understanding the words of this bold stranger, who seemed very relaxed and talkative in her presence.

"He was governor of all New Mexico. Lived in a palace at Santa Fe. He was born in 1624 in Lima. Do you know about Peru?"

She shook her head.

"Someday I will tell you about the great Francisco Pizarro, and Peru. But today I tell you about my grandfather. As a young man, he was an *alcalde*, a justice, a captain of infantry, and eventually governor of the province of Omasuyas. That's when the Duke of Albuquerque persuaded him to come to Santa Fe and become governor and captain-general of all New Mexico."

Isabella would have been impressed had she been able to comprehend fully what he was saying. She had never heard of Peru or Omasuyas, but she knew of Santa Fe. That's where Oslero's mercury was coming from. She had no concept of what a justice, governor or captain-general might be. Still, she listened intently, hoping to glean as much as possible from Del Negro's words.

"In 1662, my grandfather set out to discover Teguayo. Surely you've heard of that." She had not.

"The legendary homeland of the Aztecs, far to the north of Mexico City, the place where much of their gold came from. In 1662, my grandfather went looking for that place. He headed north from Santa Fe, but when the Zunis told him there were Frenchmen out on the grassy plains to the northeast, he went in that direction."

"What is Frenchmen?" she asked.

Chapter 9

"A bunch of dirty, thieving *hijos de puta*," he said. She still didn't know what a Frenchman was, but by the tone of his voice, she guessed it was something undesirable. She shrugged her shoulders. Del Negro continued his narrative.

"He didn't find the French, but as he started west near the headwaters of the *Rio Tizon*, Indians told him about the land of Teguayo and the great lake, Copalla, just south of the salt sea, where the richest mines of Moqtegsuma (Montezuma) were located."

"Before they could reach Teguayo, they ran short of food. There was much arguing between my grandfather, Fray Freytas, the Jesuit chaplain for the expedition, and Michael de Noriega, the captain of my grandfather's troops. They decided to return to Santa Fe for more supplies."

"Upon reaching Santa Fe, without warning, my grandfather was arrested by the inquisition for using unrestrained language against Fray Freytas, and what they called blasphemy. He was taken to Mexico City in chains, where he was thrown in jail for 32 months. Upon his release, he was fined all his gold, silver, land, horses, cattle--all his personal possessions and wealth, and banished to Spain, forbidden to ever return to the New World."

Isabella wondered why Del Negro was taking the time to tell all this to a slave girl. She thought she understood most of what he was telling her, though she didn't know what the inquisition was. She didn't want to interrupt what she thought was an eloquent narrative by asking a lot of questions. Later, she could ask Fray Carlos.

"A yellow robe with a red cross on it," he continued, "The banner of Diego Penalosa's shame, still hangs in the cathedral at Cordova."

"Cordova?" she asked, unable to restrain her curiosity.

"The place of my birth, the place I come from in Spain," he explained, not annoyed by the interruption. "A beautiful place to some--many olive, pomegranate and orange groves. But it has not been a beautiful place for me and my family."

73

"I do not understand," she said.

"You do not understand the power of the Catholic church," he said. "The yellow robe is supposed to hang in the church for 500 years or more. During that time none of my grandfather's sons, grandsons and great-grandsons can hold public office, be officers in the military, or own land."

"What does it mean to own land?" she asked.

Del Negro was not surprised at her response. While the native peoples of the New World lived on the land and recognized somewhat vague territorial boundaries, they only used the land. They did not own it. They did not buy and sell land. They thought no more of owning the land than they did owning the sky or one of their gods.

"I own this sword," he said, quickly drawing the polished blade from its sheath. "If someone tries to take it from me, I fight." Without warning he made a quick, slicing motion with the blade, removing the wick from a lighted candle on a shelf above her head. Just as quickly, he returned the sword to its sheath.

"I own that magnificent black stallion you saw me riding the other day," he said.

"A very beautiful animal," she said. "I would like to ride him."

"Because of the yellow robe, I cannot own land, but I own you," he said, ignoring her comment about wanting to ride his horse. "You are my slave. You must obey. If I send you to the mines to work, you must go. If I want to, I can give you to a soldier, or sell you to the Comanches. If I tell you to remove your clothes and get into my bed you must do it."

Isabella looked into Victorio's handsome face, wondering if he was finally getting around to his reason for spending this time with her. She liked this man. She felt herself responding to the energy that flowed from him. She liked the articulate manner in which he expressed himself. But she did not like the way he described his ownership of her. It made her want to defy him as she had defied the priest. But she still didn't know what was inside this unusual man. Was there a capacity to be gentle and kind, or was he more inclined to selfishness and cruelty."

"Do you own Raphael?" she asked, challenging what she perceived as smugness.

"Of course, I own Raphael," he said, a tone of surprise in his voice.

"He does not work in your mines. He does not till your fields," she said, not aware her voice was getting louder. "If Raphael was a woman, he would not sleep in your bed."

"*Me cago en la hostia,*" he said. "Should have killed that man. Maybe I will today."

"Perhaps if you were kind to him, treated him like a man instead of a horse, he would do your work," she offered.

"When my horse misbehaves I dig him with spurs," he said. "When he works well for me I give him corn. If I gave him corn when he misbehaved, he would soon be a worthless horse.

"Raphael is not a horse," she said. "A horse receives better treatment."

"If I was kind to the slaves who defied me, soon they would all defy me," he said. "The work at the mines would stop, and they would try to kill me."

"Why did you come here, to this land of my people?" she asked, changing the subject.

"To save my family," he said, with an intensity she had not seen in him before. "To get gold and silver, so I can pay the church to take down that damnable robe at Cordova. So my brothers and children can hold their heads up and once again enjoy the respectability and honor that was once ours. That's why I take slaves and put them to work in the mines. Usually I kill men who refuse my orders."

"Why don't you kill Raphael?"

"I hope to find a way to make him do my work. A dead man cannot dig gold."

"Raphael is a man, not a horse," she said, gently. "Give him a reason to work for you."

"What are you saying?" he asked, frustration in his voice. He looked towards the door, obviously thinking about leaving.

"I don't know," she said. "I have to think about it."

"Why don't you do that," he growled. He turned and disappeared through the open doorway.

Chapter 10

Life fell into a regular routine for Isabella. After cleaning up in the morning, taking care of a few household chores, she usually spent time with the gentle priest learning Spanish, history, and, of course the Catholic religion from the big book the priest called the *Santa Biblia*.

In time, the pain left her foot, and she was able to throw away her cane. She was given more work to do, mainly household and garden chores. Still she was free to, more or less, come and go as she pleased. The Spanish soldiers, who often looked at her, seemed to understand they must leave her alone.

Though Del Negro's rubble stone building, which served both as his living quarters and administrative headquarters, was not far away, she did not speak to him often. Frequently he was gone, but when he was home, he seemed totally engrossed in managing his mines, smelters, and the labors of his Spanish companions and Indian slaves.

Early one afternoon, she found herself alone, and unsupervised. Fray Carlos had left on horseback with Del Negro and wasn't expected back until evening. She decided to visit the abandoned mine where she guessed the slave, Raphael, was still in chains.

Quickly, she threw some tortillas, meat, fresh vegetables and several candles into a bag. She stuffed some ruffled juniper bark and embers from the cook fire into a leather pouch. Then she headed for the mine, trying to follow the less-traveled trails, where she would not be noticed. No one had told her she could not visit Raphael. Still, she sensed the Spanish would not approve of what she was doing.

Upon reaching the entrance to the mine, she removed the juniper bundle from the leather pouch and began puffing on the hot embers. When the bark burst into flame, she lit one of the candles and entered the mine, remembering to stay left as she had done that dark night when the priest was following her.

With the light of the candle, the tunnel didn't seem nearly so frightening. Nor was it as far as she thought it would be to the place where Raphael was chained to the wall, where he had saved her from falling down the vertical shaft.

In the flickering candlelight, she spotted the slave reclining against a pine timber. He knew she was coming, having heard her entering the tunnel.

Raphael wasn't nearly as ugly as she thought he would be. In fact, she guessed he would actually have been handsome had not part of his nose been missing. His shoulder-length hair covered the scars where his ears had been removed. What made him handsome to her, she supposed, was the intensity of his black eyes, and his well-muscled body. He was remarkably healthy for a man kept on the end of a chain in a black tunnel. Though frequently tortured and abused by the Spanish, they nevertheless kept him fed.

He surprised her by greeting her in Spanish. She returned his greeting as she dropped the bag of food supplies at his side.

Raphael reached in the bag for one of the corn tortillas and began chewing on it. He didn't attempt to get up. She dropped to her knees beside him.

Chapter 10

When he finished the tortilla, he rummaged through the bag examining the various food items, and the candles.

"*Gracias,*" he said, sincerely.

"*De nada,*" she responded, surprised again at his Spanish. After a few more exchanges of words, it was apparent Raphael spoke very good Spanish. She didn't remember him speaking the language of their captors the first time they met. But she didn't know their language at that time, so even if he had tried to speak it, she wouldn't have understood him. She was pleased with her discovery. Now they could communicate.

"Why do you refuse to do the work of the Spanish?" she asked.

"I am not their slave," he said. "So I do not do their work."

"You are not their slave?" she asked, bewildered. "You are in Spanish chains, in a Spanish tunnel. You don't know from one day to the next if they are going to feed you or kill you. When you make them angry they beat you, or cut off a toe or an ear. And you say you are not their slave?"

"A slave does the work of his master," Raphael said, his voice still calm. "I do not do the work of the Spanish. I am not their slave. Yes, they can cut off pieces of me, even kill me, but they cannot make me do their work. So I am not their slave."

"Is there a reason for your stubbornness?" she responded. "Or are you stupid or lazy?"

Raphael reached in the bag for another tortilla, ignoring her last question. He rolled a piece of boiled meat in the tortilla and took a bite. Isabella sat down beside Raphael, her back against the wall, and waited for him to speak.

"Why do you think I speak such good Spanish?" he asked.

"I do not know. It surprises me," she said.

"Do you know Juan, the Navajo who helps the priests?"

"Yes."

"I used to do his work. They taught me their language, their religion. Del Negro said he was taking me back to Spain with him. They baptized me."

"I am not baptized," she said. "I refuse."

"I did not refuse."

"Why are you different now?" she asked.

"One day I was very sick," he said.

"They were mean to you?"

"No. They left me alone, to die or get well."

Raphael reached in the bag and pulled out another candle. The one Isabella had brought with her into the cave was getting short. He lit the new candle and placed it beside the one that would soon be burned out.

"During the night, I was burning with fever, and thought I might die. I crawled to the top of a little hill behind the *visita*, hoping the cool night breeze might save me.

"It was the moon of red cherries. When morning came I was on my back, looking up at the sky. The wind was strong. Many clouds had come. I could hear distant thunder. It appeared rain would come, but I could not make my body move to take me back to the *visita*.

"Then far away, I saw two strikes of lightening. They did not go away, as is usual with lightening, but continued towards me. For a minute they looked more like flaming arrows than lightening. They continued towards me.

"Just when I thought I would be struck and killed by the two flaming arrows, they turned upward in the air, and stopped. They were not flaming arrows, nor were they bolts of lightening, but two warriors, standing in the air. They beckoned for me to follow them."

Raphael stopped talking. He put the last of the tortilla and meat into his mouth, chewing slowly, thoughtfully. Isabella did not speak. A voice deep inside her told her she was hearing something very important. Patiently, she waited for Raphael to continue.

"A minute earlier, I was too weak to return to the *visita*, but now I was able to follow the two flaming warriors. I do not know if my body was able to follow them, or only my spirit. All I know is that I followed them high into the sky. We went to a place where the white clouds were as big as mountains. There was no ground, but I was not afraid of falling.

"The two flaming Indians stepped to each side of me, both pointing up high in the sky. At first, all I could see was a dark spot. But it grew larger. Finally, I could identify it as an eagle, a spotted eagle, the biggest I had ever seen. And it was flying to me.

"As the big bird drew near, I could see it was not like any eagle I had ever seen. It had only one eye, in the middle of its forehead. And it wore a headdress containing three large feathers. It spoke to me, telling me to turn around and look at the faces of my people.

"I turned, but all I could see was a huge billowing cloud. But as I looked closer, into the cloud, I began to see faces. I saw my father who had died, my mother, many friends and members of some of the Goshute clans, my women and two of my children. The faces were not happy, but drawn tight with hunger, fear of hunger, and the worry of a people who do not have enough to eat. The sadness in their faces was so powerful I thought I would die if I did not look away.

"The eagle told me to look at the clouds in front of me and behold those of my people who were not yet born. Again I saw faces, but this time they were not familiar. But I knew they were Goshute faces, boys and girls, young men and women--all young faces, glowing with hope and happiness.

"The eagle now told me to behold the warrior. At first I could see nothing. Then I saw a naked warrior, on a magnificent, bay stallion, galloping towards me. He carried a flaming lance in his right hand. His face looked strangely familiar as he pulled the horse to a halt in front of me. Finally, I recognized the face of the warrior. It was mine. He was me. He did not say anything.

"The bay horse reared high in the air, pawing at the

sky in the direction of the setting sun. The warrior, who was me, pointed his flaming lance in the same direction. I looked where he was pointing, and saw nothing. Then I saw twelve black spots coming towards me. Soon, I could tell they were horses, black horses, and they were running as fast as they could.

"The bay stallion reared again, pawing to the north. When the warrior shook his lance in that direction, twelve more spots appeared. Soon, I could see they were white horses, also running towards me. When he pointed his lance to the east, I saw twelve sorrel horses running towards me, then twelve buckskins from the south.

"When all the horses had arrived and were prancing about, the warrior who looked like me, got off the bay horse and let it roll in what appeared to be a cloud of white dust. As it rolled, its features became blurred. As it began to get up, I could see it was no longer a horse, but a bull buffalo.

"The warrior killed the buffalo with the flaming spear. When he was finished, those of my people, whom I had seen in the clouds behind me, rushed forward and began eating the buffalo. The expressions of hunger and worry disappeared. It was time for feasting and celebration.

"When they had eaten the buffalo, they crawled on the many horses, and galloped after the warrior who was me, in the direction of the daybreak star, looking for more buffalo, leaving me and the spotted eagle alone. The two warriors who had escorted me to this strange place were gone.

"The spotted eagle called me Raphael. I was surprised he used my Spanish name instead of my Goshute name.

"When I told him my name was Rabbit Runner, he said that was no longer my name. He said my name was Raphael until I brought many horses to my people. I asked him how I could bring many horses to my people when I was a slave of the Spanish."

Raphael paused in his narrative. Looking down, between his knees, he began drawing the form of an eagle in the dirt, using his finger as the writing tool. The eagle had a single eye, and three feathers in its head.

"What else did the eagle say?" Isabella asked, not about to let Raphael stop before his story was finished.

"He said I was not a Spanish slave unless I chose to be. He said I should leave the Spanish and get horses for my people."

"Where are you supposed to get the horses?" she asked.

"I do not know."

"What else did the eagle say?"

"Some things that are unspeakable."

"You can't tell me?"

"No. The eagle flew away and I found myself on the hill above the mission, on my back, looking up at the clouds. I was no longer sick."

"And you were no longer a slave," she said.

"I gathered up some food and began walking back to the land of my birth. When the Spanish found me, they brought me back here and cut off two toes. The next time I tried to leave they cut off two more. I have been in chains since that time, but they have not been able to make me do their work. When they tell me I must work, I remember the eagle's words when he said I was not a slave."

"Do you not fear the Spanish?" she asked.

"I did before the vision. Not now."

"How many horses will you bring to your people if you die?" Isabella asked, thinking it was just a matter of time until the Spanish killed Raphael for his stubbornness. "Wouldn't you have a better chance of escaping if you were a willing slave? At least you wouldn't be in chains."

"The eagle said I was not a slave unless I choose to be. I choose not to be."

"Even if it gets you killed?"

"If the Spanish were going to kill me, they would have done it by now. The eagle said I must get horses for my people. I must believe the powers of the eagle will keep me alive to do what I have been chosen to do."

"You are foolish," Isabella said. "How will you get around if they cut off more of your toes?"

"Just fine, if I am riding one of those horses I saw in the sky."

"How will you get out of here?"

"Maybe you will bring me a tool to cut the chain," he said. "And perhaps some moccasins, a shirt, some food for my journey, and a knife."

"And what will the Spanish do to me if they catch me helping you?"

"You are too beautiful to kill," he said, thoughtfully. "Perhaps they will rape you."

Isabella stood up. Enough had been said. She wanted to go. She was deeply moved by Raphael's story, but deeply troubled by his stubbornness, and his fearless attitude towards the powerful Spanish. She wondered how close she wanted to get to a man she sensed was certain to be the cause of much bloodshed and trouble. Without another word, she turned to leave.

"Will you bring me the things I need?" he asked. Without giving him an answer, she hurried down the tunnel towards the afternoon light.

Chapter 11

When Isabella returned to the settlement, she was suddenly distracted from her thoughts of helping Raphael with his escape.

Islero had returned, but his return was not the happy reunion Isabella had anticipated. There had been a slave revolt at one of the mines. Two Spaniards had been killed, and some horses and mules stolen. Islero had killed four of the rebellious savages, and captured seven more.

When Isabella arrived, the seven captives had iron collars on their necks, and were secured to a long chain at four-foot intervals. The ends of the chain were attached to two trees. There was enough slack to allow the row of prisoners to kneel, but not sit or lay down.

The mission bells sounded, calling everyone to assemble at the headquarters building to witness the fate of the prisoners. Because two Spaniards had been killed, everyone knew the punishment would be more severe than a routine lashing with a bullwhip, or the removal of a few toes.

While the people were assembling, Isabella sought out Islero who had just finished a meeting with Del Negro. It didn't occur to her to feel malice towards Islero, the man who had taken her by force from her family and friends and made her a slave. She knew only that during a period of extreme crisis she had found refuge under Islero's strong arm. He had been like a father to her. When Islero was near, she felt safe.

She hadn't seen him for what seemed a very long time. She hoped he was still her protector and friend.

"Islero," she called to get his attention. He was beginning to walk in the opposite direction. He stopped, noticing a familiarity in the voice, but unsure. She ran to him. Before the surprised captain could turn fully around, the girl was standing in front of him, smiling.

Islero's first reaction was to back away, not used to public friendliness from slaves, especially those of the female gender.

"Isabella," he said, with hesitation, gradually remembering the shy, pretty Indian girl he had befriended, and given protection. He remembered how he had let her help with the horses, and how she had become attached to him.

When she began asking questions, he was amazed at her new-found fluency in his native language. She explained how Fray Carlos had been teaching her Spanish, and a lot of other things. Islero seemed pleased, but he did not have time to renew a friendship with an Indian girl. There was pressing business at hand, the punishment of the seven slaves.

Islero asked Isabella to take his horse and put it away. He advised her to take her time, and perhaps not come back at all. The punishment of the prisoners would not be pleasant.

"What did they do?" she asked.

"Killed two Spaniards," he said, gravely.

"Did they deserve it?" she asked.

Islero did not respond immediately. It was not a slave girl's place to ask such a question. What had the priest been teaching this girl? What kind of dangerous ideas were being placed in that beautiful little head?

"No Spaniard deserves to die at the hands of a slave,"

he finally responded, authority in his voice. "Nothing can justify what they did."

"What will happen to them?" she asked, undaunted by his obvious criticism of her questioning.

"They will die, all of them."

"How?"

"That is for Victorio to decide."

She didn't say anything more. She handed the reins back to Islero, and started walking towards the chained prisoners. She felt an irresistible urge to see the men who were about to die. She wanted to see their faces, maybe even learn their names. She didn't know why. It seemed she should be afraid to face men who were about to die, but she felt no fear. She didn't understand her feelings. She knew only what she had to do, and Islero did not try to stop her.

"*Como se llama?*" she said to the first prisoner, thinking there was a better chance he understood Spanish than Ute. He was a young man with broad shoulders and shoulder-length hair. He looked taller and stronger than any of the others.

Other than giving her a quick, defiant glance, the warrior did not respond to her question, not even when she repeated it a second time. She could only guess at his reasons for being cold and distant. Possibly, he thought she was like Juan, a trusted friend and servant of the Spanish, or perhaps a mistress to one of the soldiers who was going to kill him. Or was he just feeling bad about his approaching appointment with death, and didn't want to speak to anyone, Indian or Spanish.

When he gave her that quick, defiant glance, she saw his face. It was the handsome, strong face of a young warrior who ought to be out chasing buffalo, or protecting his family band, she thought. Such a fine, young brave did not belong in a black hole, digging what to him were meaningless rocks for trespassers from across the big water.

She moved to the second captive, but before she could ask him his name, the crowd of Indian slaves and Spaniards

87

around her suddenly became quiet. Victorio Del Negro had emerged from the headquarters building and was walking towards the prisoners.

Isabella stepped back in an effort to disappear into the crowd. She wanted to watch Del Negro, the prisoners, to observe what was about to happen, but didn't want to be noticed herself.

By the time Del Negro reached the prisoners, Islero was at his side. There was a grim expression on the handsome face of Del Negro. His jaw was firm. The punishing of slaves was serious business.

Upon reaching the slaves, the two soldiers parted, Del Negro striding to the right end of the string of slaves, Islero to the left. Each turned to face the slave in front of him. Both drew their razor sharp swords. Islero looked towards Del Negro, waiting for the command to commence the work of death. Del Negro was staring into the face of the young warrior, the one Isabella had tried to talk to a few moments earlier.

"*Parada,*" shouted a voice from across the square. It was Fray Sinbad. He was running clumsily towards the prisoners, his black robes catching on his knees. When he arrived, Del Negro was impatiently tapping the tip of his sword against the toe of his boot.

"Why was I not invited to this execution?" the out-of-breath priest demanded.

"The prisoners did not request your holy presence," Del Negro responded, quickly. He was obviously annoyed at the arrival of the clergy.

"Have you forgotten the king's law?" Sinbad demanded. "Condemned slaves must be baptized before execution. Mandates from his holy majesty cannot be ignored. Or can they?"

Del Negro didn't bother to answer the last question. Fuming, he stepped back, the signal for the priest to conduct his holy business. With Juan acting as assistant, Sinbad removed the lid from his vial of holy water and approached one of the slaves, who by his cowering demeanor, seemed to have no objection to becoming a Catholic prior to execution. In fact, the condemned Indian seemed so eager to participate in the ceremony, that he reached out to Juan, in a begging gesture, offering to hold the vial of holy water while the ceremony was being performed. Juan, after receiving an approving nod from the priest, patronized the slave by handing him the vial. Sinbad was obviously pleased to see a savage so eager to participate in the saving ordinances of the Catholic Church.

As the priest began to make some remarks, preparatory to baptism, the slave suddenly raised the vial to his lips and began gulping down the holy water. Before Juan could grab it away from him, the savage tossed it to the next slave, who finished off the contents.

As Juan finally grabbed the empty vial and started running towards the *visita* to get more holy water, quiet snickering could be heard among those who watched, both Indians and Spanish. All had silent admiration for a man who dared mock a priest. Only the condemned would dare such a thing, and Del Negro.

Ignoring the snickering, Sinbad was shaking his head with disappointment, and confusion. Here he was, a man of God, going to a lot of trouble to save the souls of these savages from endless torment in purgatory, and all they could think to do was mock him and his holy calling. It didn't occur to Sinbad that the condemned men had been in the hot sun all day with nothing to drink.

When Juan returned, Sinbad ordered two men to hold the slaves' arms while the Jesuit administered the holy baptism and last rites. The condemned had no idea what the priest was trying to accomplish with his holy water and Latin prayers, and they didn't care.

When Sinbad finished, he hurried back to the *visita*, Juan close behind. Del Negro appeared, calling for the *vaqueros* to get on their horses and bring their ropes. Spanish cowboys took much pride in their skills with the *lazo* or rawhide rope. When four riders appeared, ropes in hand, Del Negro ordered them to catch the feet of the prisoners. Since the neck collars on the prisoners were attached to the long chain stretched between the two trees above their heads, it would be a simple matter, once the feet were roped, to stretch out the prisoners and kill them by strangulation or by breaking their necks.

But roping their feet was no simple matter. The prisoners, though attached to the chain with iron neck collars, were free to hop about in their efforts to keep their feet out of the rawhide loops.

The spectators stepped back as the mounted riders charged in, loops swinging, horses churning up the dust. Most of the prisoners kicked and danced their way out of the first three or four loops. Had they been free to run, some probably would have escaped, but secured to the long chain, it was just a matter of time until each of the slaves had at least one foot roped, and that was enough. Once the rider had one foot or two in his loop, he would dally the other end of the rope around the saddle horn, spin his horse away from the slave and dig spurs into the horse's sides. Some of the prisoners' necks broke immediately as the horse hit the end of the rope. Others were strangled as the horse leaned into the rope, holding the prisoners in an outstretched position until the man was dead.

The spectators began cheering as the unusual form of execution progressed. No one could be certain whether the cheering was for the Indians who were dancing to avoid being caught, or the *vaqueros* who were doing the catching.

Nevertheless, after about five minutes, the dust settled and all seven prisoners were dead. Everyone returned to their work at the mission, barracks, fields, or smelter--everyone except Isabella, who was seated cross-legged in the dust, staring at the blank, dusty faces of the men who had died.

She hated Sinbad. She hated Del Negro. She hated all Spanish. She hated this place. She longed to go home.

Chapter 12

"You do not want to learn today," Fray Castilla said the next morning. He was irritated at Isabella's uncooperative attitude. Besides, he had a headache. He didn't feel good. He had consumed too much wine following the executions the previous afternoon.

The priest was trying to teach Isabella a passage from the book of Matthew, but she was refusing to recite back to him. He read the verse for the fourth time. " 'Ask, and it shall be given you; seek, and ye shall find; knock, and it shall be opened unto you.' Now, you say it!"

"I do not want to learn anything more from your holy book," Isabella said, her voice getting louder as she continued to talk. "I do not want to learn anymore of your language. I do not want to meet anymore of your people."

"What do you want?" the gentle priest asked.

"I want the Spanish to go back to Spain. I want the slaves to return to their families and hunt buffalo. I want to go home."

"Wanting something doesn't make it so," he cautioned.

" 'Ask, and it shall be given you; seek, and ye shall

find; knock, and it shall be opened unto you,' '' she said, reciting perfectly the passage the priest had been trying to teach her.

For the first time that morning, Fray Castilla smiled. His pretty subject had been listening after all.

"I want to go home," she repeated.

"Did you see the execution of the seven slaves?" he asked.

"Yes. I want to go home. I don't like Del Negro, or Islero anymore."

"I thought perhaps seeing those men die might motivate you to want to stay," the priest said, carefully.

"I think you had too much wine this morning," she said.

"Have I ever told you the story of Esther?" he said, ignoring her comment about his drinking.

"I do not want to hear anymore stories from your holy book," she said.

"Esther was like you," he said, pushing ahead in spite of her objection.

"Was she Ute?" she asked.

"No. Jewish."

"The same tribe your Catholic Jesus belonged to. I am not interested in this Esther."

"But you should be."

"Why?"

"Her people, the Jews, were slaves, much like the Utes, Navajos and Goshutes are slaves to the Spanish. She saved them all. Maybe you could learn something from Esther's story that could help you save some of your people, or at least make their lives more bearable."

"Why do you care about that?" she asked, still not wanting to hear the story of Esther.

"You were right when you said I drank too much wine this morning. I drank too much last night, too. Do you know why?"

"No."

Chapter 12

"Those executions bothered me as much as they did you."

"I do not believe you. Indians died yesterday, not Spanish."

"They were children of God."

"Not children of your Catholic Jesus."

"I did not come here to get gold," he said, ignoring her defiance.

"All Spanish come for gold," she said.

"Not me. I came to help save the souls of heathen peoples, to bring them to Christ, to save their eternal souls, to make their lives better and happier."

"How does making a man a slave in a mine make his life better and happier?" she asked.

"I see now that it does not," he said, humbly. "The church and the true religion of Christ are being used by greedy men to get rich. I am part of this evil game, and can do nothing to stop it. So I drink wine, too much wine."

"If you, a priest, can do nothing, then I can do nothing, either."

"Don't say that until you hear Esther's story."

"How could this Esther be more powerful than a priest?"

"She was a beautiful woman, and she had much courage. Sit down. I will tell you her story."

Isabella sat on a wooden stool, looked at the priest, and waited for him to begin.

Fray Castilla seated himself on another stool, facing the Indian girl.

"Over two thousand summers ago," he began, "Far across the big water, many moons travel beyond the land of Spain, there lived a great king. His name was Ahasuerus. He ruled 127 provinces or tribal homelands, from a place called India to Ethiopia.

"During the third year of his reign, he gathered together the chiefs from the many provinces for a huge feast or celebration. After seven days, the king ordered his queen,

Vashti, to appear before the chiefs so they could enjoy her beauty. She refused, perhaps because the king was drunk. Perhaps because she was shy.

"When the king asked his wise men what he should do about her disobedience, they said she should be punished. Otherwise, women throughout the kingdom would follow her example and show disobedience to their husbands. Ahasuerus took away Vashti's possessions and sent her away. Immediately, his counselors began the search for a new queen."

"I like this Vashti," Isabella said. "What happened to her."

"I don't know. The scriptures say nothing more about her. But the search for a new queen lasted four years. During that time Ahasuerus tried out hundreds of young women in his search for a queen."

"What do you mean when you say 'tried out?' " she asked.

"Each evening a new woman was sent to the king's palace. She would return in the morning."

"A new one every night?" Isabella asked. "Didn't the king tire of that?"

"I don't know, but after four years he picked a Jewish girl, Esther, as his new queen."

"Were all of the girls Jewish, that he tried out?" she asked..

"No. There were not very many Jews in the kingdom, and they were looked down upon, like the Goshutes are by the Utes and Shoshones."

"The Jews did not have horses?" she asked.

"That had nothing to do with it. The Jews had as many horses as anyone, perhaps more. Other tribes just didn't like them."

"If she was Jewish, why then did Ahasuerus pick her to be his queen?" she asked.

"The king did not know she was Jewish, only that she was very beautiful, and he liked her more than all the other girls he had considered to take as his wife and queen."

"How was Esther different than the others?" Isabella asked.

"I don't know, only that she was very beautiful. I suppose the others were beautiful, too. But only Esther was picked to be queen. And she was Jewish. But nobody knew it, except her stepfather, Mordecai, and her Jewish friends."

"I still don't know why you are telling me about Esther," Isabella said, growing impatient.

"You will soon. After Esther had been queen for five years, a man named Haman talked the king into passing a law that on the thirteenth day of the last moon, all the Jews in the kingdom would be killed."

"Why would anyone want that?" she asked.

"Some of your people would like to kill all the Shoshones. It was probably something like that. All I know for sure is that Haman hated Esther's stepfather, Mordecai, and somehow convinced the king that all Jews, including Mordecai, should be killed."

"So what did Esther do?"

"She told the king she was Jewish, and convinced him that Mordecai and the rest of the Jews should not die."

"Did the king agree to save the Jews?"

"Yes."

"How did she convince him to change the law?"

"He did it because Esther was his queen and he loved her."

"Why are you telling me this?" Isabella asked, already guessing what he was going to say.

"Victorio Del Negro, you might say, is king of this little part of the world."

"Victorio is no king," she argued.

"No, but hundreds of Indians, including many Utes, live or die at his command."

"I am not his queen. He does not love me. He probably doesn't even remember my name."

"I tell him everything you do. I assure you he is

interested. You could be his queen. You could help your people, more than anyone else.''

"I don't think Del Negro cares anything about me.''

"Why do you think I spend so much of my time teaching you our language and our ways? Because he commanded it. Why do you think none of the Spaniards try to take you as their woman? Because he commands them not to. Why do you think you do not have to work hard like the other slaves? Because Del Negro does not want you to. Why do you think Fray Sinbad no longer bothers you?''

There was silence as Isabella considered what the priest was telling her. She was amazed that it hadn't occurred to her why she was being treated better than the other slaves.

"But I don't love him. Yesterday, I watched him kill seven men who did not deserve to die. I can never love such a man.''

"He's killed many more than seven in his quest for gold," the priest said. "But that cannot be changed. The question I have is how many more he will kill, or how many more he will not kill, if you are at his side, persuading him to be more kind.''

"I am not Esther. I am not Del Negro's queen. You cannot make me do that.''

"I can't make you do anything," the meek priest responded. "I told you the story of Esther to help you see the power you have to help your people, if you choose to do so. If you choose not to, that is your decision.''

"I want to help my people," Isabella said, tears suddenly in her eyes. "But not the way you say. I do not want to be Del Negro's woman. I want to free Raphael, the Goshute chained in the tunnel. Will you give me a tool to cut his chain, a shirt, some food, and a knife? I want to take these things to him so he can escape and get horses for his people.''

"Do you know what would happen to me if I gave you these things, and Del Negro found out?" the priest asked.

"He wouldn't kill you, a priest. Or would he?''

"He would, in a minute.''

Chapter 12

"Will you give me the things I ask for?" she asked, persistent in her request. The priest turned from her, walked to a table where he poured some wine from a clay jar into a clay cup. Instead of sipping the wine, he gulped it down, spilling some on his brown robe. After replacing the empty cup on the table, he turned slowly to face Isabella.

"Come to my hut after dark. I will give you the things you ask for."

Chapter 13

It was well past midnight, and all the candles in the huts had been snuffed out, when Isabella approached Fray Carlos' hut. There was a half moon in the eastern sky. In her hand was a bag containing candles, moccasins, food and a bundle of bark containing embers from her fire.

Even though Fray Castilla said he would give her the things she asked for, she still had doubts that a Spaniard would really give her the things Raphael needed for his escape. She found it hard to accept at face value a situation in which a Spaniard would risk his life to help a slave. She was worried that the timid priest, upon getting sober, might change his mind.

She tapped lightly on the plank door. Almost immediately the door opened inward. She could see nothing. There was no light.

Silently, she waited until Fray Carlos appeared. He was agitated, looking first to the right, then to the left. Quickly, he handed her a hammer and chisel, a knife, and a buckskin shirt. Without a word, he disappeared behind the door and closed it tightly as she placed the things in her bag.

In the partial darkness, she had no trouble finding her way to the tunnel. She had been there twice before and the trail was becoming familiar. Every once in a while, she stopped in the shadows of a tree and watched the moon-lit trail behind her, just to make sure she wasn't being followed.

Upon reaching the entrance to the tunnel, she unraveled her bark bundle and puffed on one of the embers until it burst into flames. She lit one of the candles and entered the shaft.

Raphael already knew how to use a hammer and chisel. With little more than a word of greeting to Isabella, he went to work. She held the candle so he could see what he was doing, but not so close as to get in his way. He held a rag over the butt of the chisel to muffle the sound of iron striking iron. In about five minutes, his foot was free of the ankle bracelet.

"I'm going with you," Isabella said as he slipped into the buckskin shirt and began to button it up.

"You can't keep up," he said.

Isabella didn't like his comment. Maybe he didn't want a woman to tag along, but he didn't need to be so abrupt about it. After all, she had brought him the things he needed for his escape. She had done it at substantial risk, not only to herself, but Fray Carlos as well. Besides, she didn't think she would have much trouble keeping up with a man who was missing most of his toes.

"Don't forget who brought you the chisel and hammer. I am going with you," she said, firmly.

Without another word, Raphael jumped to his feet and headed out the tunnel, leaving the hammer and chisel behind, but taking the rest of the things. Isabella was close behind.

"I will go with you only as far as the Valley of the Yutas and the great mountain, Timpanogos," she said, but wasn't sure he was listening.

By the time the stars began to fade in the gray morning sky, the Rock Creek settlement was far behind. Even with the missing toes, Raphael maintained a steady and rapid pace. Isabella began to wonder if she really would be able to keep up with him. She began to hope he would stop for a rest. Still, it felt good to be free. No matter how weary she became, she was determined not to quit and go back.

She realized the traveling wouldn't have been nearly so hard had they merely been walking on flat ground. But they were going uphill, climbing out of the Colorado River drainage to the divide where they would begin their ascent into the Great Basin drainage.

Even though Raphael had not been happy about her coming with him, he did not try to make the journey unnecessarily difficult for her. He carried the bag containing provisions for both of them, and whenever they had to crawl up a ledge, or traverse a steep side hill, or cross an unusually deep or swift stream, he would take her by the hand.

When the sun finally appeared in a blue mountain sky, they stopped in the cover of an aspen grove to eat and rest. After drinking deeply from a cool mountain spring, they ate tortillas and boiled meat. Isabella fell asleep before finishing the last of her food.

It was mid-morning when she awakened. The muscles in her legs and back were sore. Even though she had slept, she still felt tired. But she quickly forgot about her discomfort. Raphael was gone. Her first thought was that he had abandoned her, but when she noticed he had not taken the bag containing their provisions, she was not sure.

She waited for what seemed a long time, no longer able to sleep because of the uncertainty facing her. She was seriously considering picking up the bag and continuing westward alone, when Raphael finally appeared. He said he had climbed a nearby hill so he could look back towards Rock Creek to see if the Spanish were following their trail. He said he had seen nothing to indicate they were being followed.

He said he had found a good trail headed west, but that it did not appear to be one used by the Spanish. He had decided to use the trail on their journey. Isabella offered no objection. Raphael picked up the bag and they were on their way again.

While the stiffness soon left the muscles in her legs and

101

back, the discomfort from bruises and sores on her feet remained constant. But she didn't complain. Raphael was taking her home. She was happy.

They saw many deer and elk tracks in the dust on the trail, even an occasional bear or lion track, but no horse or human footprints. Nor were there any other signs of human use along the trail--no abandoned campsites, no trail markers cut into trees, no piles of rocks along the side of the trail.

They traveled the rest of the day and long into the night before stopping again in an aspen grove. Again, Isabella fell into a deep sleep. It didn't matter that the night air carried the hint of frost. She was too tired to notice.

With Isabella settled comfortably on the forest floor, Raphael drew his new knife from his belt and went to work cutting sticks, quickly fashioning three figure-four triggering devices, two of which he placed under flat rocks, and one under a log--all on nearby small game trails.

About mid-morning Isabella was awakened by the smell of roasting flesh. Raphael had trapped a porcupine and a rabbit in his traps. He had already cleaned and skinned the porcupine, which was roasting over the fire on a green sapling.

As the smell of roasting flesh filled her nostrils, Isabella's belly began to ache with hunger. Saliva began gushing from under her tongue, forcing her to swallow again and again. She never remembered being so hungry in her entire life.

She didn't have to fight the pangs of hunger long. She and Raphael began feasting on the juicy flesh of the big rodent. The feast continued until all the meat was gone, interrupted only by trips to a nearby spring to gulp down cold, thirst-quenching water.

Raphael had thrown the rabbit in their bag to save for the evening meal. When they finished eating, he gathered up his traps, and once again they were on their way, feeling a little more confident than the day before, that Victorio Del Negro would not be able to find them.

Chapter 13

The next afternoon while crossing a grassy flat, Isabella stepped on a cactus. Several of the spines penetrated her deerskin moccasin. After making themselves comfortable in some tall grass, Isabella removed the moccasin and pushed her foot towards Raphael so he could try to remove the spine ends from her foot.

"Where will you go to find horses for your people?" she asked, as he removed the last cactus spine.

"The horses I saw in my medicine dream were larger and more beautiful than the bands of wild horses in the land of my birth," he responded, thoughtfully. "I don't know if I am supposed to get fine horses, like the ones in my dream, or be content with catching the wild desert ponies. What do you think?"

"Did those in your dream look like Spanish horses?" she asked.

"Yes. All of them looked like Del Negro's horse, except there were other colors in addition to black."

"Maybe you should get Spanish horses," she suggested.

"Where could I find such good animals?"

"At Rock Creek. Islero and Del Negro have many fine horses."

"Do you think I would go back to the place where I was in chains so long?"

"The kind of animals you want are at Rock Creek. You know where they keep the horses, and where the best trails are. Do you know a better place get what you want?"

Raphael could hardly believe what he was hearing. For years, his most burning desire had been to leave Rock Creek, never to return. Now this Ute girl was offering a very convincing argument for his voluntary return to a place that had been hell to him. It was something to think about. He would not decide now.

Raphael picked up one of Isabella's moccasins, holding it with the toe pointing upward, and nodded for her to slip her foot into it. As she did so, he took a firm grip on her ankle and helped guide her foot into the moccasin.

When the foot piece was in place, he did not let go of her foot. He maintained his grip, slowly caressing her smooth skin with his forefinger. When she tried to pull her foot away, his grip only tightened.

"It has been nearly three years since I have been with a woman," he said, still looking down at her foot.

Isabella couldn't believe what she was hearing. She couldn't believe Raphael would hold onto her foot like this. It hadn't occurred to her that the man with a sacred mission from the great spirit to bring horses to the Goshutes, would want to be romantic. Then again maybe he wasn't being driven by a romantic urge. Perhaps he just wanted to rut like a bull elk. Either way, she wanted no part of it.

"Let go of my foot," she said, her voice calm and firm.

"It has been three years since I was with a woman," he said, repeating his earlier words. He was still looking down at her foot.

"Please, let go," she said, a hint of anger in her voice. Slowly, the hand released its grip on her. As she turned away from him, to get up, she saw a boot, a big leather boot.

"It has been three days since I was with a woman," boomed a strong male voice, in Spanish. It was a familiar voice. Isabella looked up into the face of Victorio Del Negro. Raphael attempted to roll away, at the same time scrambling to get to his feet. He was too slow. Del Negro's powerful kick to the belly knocked the wind out of Raphael. He rolled onto his back in a semi-conscious state.

"Can't understand why you would rather be this man's woman than mine," Del Negro said, his voice sounding confident and arrogant. Three soldiers were standing behind him, including Islero Ramos. Another Spaniard was near the edge of the meadow holding the weary, sweat-soaked horses of the other four.

"I am not his woman," Isabella said, her initial surprise turning to anger. She and Raphael had been too careless. Why hadn't they followed a more remote trail? Why hadn't they

Chapter 13

stayed near the cover of brush and trees? Why hadn't they traveled at night, and stayed in hiding during the day? Why hadn't they made efforts to hide their tracks?

None of that mattered now. They were caught. The only question remaining, was what kind of punishment awaited them. How many toes would be cut off?

"He'll never run away again if I cut his leg off," Del Negro said, slowly drawing his sword from its sheath, taking a step towards Raphael, who by now had come to his senses.

"He might bleed to death on the journey back to Rock Creek," Islero said, speaking for the first time.

"Then I wouldn't have to worry about him anymore," Victorio said. "We don't get any work or cooperation out of him anyway. "Maybe I'll cut off both legs, and just leave him here to die. We'll all be better off."

Raphael was still on his back, helpless, but stupidly defiant, looking up at Del Negro. He did not beg to save his legs. Victorio stepped closer to do his dirty business.

"Stop," Isabella screamed.

Victorio turned to look at her, grinning, slowly lowering the tip of his sword to rest on the toe of his boot.

"So, the escaped slave girl thinks she can tell Victorio Del Negro what to do," he said.

"Do not touch him with that sword," she said.

"Is that a request or an order?" he asked.

"Both," she said.

"I am not in the habit of taking orders or advice from slave girls. Unless you can give me a very good reason why I should leave this Goshute alone, I intend to slice off both hind legs."

"I can give you two good reasons," she said, surprising Victorio with the quickness of her reply. For the first time, Raphael looked away from Victorio to Isabella.

"First, you are Catholic, are you not?" she asked.

"Of course, I am," Victorio replied, seeming content to listen to the slave girl's arguments.

" 'Thou shalt not kill' is one of your Catholic

commandments. According to Fray Carlos it was given to Moses by God himself on Mt. Sinai. You do not want to break that commandment and risk going to purgatory when you die."

"When God gave that commandment he didn't have Goshute Indians in mind," Victorio argued. There was a mild grin on his face. He was enjoying this interchange with the Indian girl.

"Fray Carlos says that is not true. He told me your God loves all his children the same, that he loves the Goshutes as much as the Spanish," she responded. "Raphael isn't worth a trip to purgatory,"

"I'm probably going there anyway, so what's the other reason I should let him live?" Victorio asked, apparently undaunted by the religious argument.

"If you take him back to Rock Creek, without cutting off his legs, I promise he will do your work. He will no longer refuse your orders."

The only one, more surprised than Victorio was Raphael.

"I will not be his slave," Raphael hissed.

"May I talk with him alone," Isabella asked, looking at Victorio.

"If you can get this stubborn slave to do my work, I believe I have witnessed a miracle," Victorio responded. He turned and walked a dozen paces away to allow Isabella a private conversation with Raphael.

"I am not asking you to be his slave," Isabella said, calmly.

"Then how can you promise I will do his work?"

"I am trying to save your life," she said, a hint of frustration in her voice.

"And if I refuse?" Raphael said.

"Then you more stupid than I thought you were. How many horses can you steal if your legs are cut off?"

"And what about the vision, and my mission to get horses?" he asked, his voice breaking, tears in his eyes.

Chapter 13

"I will help you get horses. That is a promise. But you must do Victorio's work while we wait for the right time. I believe in your vision of horses, and will help you. You must believe that. But you must also do Victorio's work."

"I am sorry I held your foot the way I did," he said, meekly.

"Do we go back to Rock Creek and go to work, or do I tell Victorio to cut off your legs?" she asked, ignoring his apology.

"You won't forget the horses?"

"Never. If necessary, I will help you steal them."

"Then I will work. It will be better than the black tunnel."

"And you will not try to escape?"

"Not like this."

"What do you mean?"

"When I leave Rock Creek next time," he whispered, being extra cautious so none of the Spaniards could hear his words, "I will be riding a beautiful horse, and I will be driving many more in front of me."

Isabella turned and walked over to Victorio.

"Your slave, Raphael, wants to return to Rock Creek and work hard for you," she said.

Victorio turned and waved for the man across the meadow to bring up the horses. It was time to begin the journey back to Rock Creek.

Chapter 14

Fray Carlos didn't look surprised when Isabella and Raphael returned. He did look somewhat worried, however, until Isabella assured him his role in the escape had been kept secret. He felt even more relieved when she told him Raphael did not even know where she had obtained the chisel and hammer.

Before conversing with the priest, however, Isabella had a good talk with Raphael. He seemed to be having a change of heart, wanting to return to his former position of stubborn resistance to the Spanish. He reminded her that he did not fear the Spanish, and he did not fear death. The fact that Isabella might have saved his life and wanted him to be an obedient slave, was not a strong enough argument to bring about the change Isabella had promised Del Negro.

On the other hand, he was still giving serious consideration to Isabella's other argument--that an obedient slave, without shackles or close supervision, would have a much better opportunity to steal horses. What finally won him over was her suggestion that if he were sufficiently obedient and responsible, he might work himself into a position where he worked with the Spanish mounts. Not only would he learn from the Spanish how to manage, care for, and train horses, but when the time came for him to leave, he would merely take with him the animals he was already responsible for. If someone saw him stealing horses, they would merely think he was taking them out to pasture. No one would miss the animals until he didn't return in the evening. By that time he would be so far away, even the Spanish would have trouble catching up with him.

Raphael had heard enough. He threw a hoe over his shoulder, marched into the nearest corn field, and did the work of three men before sundown.

"Why did you give me the chisel and hammer to help Raphael escape?" Isabella asked Fray Carlos, later, when they were alone in the *visita*. "It doesn't seem very Spanish, as you say, to risk so much for a slave."

"Jesus gave his life for his brothers and sisters," the priest responded. "The least I can do is give a chisel to a brother."

"Raphael is a Goshute slave. He is not your brother."

"All men are my brothers. All women are my sisters."

"Your Jesus taught that?"

"Yes. My Jesus, and your Jesus, too."

"Victorio's Jesus, too? He does not treat Indian slaves as brothers. Victorio is Catholic. Why does he not believe as you do?"

"I suppose if you asked Del Negro if all men were brothers," the priest responded, thoughtfully, "he would agree that they are, because as a child, he was taught the teachings of Jesus."

"Then why does he not do what he was taught?"

"I suppose getting gold and silver is more important to Victorio than anything else."

"Did Jesus tell people to seek gold and silver?"

"No. He taught them to love one another, that gold and silver were not important."

"If all the Spanish believe in Jesus, why do they not

110

live like he told them to?''

"Because men want gold and what it will buy, more than they want to please their God.''

"But not you,'' she said, looking directly into the priest's eyes.

"Not me,'' he said, sincerely. "But I am only one man. I came here to teach religion to heathens, but it seems all I do is keep peace among the slaves so Del Negro can get more gold. So I drink.''

"Del Negro is a fool,'' Isabella said, not wanting to dwell on the priest's hopeless frustration.

"Why do you say that?'' Fray Carlos asked.

"If he lived as he was taught, if he believed Indians were his brothers, instead of dumb animals to be beaten and driven, he might find much gold.''

"You mean the Indians would work harder?'' the priest asked.

"No. There are mines with much gold that Victorio does not know about. Mines with so much gold that men don't have to work hard to get it out.''

"You know where more gold is?'' the priest asked, suddenly very attentive to what the girl was saying.

"I do not know where these mines are, but there are those of my people who do. Many wear gold bracelets on their wrists. They did not work like slaves to get the gold for the bracelets.''

"You are telling me there are gold mines that only Indians work in?''

"No. I am saying there are mines with much gold that the Spanish do not know about. Some were worked by Spanish many summers ago, but the Spanish left, or were killed. Indians covered up the openings to these mines with brush and trees.''

"You said Del Negro was a fool. Why did you say that?'' Carlos asked.

"If he lived like his Catholic Jesus taught him to live, and treated Indians as brothers, if he did not make them slaves

111

to be beaten and killed, then the Indians would be his friends and brothers. Maybe they would show him where gold is hidden.''

"Maybe you ought to tell Del Negro what you just told me,'' Carlos said.

"Perhaps he would capture and torture more Indians trying to get them to tell where the gold is.''

"Perhaps he would take your advice to heart, free the slaves, and start treating Indians like brothers.''

"I don't know if Del Negro would do that,'' she said.

"You persuaded him to spare Raphael's life. Perhaps you could persuade him to be more kindly towards all native peoples. I think you should try. Don't forget the story of Esther. You should visit Del Negro.''

"You don't think I should wait until he calls for me?''

"No. You are Isabella. You are not an ordinary slave. Go now.''

"I will.''

Chapter 15

"How can the men in the mines want to dig your gold when it is so easy for you to kill them?" Isabella asked, as she entered the stone building where Del Negro conducted his business.

"I kill only those who defy or disobey me. Keeps the rest from rebelling. Without respect and fear for me, work at the mines would stop," he responded, easily, feeling no regret for killing the seven slaves, but surprised at the boldness of this slave girl for challenging him.

"It does not bother you that they are people, that your church teaches you they are your brothers?" she persisted.

"I am a saint, compared to those before me," Victorio said, his voice growing louder with a hint of anger. He was not accustomed to slaves talking this way.

"You are no saint."

"You think taking the lives of seven savages is a big matter?"

"I do."

"When Coronado first came to this land in 1540 he ordered 300 rebellious slaves tied to stakes and burned."

113

"I don't believe 300 Indians would let the Spanish do that to them," she said.

"You are right," Del Negro said, his tone softening. "When the Indians heard what Coronado intended to do to them, they tried to run away. Unfortunately for them, they were in the middle of a vast plain with no hiding places. The Spanish, mounted on horses, ran them down and slaughtered them with swords."

"This Coronado was an evil man."

"He was no more than a moth in a tornado next to Hernando Cortez and Francisco Pizarro."

"These Spaniards killed more than 300 Indians?" she asked.

Del Negro began to laugh. It was hard for him to believe that someone, supposedly educated in the ways of the Spanish, did not know all about Cortez and Pizarro. He would have a talk with Fray Castillo. The girl's education was far from complete if she was not familiar with the expeditions of Cortez and Pizarro.

"When Pizarro's 180 men did battle with the Inca army in 1532, in one afternoon they killed 3,000 Inca warriors. They captured the Inca, Atahualpa, who was about to be crowned king, and held him for ransom. Instead of working for his gold as I do, Pizarro just sat around while Atahualpa's servants filled big rooms with gold and silver, enough to fill many ships, including a pure gold chain that was 214 meters long, so heavy 200 men could hardly lift it. When the ransom was complete, Pizarro killed Atahualpa anyway. And you think I'm a hard man."

Isabella was speechless. She had no idea so many Indians had been killed by the Spanish in their quest for gold. But the worst was yet to come.

"When Hernando Cortez completed his conquest of Mexico City in 1521 he had killed 100,000 Aztecs. The city stunk so bad from all the dead bodies that Cortez and his men had to leave. And you are concerned about seven rebellious slaves killed by Victorio Del Negro. I am nothing next to

Pizarro and Cortez.''

"Fray Castillo told me the souls of men who kill, burn in purgatory forever," she added.

"I don't think so. When Cortez entered Mexico City the Aztec priests were offering human sacrifices. Daily, the hearts of young women and men were ripped from their bodies and, still quivering, offered to the Aztec gods. Then the priests ate the hearts. Cortez and his men saw a pile of human skulls higher than this building. In the long run, Cortez may have saved more lives than he took, by putting a halt to Aztec sacrifice. You don't seem very fond of our Catholic religion. Next to the religion of the Aztecs, it looks pretty clean to me.

"In addition to paying their *quinto* to the king, a one-fifth share of their conquered treasures, Cortez and Pizarro also saw that the pope in Rome got his share. There are no yellow cloaks hanging in cathedrals to announce their shame, and any sins they may have committed have been paid for many times over."

"In Spain, then, a man can pay for his sins with gold," she surmised.

"You learn fast," Del Negro added.

Isabella seated herself on a chair next to a table of split pinion logs. Her legs felt weak, and she wasn't sure why, except that she felt overwhelmed by the sudden exposure to a breed of men who found it easy and profitable to kill many thousands of Indians.

Del Negro picked up a clay jar and poured wine into two cups. He sipped from one, while handing the other to Isabella. She drank deeply.

"What do you want from me?" she asked, almost trembling. Del Negro seated himself on another chair, across the table from her. He looked directly at her, with the most earnest expression she had ever seen in a man's face.

Isabella couldn't help but think how handsome his face was. Not just his face, but his entire being--his intensity, his energy, his focus, his strength. If this man were not so cruel, he would be easy to love, she thought.

"When Cortez was finished with the Aztecs he had 150,000 castellanos of gold, and 88,000 pesos in gold bars. In addition, he melted 600,000 ducats worth of gold into bars three fingers wide. During a two-year period he sent ten tons of gold back to Spain to pay his *quinto* to the king. He had fifty tons of gold for himself, more wealth than all the countries of Europe possessed together, except Spain."

"Why are you telling me this?" she asked. "I care nothing for the blood-soaked gold this Cortez took from the Aztecs."

"It took several years for Cortez to finish his conquest of Mexico City," Victorio explained, patiently. "The Aztecs stoned Montezuma for letting the Spaniards into their city. Before the final assault on the city, Montezuma's servants carried off most of the royal treasure, to keep it out of the hands of the Spaniards."

Del Negro stood up, his fist clenched, the veins standing out in his neck. His eyes were fire as he continued to look directly into hers.

"The vast wealth I already described, captured by Cortez for himself and the king, was only a small piece of Montezuma's treasure!" He slammed his fist on the table. Both cups bounced off the table and broke into many pieces as they fell to the floor.

"Montezuma's servants carried most of the treasure far to the north and hid it, possibly in these mountains, possibly in a valley where their ancestors came from, a place called Teguayo, near a lake called Copalla, by a mountain called Timpanogos.

"When Cortez and his men asked the conquered Aztecs where they obtained so much gold, they always mentioned this valley far to the north, the ancient home of their ancestors. Cortez guessed at the time of his arrival, the Aztecs were receiving several tons of gold a year from this land, or somewhere nearby.

"There is a mountain called Timpanogos where I come from," Isabella offered.

116

Chapter 15

"I know, I have been there four times. I have found no signs of rich mines. I have killed some of your people, but they will tell me nothing."

"I do not know where a rich mine might be," she said. "Even if you tortured me, I could tell you nothing."

"I do not torture women."

"If I were a man, then you would torture me?" she asked.

"If I thought you knew where a mine was, and would not tell me, yes, I would torture you," he said, simply.

"And there are other Spanish mines," he continued. "There is the Pish-La-Ki in the rough canyon country between the lands of the Utes and Navajos, on Cerro Negro (Navajo Mountain). The Spanish used to work it, before the revolt of 1680 when the Indian people pushed the Spanish back to El Paso. After that, former slaves covered up many of the mines so they could not be found. I have looked for the Pish-La-Ki many times, and cannot find it. Neither can I find the Josephine de Martinique mine in the rugged Henry Mountains north of Cerro Negro, across the Rio Tizon (Colorado River). Your people who worked in these mines covered up the entrances, destroyed the trails, planted brush. I have found parts of the old trails, piles of ore, some of the *arrastras* where ore was crushed, and one of the stone cabins where the miners lived, but I cannot find the mines. I cannot find mines my people worked for nearly 200 years."

"I cannot show you where those mines are," Isabella said, beginning to wonder why Del Negro was telling all this.

"Maybe you can't, but there are those of your people who can, especially the old men. Maybe they will be more inclined to talk to you than to me. You know their language. You know Spanish, too. You can translate what they tell you."

"I have never heard of these Pish-La-Ki or Josephine mines," she protested.

"They are just two of many. There's the lost Mina de Tiro in the San Juan Mountains. Others are in the land of

117

Teguayo, and further north along the Platte, Snake and Humbolt rivers. And then there's an Inca treasure.''

"You told me Pizarro took the Inca treasure," she said.

"Only part of it. While Pizarro was holding Atahualpa prisoner, waiting for the ransom to come in, the servants of Atahualpa's brother, Huascar, carried the main part of the Inca treasure down to the coast of Peru, loaded it on ships, and sailed north along the coast for many days. They carried the treasure far inland, and hid it. Some say they took the gold chain with them.''

"Why should I help you find these treasures?" Isabella asked, not caring that she was interrupting his fiery narrative.

"It should be enough for you just to get to see some Inca or Aztec treasure," he said.

"It is not enough," she said, coldly. "I care nothing for piles of gold.''

"But you care for Indian lives, do you not? You don't like to see your people die while working in Spanish mines.''

"This is true.''

"If you help me find one of the great treasures, I will close the mines, and let all the Indians go home. I will take the treasure back to Spain and never return.''

"But will other Spanish come to take your place?" she asked. "Perhaps men who are even more cruel, men like Cortez and Pizarro.''

"That will not happen," he said. "Mexico has declared independence from Spain. I am the last of the Spanish gold seekers. No more can come. Perhaps some day the Mexicans will come. And the Americans have already built forts east of here. The closest is Fort Robidoux. Sometimes we buy supplies there. But the Americans seem more interested in trapping and trading furs than digging gold. Yes, I am the last Spaniard. Help me find the treasure, so I can give this land back to your people. You need to start fighting the Americans before they become too numerous.''

"I do not know if I can help you find treasure," she said.

"Nobody knows that, but we must try. Will you help me?"

Isabella rose from her chair, never taking her eyes from his face. She could feel his intensity, the force of his will, the animal passion that consumed his powerful body. She could not help but wonder, if this man had been born in one of the Ute bands, he would have been a great warrior, hunter, and horse thief--probably even a chief. Too bad he was wasting his life in the quest for yellow metal.

"Yes, I will help you find your treasure," she said.

"Good. We will leave on a search expedition tomorrow. In the meantime, I want to show you something."

Turning from Isabella, Victorio shouted through the open door, calling for two horses. By the time he and Isabella stepped off the porch into the plaza, a slave was running towards them, leading two saddled horses, including the same black stallion Victorio had been riding the first time Isabella had seen him, when he rescued her from Cigarro Sinbad.

It felt good to Isabella to be on a horse again as she followed Victorio through the gentle pass and down through the bean and squash fields towards Rock Creek. Upon reaching the water, they headed downstream until they came to a small, but steep-sided hill, its rocky slopes covered with sage brush and juniper.

After tying up the horses, Victorio took Isabella by the hand and led her through the stream. The melted snow-water was refreshing, and both were wet well above the knees as they approached the far side of the stream.

Instead of climbing up the bank, Victorio led Isabella around a clump of river birch which shielded the opening to a partially submerged tunnel. Without a word, he led her inside. They were wading through knee-deep water.

They hadn't gone far when the water became shallower. Isabella saw burning candles, the feeble light flickering on the black walls. When they emerged from the water they were greeted by two of Del Negro's Spanish guards.

After exchanging a few words with the guards, Victorio

led Isabella ahead. Once again they were wading in water up to their knees. It seemed to Isabella, they were in the very center of the small mountain.

Upon reaching the end of the partially submerged tunnel, they found themselves in a huge cavern. Candles were burning at regularly spaced intervals in little pockets carved in the side walls.

For the first time, she realized Victorio was taking her to his treasure room. On her right, there was a neatly stacked horde of silver bars, each one the width and thickness of a big man's hand, and about 30 inches long. She guessed there were several hundred bars in the waist-high pile.

Beyond the silver, was a pile of gold bars, which were smaller than the silver bars. Most were about the thickness, width and length of a man's foot. The gold bars were smaller in number. A cross was stamped on each bar.

On her left, was a pile of small leather pouches containing what appeared to be gold nuggets.

"I have struggled ten years to gather this tiny fortune," he said, almost apologetically.

"It appears to be a big fortune to me," Isabella said. "It is not enough for you to live comfortably in Spain?"

"Yes, I could live very well on this. In fact, with the gold and silver in this room, I am already one of the richest men in all of Spain. But, by the time I give the king his *quinto*, and make donations to his holiness in Rome to have the yellow robe removed from the cathedral, I may not have very much left over. While this pile of gold and silver may seem large to most people, it is nothing compared to the shiploads of treasure brought back to Spain by Cortez and Pizarro. There is hardly enough here to pile under the captain's bunk in a small ship."

"Tell me again why I must help you find more treasure," Isabella said.

"If I don't find treasure, I must stay until I double the piles of gold and silver in this room. Another hundred slaves will die in the mines."

Chapter 15

"If I go with you in this search for treasure, what else will I be required to do?" she asked, suddenly changing the subject, wondering if her days of being left alone by the Spaniards had come to an end.

"You will not be required to do anything against your wishes," Del Negro responded, catching her meaning. "We ride back to headquarters, I want to show you something else."

Taking her by the hand for the second time that day, he led her back through the partially submerged tunnel and across the stream to the waiting horses. Side by side, they galloped back to the group of buildings Victorio called headquarters.

As they dismounted in front of the stable, Victorio handed his reins to an Indian servant. Another Indian took Isabella's horse.

Instead of walking away, Victorio motioned for Isabella to follow him behind the stable building where the servants were caring for the horses that had just been brought in.

"Watch," Victorio said, stopping by a fence post. Isabella thought this a strange request, watching slaves care for horses, but she complied without further questions.

The servants had already replaced the bridles with hemp halters and tied the animals to a fence rail. After the saddles and blankets were removed, each horse was washed down with several buckets of water.

"Why do they put water on the horses?" Isabella asked.

"Washes the salt away so there is less chance of wearing sores," Victorio explained. "And cools them down faster, so they will have more time to rest up for tomorrow's journey."

"Raphael loves horses," Isabella ventured, remembering her promise to the slave. "He would be a good stable servant."

"When we need another, I'll send for him," Victorio promised. It didn't bother Isabella, not even a little, planting the seeds that would place a horse thief in Victorio's stable.

After the horses were rubbed down and brushed, and

121

their feet checked, they were placed in clean stables with plenty of hay, drinking water, and a fresh portion of the big seeds the Spanish called oats.

"Do you know why I wanted you to watch the horses?" Victorio asked, as they turned to walk away.

"I do not," she said.

"I own these horses," he explained, his tone quiet and thoughtful, selecting his words carefully. "You might say they are my slaves. You did not see me beat my horses today, nor is there any blood on my spurs."

Isabella still wasn't sure what he was trying to say.

"I treat my horses kindly, and they serve me well," he continued. "But I don't hesitate to use the spur if it is needed. I treat my Indian slaves with kindness, too. I don't enjoy beating or killing them."

"Then why do you kill them?" she asked.

"Sometimes I have to maintain order, but I don't enjoy it." he responded, his voice still calm. "An Indian with a good night's sleep behind him, and a full belly, can dig a lot more ore than one who has been chained to a tree all night then driven to his work with a whip."

"If your horse runs away, you do not cut his feet off or kill him."

"I might if I thought it would prevent other horses from running away in the future," he responded. "But horses are different than men, much dumber, less independent. Do you understand what I am trying to tell you?"

"Yes," Isabella responded. "If I help you find treasure, you will treat me like a horse."

Victorio laughed.

"But if I help you find treasure," she continued, "don't have your servants throw buckets of water on me, and bring me a pan of those oats."

He laughed again.

"Tomorrow, we begin a great adventure," Victorio said, in parting. As Isabella returned to her quarters, she didn't know why she felt so uneasy. She didn't know why the

Chapter 15

thought of sharing Victorio's great adventure frightened her so much.

Chapter 16

Islero was angry with Victorio, and frustrated too. It was well past the time when they should be leaving the Rocky Mountains and returning to Spain. In the past ten years they had accumulated sufficient wealth for Victorio to buy the yellow robe, and for his men to live comfortably for the remainder of their lives, even after the king received his *quinto*. Why did Victorio have to have more?

Islero felt like he thought the Egyptian soldiers must have felt, who followed Moses and the children of Israel through the parted waters of the Red Sea. Surely, they looked at the walls of water on each side of them, wondering when they would come splashing down and drown everyone.

Islero wondered about the walls around him and Victorio. They were already beginning to collapse. The Indians working the mines were more surly and quiet than they had ever been, too quiet. Victorio said this was the result of increased disciplinary action on the part of the Spanish against the rebellious attitudes. But, a voice deep inside told Islero the Indians were on the verge of revolt. It was just a matter of time until much blood would be shed.

During an earlier revolt, in 1680, every mine and *visita* in the region was overran, and the Spanish were driven all the way back to El Paso. Many lives were lost and it took 12 years for the Spanish to fight their way back to Santa Fe. The Indians did such a good job of hiding some of the mines, they were never found again. There were fewer fighting Spaniards in the area now than before 1680. It would be easier for the Indians to succeed in a revolt. Also, they had a memory of succeeding once before. It was just a matter of time. The Spanish hold was weakening. And Victorio was off with the pretty Indian princess, Isabella, looking for Aztec and Inca treasure. Islero wondered if Victorio was losing his mind. Sure, he believed the treasures really existed, but the chances of finding them were slim at best.

And the Americans were a constant worry. Already, three trading posts had been established in the area--Fort Davy Crockett at Brown's Hole on the Green River, Fort Kit Carson where Rio Damian (Duchesne) entered the Green River, and Fort Robidoux where the Whiterocks and Uinta Rivers joined, only a two-day ride from Rock Creek. While the forts were initially established to supply American fur traders, the Americans seemed more than a little interested every time a Spaniard or Indian came in with gold or silver, instead of furs, to buy supplies. The American traders always wanted to know where the precious metal came from. With the fur trade declining, it was just a matter of time until the Americans started mining. Hundreds more, perhaps thousands would come. There would be war with the new Mexican government. The Spanish would be caught in the middle.

And now that Mexico had declared independence from Spain, the Spanish were no longer welcome in Mexico and its' northern territories, particularly those who maintained loyalty to Spain and wanted to ship gold and silver back to the mother country. Already, it was necessary to pack the gold and silver at night, the last few hundred miles to the seaports on the gulf. Spanish ships deceptively showed flags of other countries while cargos of precious metals were loaded. Shipments had already been seized at Galveston. The Mexican police and soldiers were becoming better manned and organized all the time. Soon it would no longer be possible to use the gulf ports to ship wealth back to Spain. Islero felt strongly that Victorio should stop dreaming of lost treasure and face the immediate challenge of getting his men and wealth home before it was too late, but Victorio would not listen.

Islero was weighing these concerns as he approached the Mina de Perdito Alma (Mine of Lost Souls) on Ashley Creek, a tributary to the Green River. He visited this mine frequently. The deeper the shaft followed the vein into the mountain, the worse the problems became.

Unable to break away the solid rock with primitive tools, the Indian workers were required to chop wood in the nearby hills and haul it into the mine. Fires were built against the vein at the end of the shaft until the rock surface was hot enough to put blisters on a man's hand. Then, Indians, holding their breath against the bitter smoke, would rush to the end of the tunnel carrying pigskins full of cold water, which they would empty on the hot rock surface, causing it to crack. Now, the Indians could break free pieces of ore, which boys carried out of the tunnel. Men and boys tired quickly, with the fire consuming most of the oxygen in the tunnel.

The most plentiful wood in the area was juniper, which burned hot, but also produced a bitter smoke containing pitch and tar. Indians, who worked in this mine for any length of time were as black as the blackest negro slaves from Africa. The inside of their lungs and throats became black, too. Every Indian who worked very long at the Mina de Perdito Alma, had breathing problems. All coughed. It was not unusual for a healthy young man to be dead within six months of coming to this mine. And the deeper the mine penetrated the mountain, the worse the breathing problems became.

When Islero suggested to Victorio that perhaps they should close the mine, that the cost in Indian lives was too high, Victorio replied that as long as they could maintain a supply of new Indians, they would keep digging. The subject never came up again. But Islero was loyal. He somehow was able to maintain a fairly constant supply of fresh Indians, but in order to do it, the number of Indians in the area diminished, and the age of the average worker was getting younger and younger. Some of the boys entering the mine were less than 10 years old. But at least Islero had not found it necessary to put girls in the mine, even though some were used to bring firewood to the entrance.

Ten years ago, this work had been a great and grand adventure for Islero. Now, he hated his work. And feared with Fray Castilla, that the future of his eternal soul was in serious danger.

As Islero approached the mine late in the afternoon, following the main trail beside the edge of a sandstone cliff, he began to sense that something was wrong. It was too quiet. The usual strings of Indians winding down through the trees, carrying firewood, were absent. The crew, responsible for carrying pigskins of water up from the stream, was absent, too. It was too early in the day to halt work. No smoke was coming from the mine entrance. Something was wrong.

Islero pulled his horse to a halt. The five men with him did the same. No words were spoken. All were looking and listening for any clue as to what had happened. One Spaniard slowly drew his sword.

Suddenly, there was a dull thud in the dust beside Islero. First, he looked down to see the melon-sized stone that had fallen from the sky. Then he looked up to see half a dozen more stones in mid-air. Indians were throwing rocks over the top of the cliff.

Islero and his men spurred their horses ahead, away from the cliff, into a clearing where the stones could not hurt them. By this time all the men, including Islero, had drawn their swords.

Islero concluded there had been a revolt at the mine. The Indian slaves, possibly with the help of outsiders, had overthrown their Spanish overseers. The fact that the Indians were still in the vicinity and willing to attack Islero, was evidence the insurrection had been fairly recent, probably within the last 24 hours. Islero guessed the 12 Spaniards who oversaw work at the mine had been killed. He also guessed that the stones had been thrown from the cliff to force him and his men to flee into the clearing, where they were now surrounded by their former slaves.

Islero had two regrets. First, that he hadn't brought more men with him; six was hardly a formidable fighting force. Second, upon leaving Rock Creek, the men had complained so vigorously against wearing armor in the summer heat, that he had allowed them to leave their armor behind, except for their steel helmets. If the enemy began shooting arrows, his men would be extremely vulnerable.

It was as if the ambushers could read Islero's thoughts. Dozens of stone-tipped arrows began falling from the sky. They were coming from the cliff behind them, from the mountain in front of them, and from the forests and brush on both sides of the clearing.

Islero remained calm. This wasn't the first time he had been ambushed by angry Indians. He knew it would be foolish to remain in the clearing where his men were easy targets for the arrows. It would be just as foolish to charge ahead and seek cover in the mine where they would be trapped like animals in a cage. The most obvious avenues of escape were on the trails leading through the trees, both to his right and left. Undoubtedly, the Indians expected Islero and his men to try one of these trails, and were waiting in ambush. He guessed, after the barrage of stones had nearly killed his men, the Indians didn't think the Spaniards would go back the way they had come, following the trail along the cliff. So Islero decided to do just that.

He spun his horse around, calling for his men to follow, and charged back down the trail, directly away from the mine. By the time his horse reached a full gallop, he could see dozens of Indians appearing along the edge of the cliff, some armed with bows and arrows, others holding large stones above their heads.

129

It didn't occur to Islero to turn back. He had been a soldier long enough to know that indecision at a time like this could be more dangerous than the enemy. Right or wrong, he had decided to risk the dangers of the cliff, and there was no turning back now. He spurred his horse to greater speed, returned his sword to its sheath, and reached up with his free hand to tighten the chin strap on his helmet, realizing he was riding into a virtual hailstorm of stones and arrows, all coming straight down from the sky.

Islero could tell by the cries behind him that some of his men had already been struck with arrows. He looked back to see one of the horses go down. The cliff was still 20 meters away.

Islero decided it would not be wise to look up as he raced beside the cliff. Looking straight ahead, he urged his horse to even greater speed.

It was fortunate for Islero that the Indians on the cliff misjudged the speed of his horse. But this inability to judge Islero's speed resulted in havoc for the men following after him. The rocks and arrows aimed at Islero found their marks on the men and horses following close behind.

By the time Islero raced to safety behind the end of the cliff, he was alone. The men who had not been killed, were lying broken and bloody beneath a continuing barrage of stones and arrows. Islero knew it would be suicide to go back. His only option was to continue alone.

He marveled that his horse, the bigger target, had come through unscathed. Islero was not so fortunate. A rock had struck his right thigh above the knee. From the pain, he guessed the bone might be broken, but there was no blood.

An arrow had struck the top outside of his left shoulder, and had passed under the skin, clear to the elbow where the resistance of the stone tip, pushing through the skin a second time, stopped the momentum of the shaft.

Dropping the reins, Islero reached up with his right hand, where the feathered end of the shaft was sticking out the top of his shoulder, and broke it off. Then he grabbed the tip at his elbow and pulled the shaft out of his arm. Severe bleeding followed, but he didn't stop. He knew the Indians would follow him. If they were on foot, they wouldn't follow far, but if they had horses, they might follow him all the way to Rock Creek. He had to keep his horse moving.

Apparently, the arrow did more damage inside his arm than he first thought. Not only did the pain persist, but the bleeding continued until he tore off two pieces of his shirt-sleeve with his teeth, and shoved one piece into each end of the wound.

After a few miles, he let the horse slow to an easy trot. He guessed he could maintain this pace through most of the night. The sun was low in the sky. In the dark, he knew his pursuers would find his trail hard to follow. His horse had been over this trail several times, and he guessed that even in the darkest night, it would know the way back to Rock Creek. He didn't like trusting his life to the judgement of a horse. Still, he knew his horse well, and believed it would take him home.

It hadn't been dark very long when Islero began to feel dizzy. He nearly fell off the horse. He was forced to drop the reins and hang onto the wide, flat-topped saddle horn with both hands. He guessed the loss of blood in the arm, and the pain from his wounds was the cause of the dizziness. His biggest fear was of passing out, falling off the horse, and being found by his pursuers.

He knew, in the event of capture, he would receive no mercy. He also knew his death would not be quick. Parts of his body would probably be skinned, burning sticks would be pushed into his eyes. They would keep him alive as long as possible while they continued to torture him. But he did not feel anger or hate towards them, not after so many of them had died at the mine. He couldn't condemn them for anything they might do to him. But maybe God would. Unlike the Spanish, the Indians didn't have access to a priest who could absolve their sins through confession.

But they hadn't caught him yet. He was still conscious,

and he was mounted on a good horse, one he could trust to go the right way, even in the blackest night. All he had to do was remain conscious, and avoid falling off. That, he was determined to do.

Islero's battle to remain conscious was not easy. When he felt himself slipping away, he found the only thing that would bring him back was striking one of his wounds. Sometimes, the pain, like smelling salts, would revive him. But with the passing of the night, even the pain began to lose its edge. Knowing it was just a matter of time until he lost consciousness, he tried to tie one of his hands to the saddle horn, using the ends of the reins.

Islero did not know if the horse lost its way, or if it made a conscious decision, sensing the desperate condition of its rider, but it left the trail leading to Rock Creek.

As the blackness of night gave way to the gray of dawn, the tired animal was standing in the center of a cluster of brush huts. The semi-conscious Islero continued to hang on, seemingly unaware the animal had stopped.

With the arrival of daylight, the reason for the extreme blackness of the night became apparent. A storm system had moved in, and gray-black clouds covered the sky from one horizon to the other.

As Islero's horse waited for the dawn, a few raindrops began falling, then many. In the dry mountain air, even though it was summer, the drops were icy cold and had a reviving effect on Islero.

He looked around, hoping to see something he recognized, but nothing he saw was familiar, especially the circle of brush shelters. Even in his half-conscious state he knew he was in trouble, but when he touched his spurs against the sides of his weary horse, it refused to move.

He guessed the animal, after nearly 24 hours of continuous travel, was simply too tired to go any further. Or did the dumb horse sense there was some kind of haven or security among the circle of crude huts. Islero desperately wanted to do something, but his body wouldn't cooperate. All

Chapter 16

it wanted to do was fall to the ground and drift back into the peaceful world of unconsciousness. His body won. He slipped from the saddle to the rain-soaked ground, his right hand coming last as it untangled from the reins.

The jar of the fall, along with the cold water, brought Islero to his senses. He was trying to push himself into a sitting position when a woman emerged from one of the huts. First, she saw the horse, then Islero. Their eyes met in a gaze of mutual fear. He guessed as soon as she sounded the alarm, men would rush from the huts and kill him. The woman was frightened because she thought she saw a crouched man, ready to spring upon her.

Reality fell far short of both expectations. Islero, instead of leaping upon the woman, with no more strength to hold his crouch, rolled over sideways into the mud. When the woman sounded the alarm by screaming, no armed warriors emerged from the huts, only women, thirteen in all, and a few middle-sized children. All had weapons, though, and had Islero tried leaping towards them, he would have been under attack from all directions.

"*Buenos dias,*" Islero muttered, as he slipped back into unconsciousness.

Cautiously, the women approached the strange man, their weapons ready in the event he was feigning helplessness to get them to lower their guard. That, they were not going to do. Three had bows and arrows, four spears, and the rest, clubs, as they formed a tight circle around the stranger. One of the children led his horse away.

When one of the women nudged Islero with a spear point, he did not move. Several more tried it with the same result. The steel helmet told them he was a Spaniard, and probably a slaver, a man to be feared, an enemy, a man who must be killed before his strength returned.

One of the women drew back an arrow on her bow, and aimed it at Islero's chest. Before she could let the arrow fly, however, a girl who seemed ignorant of the threat to her own safety, stepped in front of the woman with the bow, dropped

133

to her knees and began removing one of Islero's boots.

To a savage living in a brush hut, a pair of boots was a treasure, and the girl saw a chance to get the boots before someone else did. But she started a stampede. Another woman started removing the other boot. Two more started pulling at the shirt. Another removed his helmet, while four or five were tugging at his trousers.

The woman who had intended to kill Islero, let the tension out of her bow. A minute later, Islero was as naked as at the moment of birth, still unconscious, stretched out on his back on the wet ground.

What earlier had been a cooling sprinkle from the heavens, was now a downpour. Now that he was naked, they could see the ugly wounds in his arm. Wounded, soaked and unconscious, Islero didn't look nearly so threatening. Without his helmet and bulky Spanish clothing, he didn't intimidate them any longer. Motherly instincts began to take over. One of the younger women suggested they carry him out of the rain and dress his wounds.

One of the older women reached out with her spear and moved a part of Islero he would have preferred to keep private. Some of the women began to giggle as it occurred to them there might be something better to do with this Spaniard than merely kill him.

Four of the women carried Islero into the largest wickiup. They wiped away the water and dressed his wounds. A half hour later he was wrapped in a heavy buffalo robe beside a small but warming fire.

Six hours later he was awakened by the aroma of rabbit stew simmering in his steel helmet which was hanging upside down by its chin strap from a small tripod placed over the fire.

When he tried to move, throbbing pains shot through his arm and down his leg with so much intensity that he almost passed out again. He decided to remain still. There was an uncomfortable tightness in his left arm which he didn't understand until he noticed it was swollen to about twice its normal size.

Across the fire, three of the women were sitting cross-legged. They were watching closely to see what he would do. None of them held weapons, giving him hope they were not going to kill him, at least not right away. Maybe they were waiting until the men came home.

In the meantime, Islero had a terrible appetite that needed satisfying. He nodded towards the simmering stew. A minute later, one of the women was helping him sip broth from a clay cup.

The next day, Islero began to move about. The broth had given him strength, and the swelling in the arm hadn't gotten any worse. He guessed he would live until his hosts decided otherwise.

After a few days, Islero began to realize this was no ordinary Indian village. He noticed that some of the women were making arrows, normally a task reserved strictly for men. Some of the women went hunting, and brought home three rabbits and a deer. Normally women waited for men to bring in the game. And while there were some children in the village, there were no babies. Most of the women were Ute, but the prettiest was a Navajo. There were also two Shoshones, a Paiute, and a Goshute named Mud Woman who spoke passable Spanish.

"When will your men return?" Islero asked. Mud Woman looked at him as if she didn't understand his question.

"When will your men return?" he repeated.

"Perhaps when the Spanish leave," she said, carefully.

"How long have your men been gone?" he asked.

"No man in village for two summers," she said.

Islero was amazed. He had stumbled upon a village of women. The men he feared would not be returning. Maybe he would not die after all.

He had heard stories about one of Sir Francis Drake's men who had walked across Peru, over the Andes Mountains and into the Amazon River country where he found a tribe of women. They were later called Amazons.

What amazed Islero most, was the fact that the Indian women were being left alone by all the Indian and Spanish slave traders, and the American traders and trappers in the area. Some of the women were attractive, especially the Navajo, also the Goshute named Mud Woman. The only reason he could guess for them being left alone by the men in the area, was the remote location. Islero did not know exactly where the horse had taken him during that long night, but apparently it had taken him into a remote pocket of wilderness unknown to the local slavers, miners, traders and trappers.

Islero realized he had stumbled onto a potential source of wealth. He could take these women to Fort Robidouix and sell them for more than he could earn working two or three years for Victorio Del Negro. But no sooner had this thought entered his mind than he began to feel guilty. He knew he would never seriously consider selling into slavery the women who had saved his life.

Islero knew Victorio would be furious when he found out about the revolt at the *Mina de Perdito Alma*. Victorio would insist the rebellious slaves be caught and punished. He would insist the mine be reopened. The responsibility of making all this happen would fall squarely on Islero's shoulders. Several years earlier, he would have responded with enthusiasm to such a challenge. Now, the thought of such an undertaking made him weary. Was he getting old, or was he in need of a good rest? Either way, he was in no hurry to leave this welcome sanctuary.

The wound on his leg turned out to be nothing more than a bad bruise, and would soon heal. His arm, however, was another matter. It was still swollen, and both puncture holes were still draining. Pain shot up and down his arm whenever he tried to move it. This wound would take time to heal, and he couldn't think of a better place to let that happen than with these wonderful women.

He had a Spanish wife in Spain he hadn't seen in nearly ten years. He also had an Indian wife in Santa Fe. While the church didn't condone polygamy, it didn't seem to mind a man taking extra Indian wives, as long as they were across the ocean in the New World. Islero didn't understand this doctrine, neither did he complain.

For the first time since the ambush at the mine, he was glad he had taken the arrow in the arm. Waiting for the arm to heal was the perfect excuse not to hurry back to Rock Creek and the insane quest for gold. In fact, he wondered if he was beginning to hate gold, considering the terrible prices people paid to get it.

Islero had found a brush hut haven where he could escape, at least temporarily, the gold seeking insanity that had occupied and consumed his life for nearly ten years.

"Mud Woman," he called. "What will we eat tonight?"

Chapter 17

Isabella and Victorio had been on the trail many days when they finally began to wind their way down the last long canyon leading to Teguayo, the legendary homeland of the Aztecs, the lush valley where sky-blue Lake Copalla rested in the shadows of the majestic Mt. Timpanogos.

The canyon was called Spanish Fork, because it was a frequent and preferred route for Spanish miners, slave traders and priests. While Fray Silvestre Escalante recorded the daily events of his journey through the canyon in 1776, others did not.

In addition to Victorio and Isabella, the treasure-seeking caravan consisted of approximately 15 soldiers, half a dozen Indian servants and guides, and Fray Carlos Castilla.
Nine pack mules carried the supplies and food.

Victorio and Isabella were riding at the head of the caravan, side by side through a meadow where the trail had widened, when she asked why the soldier directly behind them carried the Spanish flag on a long pole. Victorio said this was done to impress the savages.

"Why do you care about that?" she asked. "You buy

these people with gold, work them until they die, then buy more. Why do you wish to impress them?''

"The more familiar a red man feels towards you, the more inclined he is to steal from you, or even kill you,'' Victorio answered. "If an Indian fears and respects you, he is more likely to keep distance between you and him. If he thinks you are tired, dumb and sick with diarrhea, just like him, he will have courage to steal your horse. But if he stands in awe of your helmets, breastplates, swords, and flags, he will probably leave you alone.''

He stopped talking and looked at her as if he were about to share a great and grand secret with her. She waited for him to continue.

"More battles are won in the mind than on the battlefield,'' he said. "I work very hard trying to convince the savages that I am invincible.''

"Are you saying you and your men are more vulnerable than my people think you are.''

"I will tell you a secret,'' he said. "But you must never tell it to any of your people.''

"I won't,'' she said, but she was not sincere. She was Victorio's slave, and slaves lied to their masters, especially in matters like this.

"If a stone-tipped arrow penetrated my chest, I would die as easily as any elk or deer. I would like to pretend that God is watching over me, but deep inside I know I am no different than any other man, including my slaves. If an arrow pierces my heart, or causes my lungs to fill with blood, I am a dead man. If more of your people believed that, I would be dead already.''

Isabella had been wondering for some time how a few hundred Spanish men could control many thousands of Indians. There was much talk among her people about the strong medicine of the Spanish, and how this medicine made them superior in battle. Now, Victorio was telling her, this was not so. To a large degree, it was through trickery and intimidation the Spanish controlled the Indians.

Chapter 17

"But your shields and helmets stop the arrows," she said.

"Some of the arrows," he reminded her. "But if ten hostile savages are in front of me in the trail, and I charge, they usually turn and run. I gallop up behind them, one by one, and hack them down with my sword. They don't seem to understand that all together, they could turn on me and overpower my horse, pull me to the ground, and shove a knife or spear behind my breastplate and I would be dead. Sure, one or two or three of them would die while they did this, but when they turn and run, I can kill all of them, without receiving a scratch on my own body. I prefer to do battle that way, but I need intimidation on my side to succeed. Pizarro did the same thing when his 160-man army defeated the 9,000-man Inca army. Do you now understand why we carry flags?"

"I think so," she responded. They rode in silence for a while, Isabella trying to digest what Victorio had just told her. Had Victorio really revealed the great secret? Or was he teasing her? She guessed he was probably telling the truth, or at least what he perceived as the truth. Why did he tell her, a slave, his secret? Did he not fear that she would tell other slaves who might be more inclined to fight the Spanish? Maybe it didn't matter. Perhaps fighting was more a thing of the heart than the mind. The words of a woman would not change the hearts of the men of her people. They would still fear the Spanish, even if she told them the Spanish were only men, with no powerful medicine. Maybe someday she would know the answer to these questions. Maybe someday she would be wise. She was not wise now.

After descending the steepest part of the canyon, they entered a narrow valley where two small streams joined to become the Spanish Fork River. One of the soldiers galloped up to Victorio, announcing he had found a small cluster of brush huts a short distance up one of the canyons. He has seen a few old people, both men and women, but no warriors.

"Let's see," Victorio announced, leading the caravan

141

towards the canyon. Without receiving orders to do so, the Spanish soldiers secured the chin straps on their helmets, and drew their swords. They didn't know if they would be rounding up a few more slaves, or engaging in battle. Either way, they would be ready. The Spanish were hardened troops. None of the men looked particularly nervous or afraid. This was routine duty. All of them had been in similar situations many times.

Isabella, on the other hand, had never ridden with soldiers into battle. She didn't know whether she should stay at Victorio's side, or fall to the rear. Victorio was so occupied with leading his men up the canyon that he did not tell her what to do. Apparently, he was not concerned for her safety, she concluded. She realized she was now on the other side of a slave roundup, like the one in her home village when she was taken captive by Islero. She wished Victorio would say something. She pulled her horse back, letting herself fall to the rear of the advancing Spaniards.

As soon as the village of brush huts was in view, Isabella realized there would be no great battle. The brush huts were small, and she could tell at a glance they had been hastily put together. They were no better than the huts children made to play in. This was no village of fighting men who might challenge the Spanish soldiers, but rather a ragtag bunch of misfits and stragglers--the leftovers of the Spanish slave trade.

An older man crawled out of the nearest hut and stood to face the approaching Spaniards. He was wearing tattered leggings and moccasins. His hair hung loose about his shoulders. He was thin, and he did not carry a weapon.

As Victorio and his men pulled their horses to a halt, more people began emerging from the huts, old women and older men, a boy with only one leg, all shabbily dressed. Most of the Spaniards returned their swords to their sheaths. There was nothing to fear in this village.

A dead elk, covered with flies and maggots rested by one of the huts. It was a young bull with antlers still in the

Chapter 17

velvet. It looked like it had died of natural causes before the Indians found it and dragged it to their camp. It was beginning to smell.

"Read the *requerimiento*," Victorio shouted. Fray Carlos pushed his horse forward through the men until he was at Victorio's side. The priest pulled a black, leather-bound book out of his saddlebags, and slowly opened to the right page. He hesitated.

"Read!" Victorio ordered, impatience in his voice. The gentle priest never did things quickly enough to please Victorio.

"There is nobody here we want to take as a slave," the priest objected.

"Nothing has been said about taking slaves," Victorio explained, increasingly frustrated at the priest. "Read!"

"We certainly don't want to make war on these poor people..."

"Read!" Victorio shouted. Reluctantly, the priest began reading, without feeling. He read too fast for his words to be clearly understood. But that didn't matter. He knew the poor savages couldn't understand anyway.

"I certify that with the help of God we shall make war against you in all ways and manners that we can, and shall take your wives and children and shall make slaves of them, and we shall take away your goods and shall do you all the harm and damage that we can, as vassals who do not obey their lord, and that the death and losses which shall accrue from this are your fault and not that of his highness."

Fray Carlos slowly closed the book and returned it to the saddlebag. When he was finished, he merely stared down at his saddle horn.

"Poor wretches," Victorio said. "Probably starve to death this winter. Not much game here. If we put them out of their misery, others down the canyon will have more respect for us. Men, draw your swords." All the swords came out of their sheaths. The men waited for the order to charge the unarmed Indians.

143

"No," the priest shouted.

"Hold back," Victorio said to his men with a forced calmness. "I almost forgot the proper order of things. The priest wants to baptize these savages, write their names on a piece of paper. He'll send it to his superiors in Spain to put in his file. Wants to be cardinal someday. Go ahead, Bishop, sprinkle your holy water on them before we cut them down."

"I am not a bishop," the priest protested.

"But you will be, if you continue sending names across the ocean. They'll think you are converting all of New Spain to the true gospel."

"I will not send the names of these poor people to Spain," the priest protested.

"Then you can give the list to His Holiness of Rock Creek, Cigarro de Sinbad. He will send it to his superiors in Rome."

"There will be no list," the priest said, his voice growing firmer.

"Do you want to baptize them, or not?" Victorio asked, growing more impatient.

"I will not baptize these poor souls so you can kill them," the priest said. Everyone was looking at him, all surprised the gentle priest had the nerve to stand up to Victorio Del Negro.

"They will die anyway when winter comes," Victorio argued. "We are merely putting them out of their misery, saving them the pain of starvation."

"You have no right," Carlos said.

"Since when does a priest tell Victorio Del Negro what he can and cannot do?" Victorio countered.

"They don't need to starve. Give them food instead of killing them," the priest persisted.

The Indians watched with helpless curiosity as the discussion continued. Victorio seemed to be indulging the priest, toying with him. When the priest exhausted himself, Del Negro would go ahead and kill the Indians anyway.

"We should feed them, not kill them," Carlos argued.

"That is the only Christian thing to do."

"Giving them food is a temporary solution to their problem," Victorio said. "Killing them is a permanent solution. I intend to kill them all right now. And I think we should have brought Fray Sinbad instead of Fray Castilla on this expedition. Sinbad would have no problem with the killing as long as he could sprinkle water on them and add a few more names to his conversion report."

Fray Carlos got off his horse and knelt down in front of Del Negro's horse. With his hands clasped in front of his chest, as if he were praying, the priest looked up earnestly at Del Negro.

"I beg you to spare the lives of these poor savages," he cried. "If you do, I will stay here with them. I will build a *visita*. I will teach them how to grow food. I will teach them the true religion. And I will baptize them. Let me stay. I beg you to spare their lives, and let me stay with them."

"Alone?" Del Negro asked, surprised at the priest's offer, but moved by how much the gentle priest was willing to do for a handful of worthless savages. Maybe this priest really was a man of God.

"Isabella, come here," Victorio roared. Quickly, she rode to his side.

"Should we leave Fray Castilla with these savages?" he asked. She didn't know how to answer, wondering why Victorio was suddenly including her in the conversation. Maybe he thought she would say something funny. Surely, the great Victorio wouldn't be seeking wisdom from an Indian girl. On the other hand, she was the one who had gotten Raphael to abandon his stubborn ways, and become what appeared to be an obedient slave. Victorio knew nothing of Raphael's desire to get close to the horses so he could steal them.

"Your own grandfather, Diego Penalosa, was rude and insulting to a priest on an expedition such as this," she said. "The inquisition found him guilty, took away his possessions, sent him back to Spain, and his yellow cloak of shame still hangs in the cathedral. You told me this."

"I did," Victorio said, his voice suddenly soft and thoughtful. He was amazed that such words were coming from a slave girl. If he were in Spain, this is the kind of thing his mother might say. "Please continue," he said.

"Maybe you could learn something from your grandfather," she said. "Instead of insulting the priest, listen to him. Be kind to him. He is not Cigarro de Sinbad. Fray Carlos has a good heart. He wants only to help these poor people. And maybe he will help you, too."

"How might he do that?" Victorio asked.

"This is a well-used trail," she said, slowly, thinking carefully as she spoke. "Many people come this way. They will stop at the new *visita*. Some of them may have gold. Because the priest gives them food, perhaps they will tell him where the gold came from. Because the priest does not want gold for himself, he will tell you what he has learned."

Victorio rubbed his chin, looking at Isabella, wondering how such wise words could come from a beautiful savage. Her words made sense. He could not find anything wrong with her logic. He certainly would not miss this priest if the man stayed behind to build a *visita*.

Victorio ordered his men to put their swords away and break out some food to leave behind with the priest.

"May God bless you, both of you," the priest said. Tears were streaming down his cheeks. "This is why I came to New Spain. Thank you. Thank you." He kissed Victorio's hand.

"But there is one condition to all this," Victorio said, pulling his hand away. "If you see anyone with gold, you must ask them where they obtained it. Then you must tell me what they said. Promise me in the name of the Virgin Mary and her son Jesus you will do this for me."

"I promise," the priest said.

After the supplies for the priest were unloaded, the caravan resumed its journey down the canyon, but not before Victorio made sure Isabella was riding at his side.

Chapter 17

No one in the caravan noticed the group of Indian men sitting cross-legged under two juniper trees on a nearby hill, quietly watching all that had happened. Their faces were silent and expressionless, but all carried weapons, bows and spears, and one wore a Spanish helmet.

Chapter 18

It was a beautiful summer morning at Rock Creek as Raphael walked towards the bean fields, a hoe over his shoulder. There were no clouds in the sky. There was no wind, but the morning air was cool. He was glad he was not in chains at the end of the dark tunnel. He was glad Isabella had persuaded him to be more obedient. He hoped he would have a chance to get closer to the horses, but had no idea how that opportunity might present itself. But he was determined to be patient. Anything was better than sitting in chains in a dark gold mine.

Actually, he was growing to like the work in the bean, squash and corn fields--hoeing weeds and diverting water from the stream to let the plants drink. The exercise, fresh air, and sunshine felt good, and he did not mind being alone most of the time.

He was surprised at the lack of supervision. The Spanish guards had watched him closely the first few weeks, but when it became apparent he was not going to run away, and when they saw that he could work all day without being pushed and prodded, they left Raphael to himself more and more.

The biggest diversion from the work in the fields, was an occasional assignment at the *arrastra* or rock crusher, when pack trains, with as many as 40 mules, carried in heavy loads of ore-bearing rock from half a dozen different mines.

As Raphael was finishing hoeing a row of beans, the church bell sounded, announcing the arrival of another pack train. Quickly, the slave finished the row, dropped his hoe on the ground, and headed towards the *arrastra*.

When he arrived, he noticed about 25 mules tied to the long hitching rail in front of the building. Without waiting for orders, Raphael joined two other Indians who were removing the heavy pigskin packs from the mules and carrying them inside.

Raphael emptied his first bag on the ore pile at the upstream end of the long, narrow building. Coming in from the bright sunshine, it took a few seconds for his eyes to adjust to the dim light.

Several Indians were grabbing rocks from the ore pile and pushing them under the heavy millstone, powered by a horizontal shaft which passed through the side wall to a water wheel in the stream.

Two Indian boys were using flat pieces of wood to push the crushed ore into one of two stone tubs large enough to bathe in. When one of the tubs was about half-full, a Spaniard poured in a measured amount of the quicksilver Islero had brought back from Santa Fe. Immediately, two Indians waded into the tub, using their bare feet to mix the mercury with the ore.

This job looked fun to Raphael. He guessed the pasty amalgam created by the quicksilver and ore would feel good on his feet. He hoped he would get a chance to do that job someday. He didn't notice that the two Indians who were mixing the quicksilver were coughing, and he didn't know both would die of mercury poisoning within the year.

Next, water was channeled into the tub via a wooden trough to wash away the excess ore. Then the amalgam was scooped into pans which were placed over a big fire outside one of the doors. The quicksilver was boiled off, leaving pure metal in the pans, usually gold and silver. The slaves involved in this work were constantly breathing the mercury vapor, and if they stayed at the work long enough, were doomed to die of mercury poisoning, too.

Raphael observed the workings of the *arrastra* as he carried in bag after bag of the heavy ore. The grinding millstone filled the air with rock dust, which mixed with the pungent smell of human sweat and the toxic mercury fumes.

When Raphael was almost finished, he noticed the black-robed priest, Sinbad, enter the building and walk up to the crusher. Silently, the man of God watched the huge stone crush the ore. Occasionally, he would reach under the stone and retrieve a piece of virgin gold which the crusher had broken free from its bed of rock. The priest would bite the piece of metal, then with a thoughtful expression, announce its purity, in percentages. He was still doing this when Raphael left the building to return to the bean field.

In front of Raphael, a mounted Spaniard was fighting with one of the pack mules that had just been relieved of its load of ore. The rider was trying to lead the young mule away, but it refused to go. Apparently, the beast thought it was going to be burdened with another load, or perhaps it just didn't want to leave its companions. Either way, it refused to be led.

With the mule's lead rope dallied around his saddle horn, the Spaniard was trying to drag the mule away from the *arrastra*. All four feet were buried deep in the soft dirt. The horse could not drag it. Repeated lashings from the Spanish whip seemed only to make the beast more determined to resist.

The exasperated Spaniard looked at Raphael and shrugged his shoulders. He was a small, wirey man, obviously hardened to the rigors of the trail. But he was tired after a long day working with the mules, and wasn't in the mood for any nonsense now. The easiest and simplest thing for him to do would be simply to draw his sword and kill the animal, but that would make Victorio angry. Mules were valuable and in short supply.

Raphael stepped forward to help, but he wasn't sure what to do. He didn't want to get behind the mule and push, fearing he might get kicked. It occurred to him the animal might be hungry, and that if he held a clump of grass in front of its nose, it might step forward to eat the grass. After all, it had been packing all day, and ought to be hungry.

Raphael grabbed a handful of grass and held it in front of the mule. The weary beast wasn't about to be tricked with food. Upon seeing the grass, it laid back its long ears and dug its feet deeper into the soil.

The Spaniard seemed amused at Raphael's childlike attempt to persuade the mule. It seemed obvious to the Spaniard that this slave, though wanting to help, didn't know much about pack animals. The rider uncoiled his bullhide whip in preparation to giving the mule another whipping.

Raphael dropped the grass from his hand. Bending his knees, he reached down and scooped up a handful of dirt. He had never worked with mules before, but it occurred to him the stubborn, but stupid animal, needed something else to think about, something besides fighting the Spaniard. The animal was obviously too upset to be interested in food. And it seemed to Raphael that more whipping would only make it more determined to resist.

He didn't know if his new idea would work or not, but it wouldn't hurt to try. After motioning to the Spaniard to put down his whip, Raphael stepped forward and shoved the handful of dirt into the animal's mouth. He did it quickly, before it realized what was happening, before it had a chance to resist. Raphael stepped back, watching the surprised mule working desperately with its mouth to dislodge the dirt.

The Spaniard didn't know what to think of all this, until Raphael took hold of the mule's halter rope and started leading it down the trail. It was so occupied with spitting out dirt that it didn't think to pull back on the rope. After about

Chapter 18

20 meters, Raphael handed the rope to the Spaniard who had been riding at his side. The mule followed obediently, its tongue working vigorously to remove the dirt and silt from its mouth. Raphael returned to the bean field to continue his work, finding satisfaction in the clever way he had persuaded the mule to change its mind.

The next day, the same Spaniard rode into the fields to find Raphael.

"My name is Julio," he said. "I am boss of the horses and pack animals. I am short-handed at the stables. You are going to work for me now."

Raphael beamed. He had learned enough Spanish in recent weeks to know the opportunity he hadn't hardly dared hope for, had fallen into his lap. He knew the one-eyed eagle from his dream, the one with three feathers, was watching over him, and Isabella, too. Thanks to her, Raphael was now one huge step closer to accomplishing his mission of bringing horses to his people.

"My name is Raphael," he said. "Me and my people thank you." Julio turned his horse towards the stables. Raphael followed on foot.

Before reaching their destination, they passed the stone hut where Fray Sinbad lived. Julio stopped his horse and waited for Raphael to catch up.

"The holy man don't crap with us commoners," Julio said. Raphael did not understand. Julio nodded towards a little outhouse behind the hut.

"I'd like to run over and use it a minute, but His Highness would excrete holy wafers. Won't let anyone else use his *mierda visita*, not even Spanish bloods. We call it the *santa mierda* shrine."

Raphael thought he understood what Julio was saying, but he did not respond.

"I'd like to dump a load on his holy collection plate," Julio continued, allowing his horse to start walking again. "I'd burn in purgatory before I'd go to mass or confession with a priest too holy to mix crap with the rest of us."

153

Storm Gold

Upon reaching the stables, Julio showed Raphael where to sleep and eat. He showed Raphael some stalls that needed cleaning.

"I want you to treat these horses as if they were your own," Julio said as he turned to walk away. Raphael thought that was the easiest thing he had ever been asked to do. Of course he would treat the horses as if they were his own. Someday they would be. Of that he was becoming very confident.

Chapter 19

Several weeks had passed before the pain and swelling in Islero's arm subsided to the point where he could begin using it again. But he didn't mind the slow healing process. The Indian women were taking good care of him. And he was enjoying the vacation away from Del Negro. In fact, he liked being away from the mines more than he dared admit. Occasionally, he toyed with the idea of not going back, at least not right away. He didn't know how long he would be content staying in an Indian village full of women, but it would probably be a long time.

Life was comfortable. At least there was plenty to eat. The women were tilling and irrigating several patches of corn and squash. Some of the corn was already drying in preparation for winter.

Every few days, in the morning, some of the women would leave, following downstream the little creek that ran near the camp. In the evening, they would return carrying baskets of fish. Some they would eat, the rest they would dry for winter.

Islero began rethinking some of his opinions about the

opposite sex. He had always thought women had to be dependent on men for their daily sustenance. These women obviously were not dependent on men for anything. If they had a vulnerability, it would be protecting themselves against men. He guessed these women would be in serious trouble if discovered by wandering bands of trappers, slave traders and warriors. It was good they lived in such an isolated, remote spot. As long as they were not discovered, they could exist in relative prosperity--if they could get along with each other. There seemed to be a lot of arguing and bickering, but since native tongues were being spoken, Islero could only guess the source of the conflict, or conflicts.

He liked the Goshute squaw, Mud Woman. More than anyone else, she seemed to be the one in charge. Most of the time, when she gave an order, she was obeyed. Once, when Islero watched her argue with another woman, Mud Woman suddenly struck out and slapped the other woman across the face with the palm of her hand. The woman turned and slithered away, much like a whipped dog would have done.

It was Mud Woman's hut where Islero had been carried the morning of his arrival, and he had been staying there ever since. During the day, women would come and go, frequently staying for a meal, or just to talk. Occasionally, one of them would bring back a portion of his clothing--the items that had been stripped from him the morning he arrived. Eventually, everything was returned.

But at night, he was alone with Mud Woman in the hut. While his wound was healing, there had been no signs on her part of a romantic interest. He wondered, now that his wound was almost better, if that might change. Over the weeks, a sense of familiarity and mutual like had developed. The other women seemed to understand that he belonged to Mud Woman, and they left him alone.

In Islero's society, it was normal for a soldier to take liberties with Indian women when and how he chose. Permission from the woman was not usually sought, and certainly not required. But it was different here. These women

Chapter 19

had saved Islero's life. They had dressed his wounds, fed him, and nurtured him when he could not take care of himself. He was in their debt, and he was willing to wait patiently for Mud Woman to make the first move, when she was ready. If she did nothing, Islero would respect that, too. In the meantime he would be patient.

It was a partly cloudy morning, a gentle breeze coming from the west, when Mud Woman invited Islero to join her and two other women on one of their regular fishing expeditions. He readily agreed. A change of scenery would be pleasant after weeks of confinement in the camp.

They followed the creek downstream for what seemed several miles to where it entered what he was sure was the Green River. Islero had guessed this river couldn't be very far from the camp, but had no idea it was this close. It amazed him even more that these women were able to keep their camp location secret. It was not as remote as he had supposed.

The women welcomed Islero's strength in helping them pull their fish traps from the water. The traps were made of reed grass and willows which were abundant in the area. They were long and narrow, about the width and length of a human torso. At one end the reeds were sharpened and pointed inward to form a circle. It was easy for fish to enter the trap, but almost impossible to get out, particularly the large fish. Most of the fish they caught were catfish and squaw fish.

After all the traps were checked, emptied, and returned to the water, the women started a fire in some soft sand under a huge cottonwood tree. They began cooking some fish. A gentle breeze blew in from the water as Islero stretched out on the warm sand and went to sleep. There was a smile on his face. He hadn't felt this content in a long time.

Islero awakened with a start. He could hear the excited chatter of the women. When he opened his eyes, the women were standing at the edge of the sandy shore, looking out over the water. One of them was pointing at something floating in the current.

Islero jumped to his feet and joined the women. Fifty or

sixty feet out, a cottonwood log was floating by. Something was clinging to the log. Perhaps an animal. No, a man. But he was not moving. Islero guessed he was either dead or unconscious. Still, the man's bare arm was wrapped tightly around the floating log.

Islero had removed his boots before taking his nap, so without hesitation, he ran down to the water and plunged head-first into the river. Islero knew many Spanish sailors who did not swim, but he was not one of them. Where he grew up in Toledo, there had been a deep pond. Many fond memories of his youth involved water games and swimming races with his friends. He was a strong and confident swimmer.

Upon reaching the floating log, Islero could see from the sandy hair on the head and face, and white skin, that the man was not an Indian, even though he was wearing a soggy buckskin shirt. Islero guessed the man was probably an American trapper, perhaps British, and possibly even a Spaniard. The man's head was cocked to one side. His partially opened eyes were glazed over and expressionless, and remained so even after Islero said, *"buenos tardes."*

There was no time to attempt to revive the man, or to exchange anymore greetings or pleasantries. The swift, brown current was carrying them downstream beyond the women, towards a distant rumbling sound which Islero knew was a rapid. He jerked the man free from the tree and began towing him towards shore. Though the body felt cold, Islero knew the man was alive because he coughed whenever water entered his nose or mouth.

Islero was breathing deeply from his exertions when he finally reached shore. The three women were there to meet him, all of them grabbing the unconscious man and dragging him out of the water onto the warm sand. In addition to the buckskin shirt, he was wearing wool trousers, but no boots or shoes. A leather pouch hung from his belt. Inside the pouch was a soggy, black book, not as thick as a Bible. Islero could not read the writing on the book. It was not Spanish.

Chapter 19

The warm sun revived the man. In fifteen minutes he sat up. His blue eyes became alert and intense. Cautiously, he looked at each of the women, then at Islero.

"Am I your prisoner?" he asked. His English was perfect. There was no British accent.

Islero had crossed the Atlantic several times on British schooners. He had learned to speak passable English, though he could not read it.

"No, not mine. You are the prisoner of these women," Islero said, his speech somewhat hesitant, but clear.

"Are you their chief?" the man asked, not sure what to make of Islero's comment.

"No. I'm their prisoner too."

The man shook his head, and slapped himself on the side of the face in an effort to come to his senses, as if to bring himself out of some silly dream and back into the real world. But the three women, and the Spaniard who saved his life, would not go away.

"Who are you?" Islero asked.

"Samuel Johnson," the stranger replied.

"You are American?"

"Yes."

"Trapper or trader?"

"Neither."

"Americans who come here are trappers or traders."

"Not me. I'm on an errand for the Lord."

"I do not understand."

"Sent by a prophet of God. Looking for the promised land, a place for God's people to settle--where they won't be kicked around by the United States."

"You're a priest?" Islero asked.

"No. I'm a Mormon elder, a member of the Church of Jesus Christ of Latter-day Saints. Ever hear of Joseph Smith and the Book of Mormon?"

Islero had not. He had no idea what this strange fellow was talking about, only that it had something to do with religion, some kind of belief other than Catholicism. This man

159

was some kind of heretic.

Before Islero could answer, one of the women who had walked back to the fire, returned with a slab of cottonwood bark covered with pieces of fresh roasted fish. Sam Johnson didn't need to be invited to partake. As soon as the bark platter was placed on his lap, he bowed his head, closed his eyes and muttered the fastest prayer Islero had ever heard, then began shoving the fish into his mouth faster than he could chew and swallow. The women seemed pleased, and were thinking they would now have two men in their village. The great spirit had been kind to them.

"Never tasted anything so wonderful. Not ever," Johnson said, his mouth still stuffed with fish. "I swear I can feel the strength spreading from my stomach to the rest of my body. Oh, thank you. Tastes better than any roast beef, potatoes and gravy, and apple pie I ever et." His words were mostly meaningless to Islero and the Indian women who had never tasted such things, but Johnson's meaning was clear. He had the hunger of a man who hadn't eaten in several days.

"Why were you floating down the river?" Islero asked when it appeared Sam's appetite was finally beginning to be satisfied, and there was no cooked fish remaining for him to devour.

"Was traveling with some trappers who said they would show me the Great Basin and a big chunk of fertile land near the Great Salt Lake. We were following the Platte, then made a detour down to Brown's Hole to trade some stuff. That's where the Crows attacked us. Trailed us for a couple of days. I finally lost them when I jumped into the river and latched onto the big tree you saw me hanging onto. Think everybody else was killed and scalped."

"Lucky to be alive," Islero said.

"Didn't tell you the worst part," Sam said, thoughtfully.

"What's that?"

"Can't swim a lick. Never could. That's why I was still hanging onto the tree when you found me. Couldn't get to

160

Chapter 19

shore."

Islero looked at Sam Johnson with new respect. It took a lot of courage for a man who couldn't swim to jump into the Green River.

"How long were you in the water?" Islero asked.

"About three days, I reckon. Three longest days of my life. Made a sacred vow to the Lord."

Islero had been with a number of men over the years who, when facing death, had made promises to God. Usually they promised to mend their sinful ways if God saved them. And when their lives were spared, which was not always the case, they usually went right back to doing the same old things they had always done.

"What did you promise?" Islero asked, figuring he already knew the answer.

"Didn't promise to be a good boy," Sam said, grinning, knowing what Islero was thinking. "Already a good boy. Don't drink. Don't chew. Don't cuss. And don't fornicate."

"Then what did you promise?" Islero asked. He was beginning to like this American.

"That if he'd spare my life, I'd learn to swim. And that I intend to do. Will you teach me?"

Islero began to laugh, at the same time realizing he hadn't laughed in a long time. "Yes, I'll teach you, but not today. It is a long walk back to camp. You had better come with us."

"Are we really prisoners, like you said?"

"They saved me like they did you. I don't think they will scalp us. Come."

On the way back to camp, Islero explained how the village they were approaching consisted of women only, how the women were from different tribes, that their men had been killed or taken away as slaves. The abandoned women had banded together for mutual survival and protection. Luckily, they had found an isolated valley, where no one had found them, at least not until Islero had come along.

Storm Gold

Sam Johnson explained his mission to this wild, remote, Green River country. The Mormons had been driven from Missouri after their capital city, Far West, had been taken over by state militia in 1838. The prophet, Joseph Smith, had selected several men, including Sam Johnson, to go west in search of a place where the Mormons could settle, far from the unjust government of the United States.

Two of the men had gone to Oregon and California, one to Vancouver Island, and two to Texas while Sam was trying to find and explore the Great Basin area around the Great Salt Lake.

"I have been there, several times," Islero said.

"Would you take me there?" Johnson asked, his voice suddenly very excited.

"Maybe someday," Islero answered, reservation in his voice, thinking Johnson's request was a pretty big one, considering the two had just met.

"Tell me about it," Johnson insisted.

"Fray Escalante visited the valley south of the salt sea in 1776. He said the land could support a city as large and grand as Toledo, the place of my birth. The mountains to the east of the valley catch enough snow in the winter to feed the valley with water all year. The biggest mountain is called Timpanogos. The rivers dump into the legendary lake the Aztecs call Copalla. It is full of speckled trout and squaw fish as big as a man's arm. At the edge of the lake the grass is as tall as the back of a horse. Every summer the many bands of Ute Indians gather at Lake Copalla for their annual fish festival. Sometimes, the American traders come with plenty of whiskey and beads."

"Sounds like a wonderful place," Johnson said. "I'm going there."

"The man I work for, Victorio Del Negro, is there now," Islero volunteered.

"He wants to start a city?" Johnson asked.

"No, to find gold."

"What gold?"

Chapter 19

"Aztec gold. Or at least the mine where they got it. Victorio inherited documents from his grandfather, Diego Penalosa, indicating this land of Teguayo, where Mt. Timpanogos and Lake Copalla are located, is the same place where the Aztecs mined the gold they hauled to Mexico City for over a thousand years."

"Is the gold still there?" Johnson asked.

"Got to be, but we can't find it. That's why Del Negro is there right now."

"When will you take me?" Johnson asked.

"Maybe never, but if I don't, I know where to find some American trappers who might," Islero said.

The next afternoon, Islero and Sam sneaked away from the village, when they thought the squaws were not looking, and worked their way up the little creek to a spot Islero had discovered earlier. A rock slide backed up the water to form a long, waist-deep pond. It was time for Sam's first swimming lesson.

After removing their clothes, Islero plunged into the water and demonstrated the crawl, backstroke, sidestroke and the back float. When he was finished, Sam worked his way carefully into the pool to begin his first awkward attempts at learning to swim.

An hour later they crawled from the water onto the bank where they stretched out on the grass to bask in the sun. Islero began humming a bawdy song he had learned from some British sailors, but he could not remember the words.

Both were enjoying themselves immensely, relaxed and happy, stretched out naked on the cool grass, soaking up the summer sun.

"I think I hear some noise in the bushes behind us," Islero offered, turning to look. Sam continued to look straight ahead at the water.

"Could it be a bear?" Sam asked, no sense of alarm in his voice.

"Good choice of words," Islero said. "Bare, all right, all 13 of them."

163

Storm Gold

Suddenly the air was filled with shrieks of delight, and female laughter, as 13 stark naked squaws raced from the bushes, across the grass, and plunged into the water. Some began splashing water on the two surprised men.

Ten minutes later some of the women were still bathing in the stream. The rest were sunning themselves on the grass, Sam turned to Islero.

"I think its time for a very serious discussion on morality."

"Morality, I don't understand," Islero said.

"The rightness and wrongness of men and women, who are not married, enjoying close physical contact," Sam explained.

"You mean sex out of wedlock?" Islero asked.

"Yes. What does your Catholic Church say about that?"

"That it's wrong. You can burn in purgatory for adultery."

"Us Mormons believe about the same thing. So I guess you don't plan on touching any of these women."

"You are wrong, my friend," Islero said. "I plan on touching as many of these dark beauties as want me to, and maybe some of the non-beauties too."

"So then you are not a good Catholic. You do not take your religion seriously."

"I am insulted," Islero responded. "My religious beliefs are sacred to me."

"Then how can you say, with a clear conscience, you intend to take liberties with these women?"

"First of all," Islero said. His voice was strong, filled with conviction. "These women are heathen savages, not Catholic, Christian white women."

"Do you really think these women have any less value in the sight of God than a Christian white woman?" Sam asked. Neither man was smiling. The discussion had become very serious.

"Probably not, but I know some priests who argue

these women are not the same. Still, I don't think God judges quite so harshly in cases like this. I'm 10,000 kilometers from home and haven't seen my wife in over eight years. The Lord must understand that.''

"Still, it's adultery. I've taken sacred oaths to remain chaste,'' Sam explained.

"Then there's confession'' Islero continued. "When I get back to Rock Creek, I'll confess to Fray Castilla what I did here. I'll toss a few nuggets on his little silver plate, and he'll say, 'My son, your sins are forgiven.' Don't Mormons believe in confession?''

"Yes, when serious sin, like adultery, is involved,'' Sam explained. "But if we confess, then sin again, we are in deep trouble. The confession only works if you change and never do it again.''

"I like the Catholic way better,'' Islero said.

"Right now, I do too,'' Sam confessed.

The pretty Navajo woman, the one Islero thought might be even more attractive than Mud Woman, crawled out of the pool, walked over to Sam, leaned over him and shook her wet head, much like a dog would have after getting out of the water, playfully spraying him with the water from her body. Then she stretched out on the grass next to him.

Islero grinned as he watched Sam struggle with himself not to look over at the beautiful woman stretched out on the grass beside him. Islero figured Sam's battle would be a losing one.

"You could come back to Rock Creek with me,'' Islero offered. "Offer your confession to Fray Castilla. I'm sure he would give you the same forgiveness he would give me. You don't have to tell him you're a Mormon. He won't ask if you put enough nuggets on the plate. I'm sure he doesn't know what a Mormon is anyway.''

"I can't do that. I'm not Catholic.''

"We could get you baptized real quick.''

"You can't trick the Lord,'' Sam said. "I'll lose my eternal soul if I stay here another day. I'm leaving for Fort

Robidoux tonight.''

"But you don't know the way," Islero protested, not wanting to lose his new friend.

"You could draw me a map.''

"It would not be safe for you to travel alone. Besides, you could not follow a map in the dark.''

"What's her name?'' Sam asked, glancing quickly at the woman, then forcing himself to look away.

"Ish-na-bah. She's Navajo. She likes you very much.''

"Just point in the direction of Robidoux. I'm on my way," Sam said, starting to get to his feet, looking in the direction of the bush where he had left his clothes.

"Wait a minute," Islero said, grabbing Sam by the hand and pulling him back to the ground. "Tell me if you have a wife.''

"Yes," Sam said. "Back in Missouri. Her name is Martha. We have no children.''

"I am sorry," Islero said.

"Sorry. About what? That I have no children?''

"No, that you have a wife. If you didn't, as *alcalde* of this little village, I could marry you to Ish-na-bah.''

"What is an *alcalde*?'' Sam asked.

"The head man in a village. In Spanish villages, the *alcalde* has authority to perform marriages. But since you are already married, I guess that was a bad idea.''

"You didn't tell me you were the head man," Sam said.

"I'm the only man, at least I was until you came along. But don't tell Mud Woman I call myself the head man. She's the head woman. Don't want her thinking she's got a rival.''

"What have you heard about the Mormons?'' Sam asked. "Before I came along.''

"Not a thing. Out in this country you can't keep up with what the American sects are doing.''

"One time, our prophet, Joseph Smith, was asked how the Indians would become 'white and delightsome' as prophesied in the Book of Mormon. He said the brethren

166

would marry the squaws and produce white, or at least whiter children. Then someone asked how the brethren could marry squaws when they already had wives. He said they would do it the same way Abraham, Isaac, Jacob, David and Solomon did it, by taking plural wives."

"Mormons believe in polygamy?" Islero asked, with enthusiasm.

"Some of the brethren have already taken plural wives, some Indian wives, too. But it's all very secret. Rumors about it are already threatening to tear the Church apart. I should not be telling you this."

"Tell me no more," Islero boomed. "Sam, my friend, your troubles are over." Before Sam could respond, Islero reached across Sam's knees and grabbed Ish-na-bah by the hand.

"Ish-na-bah," he began. "Do you take Sam Johnson, Mormon elder, to be your legal and lawful husband?"

The woman looked uncertain. She hadn't understood a word that had been spoken. Islero reached out with his other hand and moved her chin up and down.

"I'd say that's a passable gesture," he said. Then looking at Sam, he said, "Sam Johnson, do you take Ish-na-bah to be your legal and lawful plural wife?"

Sam didn't respond, stunned by the suddenness of what was happening. Islero grabbed him by the chin and pushed it up and down, as he had done with the woman.

"As *alcalde* of Squaw City, I now pronounce you man and plural wife. Sam you may kiss the bride. You don't have to wait until she is dressed."

Sam didn't kiss the bride, at least not at that moment. He jumped to his feet and ran to the bush where he had left his clothes.

Chapter 20

Fray Castilla was proud of what he had accomplished in such a short time. Since the day he had begun his training in the Franciscan order, he had dreamed of establishing his own mission. Now he was doing it.

With the help of the local Indians in upper Spanish Fork Canyon, he had just completed the *visita* or church. He was the first to admit it wasn't much by European standards, but it was a beginning. The walls were of rubble stone, piled to a height of about six feet. The roof consisted of poles and brush, which was effective in keeping out the summer sun, but not the rain. The building was about three meters wide, and seven meters long, with a single entrance at one end. There were no window openings. A log cross over the doorway was the only evidence on the outside that this humble structure was a house of God.

Inside, at the far end, was a plank altar, decorated with pictures of the Virgin Mary holding her new baby, and Jesus in the garden tomb. There was a log cross above the altar. Crude candleholders lined the walls, but only two contained candles.

Storm Gold

Behind the church was Fray Castilla's private quarters, a stone hut with a roof of pine boughs. It was about eight feet wide and eight feet deep with a ceiling barely high enough for him to stand up. But it was sufficient for his needs, and he had built it himself, with the help of some of the Indians.

He persuaded some of the Indians to help clear and till several patches of good soil next to the little creek. Here he planted squash and beans. It was too late in the season for corn.

But what pleased Castilla more than his new church, home and gardens was the fact that his congregation was growing. He hadn't baptized anyone yet, but every time he held vespers or other meetings, it seemed more Indians were in attendance.

One thing he made clear. Everyone who shared his food and stayed at his new settlement was required to attend meetings. So far everyone, except the sick, had complied with this request. But he knew the time would come when verbal urgings would not be sufficient to get everyone to services.

It was common at remote *visitas* throughout New Spain to take roll at meetings and administer whippings to heathens, particularly men, who missed more than one meeting in a row. Priests all over New Spain were in agreement, that for the most part, heathen savages were not capable of using free choice to come to Christ. Sterner measures were needed. But fearing such strict measures might drive some of the Indians away, Fray Castilla decided verbal persuasion would have to suffice, at least in the beginning.

Castilla's advertising consisted of three brightly colored flags on a little hill overlooking the main trail. Everyone using the trail, mostly Indians, would see the flags and come to investigate. The friendly friar would give them something to eat, then invite them to stay for services. Some, at the priest's urgings, agreed to stay longer. The supply of corn, beans, and dried meat left behind by Del Negro was disappearing quickly, but Fray Castilla was confident when these supplies ran out, the Lord would provide another source of food. In the meantime he was doing the work of God, saving heathen souls.

Castilla felt strongly that even savages must understand the basic principles of Catholicism before they were baptized. Therefore he began courses of instruction, focusing on Spanish and religion at the same time. Most of the time the classes were held in the church, but sometimes he did his tutoring under a large cottonwood tree near the church.

Something that worried him the first few weeks was what to call the place. He felt embarrassed whenever he thought of naming it Castilla, after himself. Finally, he selected Medicine Springs as the name. There were several hot springs in the area which the natives believed had medicinal, or healing properties.

One afternoon a group of warriors entered the settlement. They were the same ones who had watched Fray Castilla from the hillside the day of his arrival. The one wearing the Spanish helmet was their leader. He was a squat, powerful man. When his helmet was removed, he looked as if a heavy weight had been placed on his head, pressing down, forcing the sides out, widening his jaws--giving him the look of a large toad. A large number of complexion blemishes only added to the comparison. His thick black hair was short for an Indian, and hung loosely about his shoulders. His name was Wahpeoop. The only thing beautiful, or graceful about the man were the two golden bracelets on his left wrist.

Wahpeoop was not Ute. He was from the rugged land of deep canyons and high mountains between the Humbolt and Snake River drainages. He was already hated by the Shoshones and most of the Paiutes, and on this expedition was hoping to establish a reputation among the Utes--but from the looks of the small string of skin-and-bones horses he was leading, it was apparent he was not enjoying very much success. Wahpeoop and the six men with him were in sour spirits. The hardships of the trail had not been rewarded. They were still a long way from home, and had nothing to eat. They had had a difficult time finding game.

Castilla excused his students from their language lesson under the cottonwood tree in order to greet the new guests. He offered them tortillas and beans, and invited them to stay for evening vespers. None of them had the slightest idea what vespers was, but since it was late in the day, and it appeared there was a good chance for another free meal the next morning, they decided to stay.

After checking the general condition of the horses in Fray Castilla's pasture, and the women in the brush huts, Wahpeoop decided the only reason to stay over was the free food. Unless... He noticed the priest's reddish-brown hair only partially covered by the little brown skull cap. A scalp of that color would be a wonderful prize to hang on his lodge. And it would be nice to get the priest's bags of beans and corn, and be well fed for the duration of their journey.

After vespers, Wahpeoop and his men disappeared into the trees, taking their horses with them, but they were back again the next morning, wanting something more to eat before heading down the trail. All the men were armed, and their mood seemed every bit as sour as it had been the previous afternoon.

For the first time, Fray Castilla noticed the golden bracelets on Wahpeoop's arm. The priest remembered Del Negro's request to keep an eye open for gold, and information about gold.

When Wahpeoop and his men finished eating, Castilla wrapped up some tortillas and beans for them to take with them on the trail, but when Wahpeoop reached out to take the fare, Castilla refused to give up the food, pointing to the Spanish helmet, indicating he wanted to trade the food for the helmet. The Indian shook his head, refusing to trade his metal headdress for food. Castilla tucked the bundle of food under his arm, and turned as if to walk away.

Wahpeoop reached out and grabbed the priest's robe, stopping him from leaving. His companions' hands moved closer to their bows and spears, anticipating a confrontation of force. Wahpeoop didn't want to give up the helmet, but he had to have the food, even if he had to take it by force. But he hesitated using force on the strange white man. Some said the black robes made strong medicine, that they could not be defeated in battle. The priest didn't appear to be carrying a weapon, unless one was hidden beneath the robe. The Indians at the settlement didn't appear to be strong enough to protect the priest. Yet the priest didn't seem to fear Wahpeoop and his companions. Why was the priest not afraid? What hidden powers did he possess? Wahpeoop wasn't sure what to do. He knew only that he had to have the food.

In a somewhat nonchalant manner, Castilla pointed at the golden bracelets on Wahpeoop's left wrist, indicating he might be willing to trade for one of them. Without hesitation, Wahpeoop tore off one of the bracelets and handed it to the priest, who in turn handed the brave the bundle of food.

In trading for the bracelet, the priest didn't see gold and the wealth it represented, but rather a few more sacks of corn and beans which he knew Del Negro would give him now that gold was involved. Castilla knew Del Negro would continue to supply the new mission as long as there was hope the source of the golden bracelets might be discovered.

Wahpeoop grunted his satisfaction upon receiving the food. He didn't care about giving up the bracelet. There were plenty more where that came from. As he turned to leave, he looked at the priest's reddish-brown hair one more time, promising himself the time would come when he would return to take that scalp, but not today. As Wahpeoop and his companions galloped away, Fray Castilla had no idea how close he had come to losing everything. As he slipped the golden bracelet on his left wrist, he knew only that he had something that would make Victorio Del Negro very happy.

Chapter 21

Isabella and Victorio's march slowed down considerably after leaving Fray Castilla behind at the head of Spanish Fork Canyon. It seemed the canyon was full of travelers, not just Indians, but Spaniards as well. Or at least Victorio called them Spaniards, though most of them now called themselves Mexicans. It had been nearly 20 years since Mexico had declared its independence from Spain.

The first evening after leaving Fray Castilla behind, Victorio shared camp with Pedro Leon, a Mexican slave trader who was returning to Santa Fe after trading the Teguayo Utes out of 23 Goshute children, mostly girls.

When Isabella saw the girls resting beside their campfires, nursing sore feet, she remembered her own journey from her home village to Rock Creek. Few, if any, of these girls would find slavery as agreeable as she had. But their life of survival among the horseless Goshutes was not easy either. Perhaps slavery would be an improvement. But these girls were not headed to the mines, but to Sante Fe. Most would become domestic servants. Some would become prostitutes.

After supper, Victorio began to negotiate in earnest with

Pedro Leon for the purchase of some of the Goshute boys. Isabella found this an excellent opportunity to slip away from the camp. She wandered downstream looking for a secluded bend in the river, where she might find a pool where she could bathe.

She was probably a mile from camp when she found just what she was looking for, a sharp turn in the river where a deep pool had been dug in the soft sand. Willows clogged the bank on all sides, except for a ten-meter sand bar at the edge of the pool.

She didn't waste any time slipping out of her clothes and sliding into the clear, cool water. It didn't worry her that it would soon be dark. By the time it got dark a three-quarter moon would be coming over the eastern hills, and there would be plenty of light for her to see her way back to camp.

She was floating on her back, paddling slowly across the pool, when she saw the first puff of smoke, on the crest of a nearby hill. She thought it strange that someone would want to build a campfire on top of a steep hill, when the best places to camp were on the valley floor where the meadows were flat, and there was plenty of water and firewood.

As she changed directions to paddle back across the pool, at the same time making it easier to look in another direction, she saw another puff of smoke on another hill. Now that her interest was aroused, she looked carefully in all directions, and found still another column of smoke. She was still floating on her back, wondering why so many people would want campfires on top of the hills, when she saw a column of men, Indians, walking along the crest of one of the ridges. There were twelve men in the column, and all were carrying bows or spears.

She guessed these men were not a hunting party. Because so many people traveled through this part of the canyon, the wild game, for the most part, had been hunted out. This was not a good place to hunt. A hunting party would not come here. And if they were merely passing through, they could travel much faster on the main trail than on the hilltops.

176

Chapter 21

No, this was a war party, and there were probably a lot more Indians involved than the twelve she had seen. It was easy to guess who in the area they intended to make war on-- Pedro Leon, the slave trader, or Victorio Del Negro, the one who bought slaves for his mines.

She paddled to the edge of the water and crawled out on the sand. Between the warm evening sun and the cool breeze, it took only minutes to dry. Quickly, she slipped into her deerskin dress, glancing over her shoulder at the hill where she had seen the warriors, hoping no one had seen her.

She didn't head back to camp immediately, guessing there would be less chance of anyone seeing her if she waited until she could find cover in the shadows of twilight.

As soon as the sun dropped below the western hills, she began her cautious journey back to camp. The thought occurred to her that instead of going back to a camp that was going to be attacked, perhaps she ought to sneak into the thick brush where she could hide until it was safe to work her way back to her people. She wondered why she should feel obligated to warn Victorio of the danger in the hills around his camp. She couldn't answer that question. She knew only that Victorio must be warned of this danger before it was too late.

Isabella tried to stay in the shadows as she worked her way upstream. The distance from camp to the bathing pool hadn't seemed very far, but now that she faced the possibility of hostile eyes watching her, it seemed the camp was a continent away.

What she didn't know was that some of the Indians on the hilltops had spotted her on the way to the pool, and that half a dozen Shoshone warriors had already abandoned their hilltop vantage point in an effort to intercept her before she could return to camp.

The men stalking Isabella were not so much soldiers as hunters--men who had grown up in remote wilderness environments, hunting deer, elk, antelope, bison and other animals. These were men who had perfected the primitive skills of stalking and tracking. They were masters at getting

177

close to game without being seen, smelled or heard. They had hunted so much, that it had become more of an instinct than a rational applied knowledge. They were wolves gliding effortlessly and silently through the primeval forest, not white men stumbling clumsily in an unfamiliar stand of timber.

Isabella hadn't gone more than a hundred yards when she was grabbed from behind and wrestled to the ground. When she tried to scream, a wad of greasy buckskin was shoved into her mouth. Quickly, her hands were tied together behind her back with a strip of rawhide. Her ankles were left unshackled, so she could walk with her captors.

Not a word was spoken as they led her up a brushy draw away from the river. She had no idea where they were taking her, but she had a pretty good idea what they were going to do to her. She wanted to tell them she was not Spanish, that she was a slave, that she was grateful to them for taking her away from Del Negro. She hoped they would let her return to her people, the Utes. But with the rawhide wad in her mouth, she could say nothing, and she wasn't sure her words would do any good, even if she could talk. These men were Shoshones, the enemies of the Utes and the Spanish. Either way, she was in trouble. At worst, she would be dead by morning. At best, they would make her their slave and take her home with them to their homeland along the Snake River.

At the head of the draw, they reached a grassy flat, circled by thick patches of oak brush. Many horses were tethered to trees and bushes. She noticed two or three cook fires. Men came from every direction to see the new captive.

One of her captors jerked the wad from her mouth, pulled her to him and began kissing her on the lips. She pretended to be giving in to him until he gave her the opportunity to bite off the end of his tongue. He pushed her away as the blood began oozing onto his bare chest.

Three other men grabbed her, untied her hands so they could remove her dress, then pushed her to the ground. When one of them tried to climb on top of her, she kicked him with

178

all her might between the legs. He rolled away, in pain and agony.

More men fell on her and held her tightly while she thrashed helplessly to get away. A stake was pounded in the ground about a foot above her head. They lashed both her hands to this stake. Two more stakes were pounded in the ground, one out to the side of each foot. Two braves pulled her legs apart and lashed her ankles to each of these stakes.

About a dozen warriors stood in a circle around her, examining their good work in securing their beautiful victim, and anticipating the pleasure she would give them during the night. The only question remaining was who would be first.

One of them produced a piece of bone, suggesting a few rounds of the bone game--that they gamble for the rights to enjoy the woman. All readily agreed, and quickly seated themselves cross-legged on the ground in two rows, facing each other.

Isabella stopped struggling, closed her eyes and began to pray. She prayed to the Ute God Towatts, begging him to free her from the approaching agony, even to take her life, if necessary. When nothing happened, she began praying to the Catholic Jesus. She had never professed belief in this Jesus, and had not been baptized, but the unwavering faith of Fray Castilla had made an impact on her. With tears streaming down her cheeks, she promised the Spanish Jesus that she would give herself to baptism and become a good Catholic if he would save her from the Shoshones. She begged with all her heart for him to help her.

She didn't know how long she prayed, but it was nearly dark when she opened her eyes. The first thing she noticed was that the braves who had been noisy and boisterous in their bone game a few moments earlier, had suddenly become silent.

For a brief moment she thought her captors might have deserted her, so complete was the silence. But when she turned her head to the side, she could see the two rows of warriors, but instead of gambling, they were all looking in the

179

same direction, towards the bottom end of the clearing.

It was almost too dark to see, when she turned her head even further to see what they were looking at.

Even in the semi-darkness she had no trouble seeing a different kind of warrior at the edge of the meadow. He wore a polished breastplate and helmet, and his muscular arm carried a glistening blade of Seville steel. The majestic warrior was mounted on a nervous black stallion. Victorio Del Negro had come to rescue her. She hoped others had come with him, but she could see no one else.

Victorio moved forward, not at a gallop, but at a walk, or more of a prance. The big black was too excited to walk quietly. The sides of his neck were wet with sweat resulting from the eager anticipation of battle.

As Victorio moved towards Isabella, the Shoshones seemed paralyzed with surprise and astonishment. They remained silent, though some rose to their feet. Some looked towards the brush, probably wondering if this strange warrior had companions.

Upon reaching Isabella, Victorio reached down with the tip of his sword and touched the rawhide bands holding her wrists. The stiff leather offered no resistance to the razor-edged steel. Then he cut free both of her ankles. Some of the warriors began moving towards the edge of the clearing to get their weapons.

Without warning, Victorio, with a tug at the reins and a touch of the spur, launched the black stallion into action. The powerful animal spun and lunged at the warriors who still remained, its ears pinned back flat on its neck. The first warrior lost his head, the second an arm, and the third, half a torso.

Isabella did not stand around to watch. She slipped into her dress and started running towards the draw at the bottom of the clearing. She hadn't covered half the distance when she heard hoofbeats behind her. The powerful arm of Victorio reached down and scooped her up, not bothering to slow his horse as she settled behind him, grasping tightly to his waist.

Chapter 21

As the powerful black raced out of the clearing and into the draw, arrows were raining from the sky.

On the way back to camp, Victorio explained that when he had finished his business with Pedro Leon he had come looking for her. One of his men had seen her heading downstream earlier in the afternoon, but had not seen her return. Concerned for her safety, Victorio continued his search. Fortunately, as he passed the draw leading to the warrior camp, he had looked up just in time to catch a glimpse of the warriors dragging Isabella up the trail.

As she thanked him, she thought of her prayer to Jesus, and wondered if it had really been answered. Her faith in the prayer was tempered by the knowledge that Victorio was already on the trail to save her before she offered her plea to heaven.

She told Victorio about the three columns of smoke and the dozen warriors she had seen before her capture. She believed there were a lot of Indians in the area, many more than the ones Victorio had encountered in the meadow. Victorio concluded the Spanish camp would probably be under attack by morning.

No one slept that night, other than an occasional nap, as everyone frantically prepared to fight. Swords and spear points were sharpened, muskets were loaded, horses shod. River rocks were piled in rows to form defensive barriers. Food was cooked, water jugs filled, prayers offered.

Upon seeing the preparations for battle, Pedro Leon gathered up his slaves and retreated up the canyon. Del Negro made no attempt to stop him. Leon's men didn't appear to be fighters, and the slaves would be in the way. If a lengthy siege developed, there would be too many mouths to feed.

Whenever Isabella had a free moment, she found herself thinking about her capture by the Shoshones, and how Victorio had boldly entered the clearing to rescue her. Even though he had been badly outnumbered, he had risked his life to save hers. She thought about the ride back to camp, her arms around his waist, holding on tightly, feeling his warmth and strength, her face in his hair, her knees against the back of his thighs. She remembered the goose bumps on her arms, even though she was not cold. She wished there was more time to talk with Victorio about what had happened, but he seemed totally engrossed in the preparations for battle.

With the first light of day, arrows began falling from the sky. They were coming from the steep, oak-brush covered hills on both sides of the camp. Because the arrows were fired from long distance, they were not very accurate, most sinking helplessly into the soft ground. But in less than an hour, some had found their mark. Three horses and one man had been wounded.

The campsite had not been selected for its strategic value in time of war. There was plenty of feed for the animals, and good water. Had Victorio known there was a risk of attack by Indians, he would not have camped in such a vulnerable place. But there was no time for regrets now.

The valley narrowed above and below the camp. Any attempt to retreat would be like running the gauntlet. Undoubtedly, the enemy had men stationed in both locations, ready for easy ambush.

What seemed unfair to Victorio was the knowledge that the hostile Indians had been pursuing Pedro Leon who frequently traded in Shoshone slave children. Pedro had slipped away during the night, leaving Victorio Del Negro behind to fight his battle.

The thick oak brush on the hillsides above the camp made it impossible for Victorio and his men to see the enemy. Victorio decided against launching an attack up the steep mountains. There was too much brush to make attack by horseback feasible, and men on foot, carrying heavy armor, uphill, would be at a huge disadvantage.

While defending themselves against the onslaught of arrows from the sky, Victorio ordered his men to be patient, to give the appearance of vulnerability, hoping the hostiles would attack. Victorio was confident his men, armed with swords and muskets, and protected with breastplates and helmets, could easily win a battle on the open, flat ground, even if the Shoshones had vastly superior numbers. But he didn't think he could effectively fight them in the thick oak brush on the steep sidehills, particularly when they had the elevation advantage. So he waited, ready for battle, if and when the Indians decided to attack.

The wait was a long one. Arrows continued to fall from the sky throughout the entire morning. Some of his men began collecting arrows, and had accumulated hundreds, many without broken tips. The siege continued into the afternoon. More men and animals were wounded. The Indians showed no signs of letting up, nor were there any indications they might attack.

By evening, the horses and mules were getting restless, having not been allowed to graze since the attack begun. The men were getting restless, too. The relentless onslaught of arrows had added anger to their frustration at not being able to see the enemy. Not only were they ready, but they were eager to fight. It was time to do something. The only thing Victorio could think to do was fight through one of the narrow passes above or below the camp. Undoubtedly, the Indians were anticipating such a move, and would be ready. Losses could be high, but perhaps could be tempered with the partial cover of darkness. With the new three-quarter moon, the darkness would not be complete.

As the sun went down, the men began saddling the horses and mules in preparation for a charge down the canyon. The evening wind was stronger than usual. Victorio couldn't see all the way through the canyon he intended to escape through, so as soon as it was dark, he sent two men ahead on foot, to make sure the trail was clear, through the narrowest part of the canyon.

An hour later, the scouts returned with bad news. The Indians had barricaded the narrowest section of the canyon with cottonwood logs. The horses and mules would not be able to get through. The Spanish would have to stop and move the logs, during which time they would be easy targets for

183

Indian arrows.

Victorio sent two scouts upstream to see if the path was clear to escape in that direction. Again, a cottonwood log jam was found. Apparently it had been put in place after Pedro Leon had made his nighttime escape.

More arrows began falling from the sky as Victorio made his way over to Isabella. He explained his predicament. The log jams would set his men up for certain slaughter should they try to escape during the night. The Indians would continue to shower arrows on them if they remained where they were. It appeared the only reasonable alternative now was to wait until morning, then wage a desperate battle fighting up the steep, wooded hills against an enemy who outnumbered them five or six to one.

She wondered why he was telling her all this. It wasn't as if he were expecting military advice from a woman, and a slave woman at that. She guessed maybe she was just someone for him to talk to, a sounding board perhaps, a chance to think out loud. She let him talk as she warmed some tortillas and meat over a small fire under a crude log shelter that had been hastily assembled as a shield against the arrows falling from the sky.

She stirred the coals to get a little more heat as Victorio paced back and forth. When she handed him a piece of meat wrapped in a tortilla, their hands touched, briefly. She felt a pleasant chill run up and down her spine, and found herself longing to touch him again. He seemed indifferent to her as he turned and walked away, chewing thoughtfully on his supper.

As she returned to the fire to warm another tortilla, a clump of dry grass next to the fire, burst into flame. It spread to a second clump of grass before she could stomp it out. One had to be careful with fire, especially when the wind was blowing so hard. And everything was so dry.

An idea entered her head, too outrageous to think about. She tried to dismiss it, but it would not go away. It was almost dark when she looked up at the steep hills on both sides of the camp. The thick brush, which offered the Indians such excellent cover, could be their undoing.

She prepared a bundle of shredded juniper bark, and scooped coals from the fire into it. She wrapped the bundle in a piece of soft deerskin and went looking for Del Negro.

She found him in heated discussion with some of the men, who argued it would be better to do battle at either of the log barricades than try to fight up the steep hills. Victorio disagreed. The discussion was intense. The lives of everyone in the party were on the line.

She tapped on Victorio's shoulder. When he looked at her, she said she needed to speak with him, and asked if he could step away from the other men for a moment. He said he couldn't until he was finished with the business at hand. He didn't say it, but the look on his face said he was too busy discussing important matters with men than to be bothered by a woman. Then he turned away from her to continue his discussion.

Isabella felt hurt and rejected. Angry too. Victorio was stupid not wanting to consider all ideas that might save him and his men from such an awful predicament.

As she walked away, she looked up at the eastern hills. There was a silver lining, indicating the moon would be coming over the hill any minute, eliminating the cover of almost total darkness. The wind was still blowing briskly, but it could stop at any moment, as it did every evening about this time. There was no time to lose. She could not wait for Victorio to make time to speak to her. She disappeared in the darkness, feeling her way towards the nearest hill.

Upon reaching the steep incline, she groped around until she found some thick brush, tangled in thick, dry grass. She dropped to her knees and unwrapped the juniper bark bundle. She nudged several of the embers onto the grass, then quickly re-wrapped the deerskin bundle. She didn't need to bend over and blow on the embers. The wind did it for her. By the time she had tucked the bundle under her arm, the grass in front of her had burst into flames. She turned and ran, knowing the new light would make her an easy target for Shoshone arrows.

Upon reaching camp, she did not stop to discuss what she had done with Del Negro, but continued straight ahead to the opposite hill, where she dropped to her knees in some thick brush and started a second fire.

By the time she returned to camp, there was no more darkness to hide her actions. The roaring flames on both sides of the camp had turned night to day. Fanned by the wind, the flames were roaring up both hills, some of the flames taller than the tallest cottonwood tree. Occasionally, an Indian could be seen, scampering ahead of the flames. Some were not fast enough, and their death cries could be heard as the fire engulfed them.

Victorio didn't waste any time taking advantage of the situation. He ordered the pack mules loaded. As soon as that was accomplished, he ordered everyone to follow him up the nearest hill, behind the line of fire. His objective was to capture a defendable position on high ground before the Indians had a chance to regroup.

Most of the mules and some of the horses were reluctant to enter the ashes and embers left behind by the raging fire. With the help of spurs and whips they finally consented to make the journey up the mountain.

The Shoshones offered no resistance to the ascending Spaniards. The enemy's line of defense had gone up in smoke. In fact, not a single arrow was fired at Victorio and his men as they struggled in a criss-cross fashion up the steep hill.

At first there was plenty of light from the fire, but as the fire burned further and further away, they depended more and more on the light of the moon which by now was in full view over the eastern hills.

Isabella rode at the rear of the column. Everyone was so engrossed in getting out of the death trap, that no one was asking how the fires got started. And she wasn't about to start bragging. But if anyone ever asked her for an opinion, she thought she would simply say she thought the men of the world would be better off if they spent more time listening to women.

Around midnight, Victorio found a flat on top of a rocky ridge he thought would be easy to defend. The sore-footed horses and mules were unsaddled and staked out to graze. None of them had any hair left around their feet and ankles, thanks to the hot embers left behind by the fire. Guards were posted. Everyone else took turns washing off soot and ashes at a nearby spring. After washing, Isabella found a soft clump of grass and went to sleep.

She awakened to a gray dawn, the air filled with the smoke of a thousand fires. Everyone had sore eyes and throats from all the smoke. Three scouts, sent out by Victorio at first light, returned with news that the Shoshone war party had retreated down the canyon. There was no immediate danger of Indian attack. Those who were awake cheered, awakening everyone else.

Victorio stepped to the center of the camp, as if he were about to make a speech.

"Who started the fires?" he demanded.

Isabella was reluctant to speak. She was still feeling hurt at having been rebuffed by Victorio. Also, she suspected some of the men might not believe her if she admitted doing it. It would be hard for some to accept the fact that a slave woman had figured out a way to win a battle, when men had failed. She remained silent.

"Who started the fires?" Victorio asked again. There was silence. His piercing eyes looked at each face, one at a time. When he looked at Isabella, she was staring at her feet.

"When you wanted to talk to me last night, just before the fires, there was a bundle under your arm," he said, slowly. "What was in the bundle?"

"Fire," she said, without looking up.

"It was you, wasn't it?" he asked.

She nodded, continuing to look at her feet, not sure why she felt so hesitant, so self-conscious. By now everyone was looking at her, waiting for Victorio to continue.

"You saved many of our lives, possibly all of them,"

Victorio said, with a quiet force that pierced every ear. She said nothing in return.

"Do you wish some kind of reward for what you did?" he asked, his voice full of emotion. "You may ask for anything."

She shook her head, indicating she did not want a reward. She continued to look down. She felt like crying, but didn't know why. She forgot her little speech about how men ought to pay more attention to what women had to say.

"You are no longer my slave," he said. Her first thought was that Victorio had sold her to Pedro Leon without telling her. Then, slowly, the realization of what he was saying filled her. For the first time, she looked up at him. There were tears in her eyes. She truly did not understand her feelings.

"You are free," he said. "I will take you back to your Ute home, if you want me to. Or you may return to Rock Creek. I will send you to Spain if you wish to do that. Or you can continue with me on this journey. You are a free women. You decide."

"What do you wish me to do?" she asked, surprising even herself with her response.

"I would like you to ride with me," Victorio responded, without hesitation. "At my side."

"I would like that very much," she said, getting to her feet, walking up to him, looking in his eyes. "If we find an Inca or Aztec treasure will you share it with me?"

"Of course," he smiled. She wasn't sure she believed him, but still, she wanted to go with him on this quest, more than she had ever wanted anything in her life.

"Thank you for saving me from the Shoshones," she said.

"Thank you for saving me from the Shoshones," he said. They laughed together, and the others joined them.

Chapter 22

It was late afternoon when Islero reached the top of the hill overlooking Fort Robidoux. Sam Johnson was with him. They were leading Islero's horse, the same one that had carried him to the squaw village. They had been taking turns, riding and walking, during the two days it took them to reach the fort.

Islero knew he was urgently needed at Rock Creek. Still, he would have been content to stay a little longer with the squaws, but Johnson couldn't put off exploring the valley of the salt lake for his Mormon leaders any longer. Sam hated to leave behind his new wife of just a few weeks, even temporarily, but duty called. He promised Ish-na-bah he would return for her later, hopefully within the year.

"I'll buy you a horse," Islero offered. "But you shouldn't go to the Great Salt Lake alone. Wouldn't be safe. Wait until some trappers or traders are going that way. Travel with them. I will give you money for food and supplies."

Islero had been to Fort Robidoux many times, and from the beginning, had not been impressed with the way the Americans did business. The normal source of supplies for the

189

Spanish was Santa Fe, but Fort Robidoux was much closer, and Islero found himself going there frequently for items such as lead, powder, iron, tools, even sugar and whiskey. The prices were outrageous, the service bad. The trader and his American companions, mostly over-the-hill beaver trappers, spent most of their time drinking, fighting, and gambling. Islero could see no discipline, no order, no pride, no class in anything these Americans did.

When fellow Spaniards or Mexicans expressed concern to Islero that someday the Americans would take over the land, Islero laughed. The only Americans he knew, the ones at Fort Robidoux, couldn't take over anything. They couldn't even control their whiskey. And the Indians who stayed at the fort were no better. Islero had seen fort Indians who wouldn't hesitate to trade a fine horse, or even a wife for a bottle of watered-down whiskey.

But Sam Johnson was different, unlike any of the Americans Islero had ever known. The Mormon didn't have the mean streak all the Americans at the fort seemed to enjoy. He had been kind to all the women at the squaw camp, even the ugly ones. Sam remained loyal to his Mormon leaders even though he was nearly 2,000 miles from them. Johnson was neat, clean and orderly in his personal appearance. He was a man of character, but also very human with a warm, personal way about him. If there were very many Americans like him, they would indeed take over the land, but not necessarily by force. Islero was certain that men like Sam didn't need to conquer by force. They just had to come, and eventually, through competence and personal charm and character, would control everything.

The trader's name was Henry, and he was glad to provide Sam with a horse, a rifle, and other supplies, as long as the greaser called Islero agreed to pay the bill. Islero didn't understand why the Americans had so much contempt for him and his people. Islero was better mounted, better clothed, better armed, better mannered, had more money and was probably a better fighter than any of these Americans, yet they called him greaser, with contempt. He hoped hostile Indians would someday destroy the fort, but in the meantime he would take advantage of the convenient location for goods and supplies.

When Sam was outfitted, and everything had been paid for, Islero asked the trader if he knew of anyone who might be headed in the direction of the Great Salt Lake. Henry said he did, some trappers from the California coast, who were in the area. They were going that way to Fort Benton, then float down the Missouri River to St. Louis.

Sam asked where the trappers were, and when they would be leaving.

"Off on some slave business. Be back in a few days."

"Slave business?" Sam asked.

"Seems one of them was out trapping last spring, found a tribe of squaws. Said he really did. Don't know if I believe him. Anyway, the hosses have gone out to round up 20 squaws to sell to the greaser, Pedro Leon. Couple of the squaws are real lookers, ought to bring some good money, especially after they been broke in a little. Been gone a couple of days. Maybe they'll be back tomorrow, maybe next..."

Before Henry could finish, Sam and Islero were grabbing up their supplies and scrambling out the door. A minute later they were on their horses, galloping out the front gate, not towards the Great Salt Lake, but back to what Sam and Islero affectionately called Squaw City.

They hadn't gone far when Islero began to wish he had asked the trader more questions, like how many trappers were in the bunch, what kind of horses they were riding, who their leader was, and how well-armed they were. Maybe it didn't matter. He would learn the answers to those questions soon enough.

Islero wondered why he and Sam had not passed the trappers on the way to Fort Robidoux. Apparently the Americans did not know the country as well as Islero did, and had not taken the most direct route to the Indian camp. This thought gave Islero hope that he and Sam had a chance to reach the camp before the trappers did. He wondered if he and Sam should try to flee with the squaws, or stay and fight the trappers.

While it took nearly two days for Islero and Sam to reach Fort Robidoux, it took only 13 hours to return. They arrived in the middle of the night.

Cautiously, they approached the camp, knowing the trappers might already be there. In the moonlight they could see the brush huts, but there were no fires. It was impossible to tell if the huts were occupied or deserted.

They stopped their horses, and dismounted at the edge of the camp. "If the trappers were here, it would not be so quiet," Islero whispered. Sam agreed as his eyes scanned the moonlit horizon for any sign of the Americans. He couldn't see any horses either.

"Ish-na-bah," Sam called in a quiet voice.

A muffled scream was heard in the direction of the huts. A moment later, Ish-ha-bah scrambled out of her hut, wrapped hastily in a sleeping blanket. She raced to the two men, throwing her arms around Sam, hugging and kissing him many times. Tears were streaming down her cheeks. By now women were emerging from all the huts.

Sam looked over at Islero, a sick, guilty look on his face. "I'll never leave her again," Sam said. "I don't know what I was thinking, just leaving her out here with no one to protect her."

By now all the women had gathered around the two men. Mud Woman had her arms around Islero's neck, as he began to explain how the American trappers were coming to get them, to make them slaves so the trappers could sell them to a mean Mexican. Some of the women started to run to their huts to get their weapons. Islero called them back.

He asked Mud Woman if she knew a place where the women could hide. She did. There were some caves, high in the cliffs, about a half a mile from camp. Some of their winter food supplies were stored there. Islero urged them to fill some water pots and hurry to the caves. He cautioned them to be

192

careful not to walk across sand and dirt where they would leave tracks, but rather follow the slick rock sidehill where they would leave no trail.

When Sam started to follow the women, Islero stopped him. "If the Americans find no one, they'll search. If we are here when they come, perhaps we can persuade them not to search for the women."

"How would we do that?" Sam asked.

"I don't know," Islero said. "But we have time to think about it. We will think of something. While the women hurried off to the caves to hide, Sam and Islero crawled into two of the brush huts and went to sleep.

About mid-morning, four shabbily dressed American trappers entered the camp. They did not attempt to surround the camp, nor could their approach be called an attack. They just rode in on horses that looked tired and thin. Each of the men carried a long rifle, balanced across the front of his saddle.

"Howdy," Sam said, emerging from his wickiup. He was wearing buckskins, and carried a loaded .40 caliber Hawken rifle.

"Howdy," one of the trappers said. He was a large man whose belly touched his saddle horn. The entire front of his buckskins was greasy from sloppy eating habits. His stirrups were too short, giving an uncomfortable and twisted look to his legs and feet. There was an unnatural curve in his back as he slouched forward. Perhaps an old injury prevented him from sitting straight in the saddle. His black beard and mustache were so thick and full that it was impossible to get a good look at his round and puffy face.

"Where's the squaws?" the big man asked.

"You don't want to know," Sam responded, a friendly tone in his voice.

"I be the judge of that," the trapper said. Islero emerged from one of the other huts. He was wearing his helmet, and carried his sword. The Seville steel glistened in the morning sun.

193

"Left the California coast to get away from the damn greasers," one of the men complained. Islero ignored the insult.

"Where's the squaws?" the big man repeated.

"Said you don't want to know," Sam repeated.

"Maybe I do," the man said, raising his rifle and pointing it at Sam.

"Ugliest bunch of sows ever to set foot on God's good earth," Sam said.

"I heard some was real lookers," one of the men volunteered. "Charlie here seen 'em, says some are lookers."

"He never lifted their skirts," Sam said.

"What?" the big man asked.

"Got the clap, and the pox, every one of 'em," Sam explained. Enough sickness to kill a man three or four times over."

Caught by surprise, the trappers were listening intently.

"Why you think they out here by themselves?" Islero asked with a stronger than usual Spanish accent. "No man would have them, not even us greasers."

The trappers looked at each other, unsure what to do next.

"Where are they?" the big man asked.

"Sent'm away. Didn't want to catch nothin'," Sam said.

"Which way did they go?"

"Down the canyon to the big river. Said they had some canoes, or a raft or something down there. Said they was going to float to California where men wasn't so fussy."

The trappers looked down the canyon, as if wondering whether or not to follow the women.

"Don't believe a word yer say'n," the big man said, turning back to Sam. "Why would you stay around and sleep in their huts if you thought they was full of disease?"

"Let's foller'm and see if they's as sick as these men says," one of the trappers whined. "Not much worried 'bout myself. Already had about any sickness a man can get. One or two more won't hurt. Let's get'm.''

Without any more talk, the trappers turned and headed their horses down the canyon. As soon as they were out of sight, Islero and Sam hurried to the caves where the women were hiding. On the way, they discussed the alternatives.

The first was to stay with the women, waiting for the trappers to return. The canyon ended at the river, and unless the trappers crossed the river, they would have to come back this way. Would the returning trappers ride on through, or would they stop and search? Would it be better not to take any chances with the trappers, and leave? And if they left, where should they go?

"Rock Creek is the only safe place for them," Islero insisted.

"They'll be Spanish slaves if we take them there," Sam protested.

"They'll be safe. They can work in the corn and bean fields. They'll have plenty to eat, and they'll have shelter."

"What will happen to them?"

"When Victorio and I return to Spain, sometime next year, I hope, they'll be free. The Indian men will be released from the mines at the same time. They can all stay at Rock Creek and live happily as long as they wish, tilling the fields we left behind, or they can return to their home villages."

"What about Ish-na-bah?" Sam asked.

"She's your wife. Take her with you back to the Mormons, or leave her with me. The choice is yours. At Rock Creek I will find a trustworthy Spaniard to take you to the valley of the salt sea."

Sam finally agreed to Islero's plan. The women had watched the trappers from their caves, and were quick to agree to anything Islero suggested. Quickly, they picked up their things and were following Islero and Sam to Rock Creek.

Chapter 23

With Isabella's blaze raging up and down the canyon, and high into the foothills, Del Negro decided to stay where they were for a few days. There was plenty of feed and water for the animals, and no immediate fire danger even though there was a lot of smoke in the air.

Victorio did, however, send a group of three men up the canyon to see if Fray Castilla was having problems with hostile Indians, or fire, and determine whether or not the priest, for his own safety, should be brought back to join the main party. He sent more men into the hills and valleys looking for ore veins that might have been exposed by the burning.

In a few days, the men he had sent up the canyon returned, but not with the priest. Instead, they brought the golden bracelet Castilla had obtained from Wahpeoop. The priest had sent a handwritten message explaining that the Indian who had brought him the bracelet was from a land of rugged mountains many days northwest of the land of Teguayo. When the Indian returned, Castilla promised to get more information about the origin of the bracelet. In the meantime, Fray Castilla needed more corn and beans for his growing *visita*. Del Negro ordered his men to take food to the "most holy submissive son of obedience."

That evening, Isabella was walking alone along the crest of the ridge above camp. This was the first time she had been by herself, for more than brief periods, since the fire. It felt good to be walking in the cool of the evening, having time to herself to think, to ponder her decision to remain with Victorio. She did not want to return to her home village, and wasn't sure why.

As she approached a large pine tree at the end of the ridge, where some steep rock outcroppings formed a cliff which provided a spectacular view of the smoke-filled Spanish Fork Canyon, she noticed someone else was already there. It was a man, sitting on the edge of the largest outcropping. His back was turned to her. He did not see her approach. Beyond him, the canyon was turning red, not from fire, but from the summer sun dropping low in the smoky sky.

Just as she was about to turn away and go somewhere else, the man turned his head just enough so she could see the side of his face. It was Victorio. Quickly, she stepped in the shadows of the large tree. She didn't want to leave now, but neither did she want him to know she was there. She continued to watch from her hiding place as the sky grew brilliant with streaks of red and black.

Victorio was holding some paper on his lap. A pencil was in his hand. He was trying to write something, but from the few words being scratched on the paper, it was apparent he was having a difficult time. She was not close enough to read what he had already written.

"From her gentle eye,
     The raging fire burst," he said, thoughtfully, reading from the paper.
     "The flames raced to the sky,
     With fire's unquenched thirst.
     But when I told her to go,
     That now she was free..."

Chapter 23

Slowly, Isabella realized what Victorio was doing. Fray Castilla had read poems to her, from the bible. Victorio was writing a poem. And it was about Isabella. She pushed closer to the tree, wanting to hear how it would continue.

"But when I told her to go,
    That now she was free..." Again he hesitated, not sure how to continue.

"She confessed her love,
    In staying with me," Isabella said, impulsively, not meaning to speak, but the lines just seemed to flow from her mouth without her intending to say anything. Once said, she could not take the words back.

Victorio spun around, seeing her in the shadow of the tree. At first, he seemed angry that his privacy had been intruded upon. Then he began to smile.

"My homeland was in bondage to the Moors for nearly a thousand years," he said. She wondered why he was saying this. Had he not heard what she had said?

"Mu'tamid was one of the greatest Moor kings during the occupation. They called him the poet king of Seville. One day he was on the bank of the Guadalquivir River, composing a poem. He was having difficulty, when a slave girl, who was washing clothes in the river, suddenly recited him the line he needed to finish his verse. I get the feeling history is repeating itself tonight. Come here and sit by me."

Cautiously, Isabella, stepped from the shadow of the tree and approached Victorio. Her heart was pounding.

"What happened to the Spanish slave girl?" she asked, as she sat beside him, her feet dangling over the edge of the cliff.

"She was as beautiful as she was smart," he explained. "Mu'tamid married her, and remained devoted to her throughout his life. He penned many poems to her, some in the thick of his military campaigns."

"Did you fight the Moors?" she asked.

"The last of them were defeated before I was born, but my ancestors fought them for many generations."

"Tell me more of your history," she said, as he took her hand in his.

"The Romans were the first to invade our country," he began. She scooted closer to him. Their shoulders touched. "They came from the north, over the Pyrenees Mountains. We were not a nation then, just city states."

"Like the many bands of Utes?"

"Except the city states were much larger than your Ute bands," he explained. "Sometimes a city would have fifty thousand people, or more. The Romans conquered us, then criss-crossed our country with roads."

"Roads?" she asked, not understanding.

"They covered the paths with stones, so people could travel even when there was much rain. They made them wide enough for carts and coaches to travel on them."

She knew what he was talking about. She had seen the two-wheeled carts at Rock Creek. The carts were pulled by oxen or mules, and were used to bring in crops from the fields and to haul ore.

"After the Romans, the Moors came--from the south, a continent called Africa. Their symbol was the crescent, a quarter-moon. The tide of their conquest swept over our country in 737. They were fierce fighters, mounted on fine horses. They were not Christians. They brought with them new crops that changed our country forever--cotton, rice, apricots, pomegranates, lemons, oranges."

"What are these things?" she asked.

"Good things to eat, that I could never fully describe to you. The only way you could understand would be to come to Spain and try them for yourself."

"I would like that," she said. "As long as the Moors are gone."

"They are gone, but it took a long time to get rid of them. Rodrigo Diaz de Vivar, whom we call El Cid, was the first Christian general capable of defeating Moors in battle. He lived seven hundred years ago. We still celebrate his victories in our songs and plays.

200

Chapter 23

"El Cid defeated Almanzor, a Moor general from Cordova, known for his ruthlessness, fanaticism, and destructive campaigns against the Christians. I once had a horse named Almanzor. In battle, he would trample, kick and bite the enemy.

"Over the centuries there were many great battles, many great leaders. Even in the church there were orders of warrior monks who fought the Moors. The greatest was the Order of Santiago. I wish we had those kinds of priests today to help us in this wild land.

"My favorite book as a youth was "The Dove's Ring," by Ibn Hazm of Cordova. He was the greatest writer and poet during the Moor occupation. If only I could write like him. There was a spirit of pride and defiance in everything he wrote. He was proud and passionate, a noble-hearted seeker of truth. The Malachite jurists burned his books.

"Ferdinand and Isabella drove out the last of the Moor rulers in 1492, the same year Columbus found this land we call New Spain. Islero named you after Isabella. She was wise, honest, deeply religious, and inspired affection from everyone. But she was not as beautiful as you."

Isabella was very aware that her hand, arm and shoulder were touching him. Her heart had not stopped pounding since sitting down next to him. Her mouth was dry. She had never felt this way before. Her entire being was filled with a pleasant itching and yearning which instinct told her only Victorio could satisfy.

"During Isabella's reign," he continued. "the universities flourished. There was a spirit of learning, adventure, and the seeking of truth. Suddenly there was light after a thousand years of darkness, bondage and war. People had grateful hearts. Spain built the greatest fleet of sailing ships in the world. Riches started pouring in from New Spain.

"Then came the inquisition. The Order of Preachers was founded by St. Domingo Guzman. At first the Spanish liked the inquisition. It required that Moors be baptized or exiled. Then it turned its wrath on the Protestants and Jews.

The Jews were hated, for the most part, because they had been the slave traders for the Moors.

"Finally, the attention of the inquisition was turned on the Spanish citizens themselves. People were burned at the stake for adultery. Bankers were exiled for charging interest on money they loaned. Men were beheaded for making jokes about the pope, or local church leaders. People who didn't attend mass were whipped and tortured. The universities became enforcement institutions for the inquisition. People were afraid. Thousands died when church courts found them guilty of heresy or blasphemy."

"What is heresy and blasphemy?" she asked.

"That's when an inquisition priest doesn't like you, for any reason, and wants to have you killed," he said, bitterly. "I told you about my grandfather, Diego Penalosa. On an expedition such as this, he argued with a priest. He was found guilty of blasphemy, imprisoned, his personal possessions taken away, banished to Spain for the remainder of his life, and the yellow cloak of his shame still hangs in our cathedral.

"But not for long. When I return with a ship full of gold, it will come down. Once again my brothers and cousins will be able to hold public office, be officers in the military and own land. Me and my gold will change all that," Victorio concluded, his voice full of passion.

"I think I understand now why gold is so important to you," she said.

"Nothing is more powerful than gold. By it, all things are torn asunder; all things are accomplished," he said, almost shouting. "This is the age of gold. The greatest rewards come from gold. By gold, justice is bought. By gold, faith is destroyed. By gold, love is won. Law follows the track of gold."

"I don't think a man could win my love with gold," she said, wanting to change the subject. His passion for gold frightened her, made her jealous. These were new feelings for her. She did not understand.

"I disagree," he said, teasingly, reaching into his

Chapter 23

pocket and removing the gold bracelet he had received from
Fray Castilla. He lifted Isabella's left hand, pulling it in front
of him. Gently, he slipped the golden bracelet onto her left
wrist. Tenderly, he caressed her hand and wrist as he did so.
Goose bumps covered her arm as they had done when
Victorio rescued her from the Shoshones.

"This gold is as pure as the love and devotion I feel for
you," he said, continuing to hold her hand and wrist. For the
first time they looked long and deep into each other's eyes.
There was silence for a long time.

"Do you believe me when I tell you I love you?" he
asked, finally breaking the silence.

"Yes," she said, warmly, "but not because you gave
me the golden bracelet."

"How then do you know?" he asked.

"I knew when you entered the meadow to save me from
the Shoshones," she said. "I remember looking behind you,
expecting others to follow. When they didn't come, when I
realized you had come alone against so many warriors, just to
save me; I knew then you loved me."

"And I knew you loved me," he said, "when you
finished my poem." He pulled her to him, gently but firmly,
kissing her on her lips. Her heart was pounding out of
control, her breath was short. But she fought desperately for
control of her emotions, and her body.

She couldn't give herself to Victorio, not totally. She
didn't doubt that he loved her. She just knew, or thought she
knew, that he loved gold more.

Chapter 24

Victorio was able to trade for two more gold bracelets before reaching the mouth of Spanish Fork Canyon. Both were being worn by Indians on the left wrist. When he questioned the Indians about the origin of the gold, with Isabella serving as interpreter, the only response he could get was that the bracelets were obtained through trade with other Indians. When asked where they thought the gold had been mined, they always pointed west or north, but could give no specific details like how far the mine might be, what it was called, or who worked it.

But Victorio wasn't discouraged. Where there was smoke, there must be fire. If he could trade for three gold bracelets traveling down a single canyon, somewhere ahead of him there must be a lot more. He told Isabella on several occasions, that he could feel this trip was different from others he had taken. He just knew something important was going to happen during their journey. Perhaps they would discover one of the Inca or Aztec treasures. The bracelets were just the bait. Somewhere ahead of them the big fish was waiting.

Isabella began to find Victorio's passion for gold

contagious. She wanted to please Victorio. She wanted to help him find it. She found herself awake in the middle of the night, trying to remember things she had heard or seen in her childhood, that might lead her to a gold mine, or a hidden horde of treasure. Still, she knew she was different than Victorio. While his passion was driven by the desire for gold, her passion was driven by the desire for Victorio. She wanted gold because Victorio wanted gold. Victorio was beginning to dominate her life, and she found herself not wanting to resist this domination. Still, deep inside she knew he loved gold more than her, but hoped someday that would change.

When they reached the mouth of Spanish Fork Canyon, while the rest of the party tied their animals to trees to take a midday break, Victorio led Isabella to the top of a red clay hill, on the south side of the river. He said it was the same hill Fray Francisco Dominguez and Fray Silvestre Escalante climbed for a view of the valley when they first entered it in 1776.

"Our missionary fathers said this valley could support a city the size of Toledo," he explained. "One of our maps shows this valley as a province of Spain. See, the great mountain, Timpanogos. It still has snow on it. Every time I come here I love to look over the sky blue waters of Lake Copalla. The great sea of salt is to the north and west of those far hills."

"This is the valley where our people have their annual fish festival," she said. "I have been here several times. We camp where the Timpanogos River enters the lake." She pointed to some open meadows, nearly ten kilometers away.

"This is the legendary land of Cibola," he said. "The *conquistadors* called it Teguayo. Somewhere in these mountains the Aztecs mined gold for a thousand years."

"It is a beautiful place, even without the gold," she said. But Victorio wasn't about to change the subject.

"I think the Indians covered up the mines. Maybe, with you as my interpreter, the old ones will tell us where the mines are. I hope they have not forgotten."

206

Chapter 24

"Look," she said, trying to change the subject again, pointing to a grassy spot not too far distant. "Many horses, and some tepees."

"Too many horses for an ordinary Indian camp," he said, seeing where she was pointing. "Must be Walkara. Have you heard of him?"

"Yes," she said. "He is Ute too. I have not met him, but my people say he stole horses in the place the trappers call California."

Victorio laughed at her understatement. "Walkara didn't just steal horses. He stole five thousand horses in one raid. This horse I am riding is one of them. Walkara is the greatest horse thief that ever lived. I have bought many horses from him, and many slaves. He is a shrewd trader. We are lucky to find him. He uses up horses the way priests use up candles. This time of year one might find him on the plains east of the headwaters of the Rio Tizon hunting buffalo, or in the lands of the Paiutes and Goshutes capturing slaves, or trading in Mexico, or stealing more horses in California. The man does not understand discomfort and pain. I think he can get on a horse and ride a thousand miles without stopping. Would you like to meet him?"

"I would," she said.

"He is probably the richest Indian in the world, if you measure wealth in horses and guns," Victorio added. "He has three or four wives that I know of."

"He has no gold?" she asked.

"He's had some from time to time, mostly bracelets, but I always trade him out of them. Maybe he'll have some today."

They pulled their horses around and headed back to the others. An hour later, they reached Walkara's camp after riding through a meadow containing several hundred horses.

When Walkara stepped out of his tepee, Isabella found herself catching her breath. Here was a man to compare with Victorio. Walkara was taller than she had supposed, and younger. As he walked towards her, with the grace of a lion, every muscle rippled in the afternoon sun. And she could see them all because he wore only a loincloth, moccasins and a multi-colored headband. He was a man who didn't sit still long enough to get lazy. There was no fat on his entire body.

Walkara's head was erect and alert, like that of a wild stallion. He had a proud nose, and a firm jaw. His glossy black hair hung loose over his muscular shoulders. The intensity of his gray eyes reminded her of the fiercest lightning bolts she had ever seen. She felt like she was in the presence of a great king.

After offering a brief greeting to Victorio, Walkara walked over to Isabella, who was still mounted on her horse.

"If this slave girl is for sale, I want to buy her," Walkara said to Victorio, in perfect Spanish.

"This is Isabella. She is not a slave. She is my woman," Victorio said, firmly.

"Navajo?" Walkara asked.

"Ute," Victorio said.

"Why have I not seen you before?" Walkara asked, this time speaking to Isabella.

"Perhaps you are lazy and spend too much time in your tepee," she teased.

"You should be ashamed of yourself," he said. changing his language from Spanish to Ute. A proud Ute has no business being the whore of a gold-digging, slave-trading Spaniard."

"You should be ashamed of yourself," she responded, also in Ute. "Trading your people to the Spanish, to die in their mines. You have betrayed your people."

"I do not trade Utes to the Spanish, only Goshutes, Piutes, Shoshones, some Bannocks, and a few Black Feet and Navajos."

"They are still Indians, and you should be ashamed. I hope you will stop doing it."

"Maybe I would if you would come back to your people. You are welcome in my family."

Isabella was flattered by the proposition, but her place

was with Victorio.

"I think it is time to go," she said to Victorio.

"No, you must stay," Walkara said. "My women are preparing a feast. Victorio agreed to stay.

By Ute standards, the feast was fabulous. There was an elk stew flavored with camas bulbs and wild onions, served in dried squash shells. There was fresh pemmican containing wild raspberries, thimbleberries, pine nuts, elk meat and rock salt all crushed together and served on slabs of cottonwood bark. There were corn cakes, flavored with a paste made from black raspberries, and watered down whiskey, flavored with brown sugar and cayenne pepper. The whiskey was from Fort Bridger.

Walkara, Victorio and Isabella enjoyed their feast in Walkara's tepee, seated on buffalo robes around a small, smokeless fire. Indian women brought in the various foods as needed. Isabella assumed the women were Walkara's wives. They did as they were told. There was no conversation between them and the chief.

For the most part, Isabella remained silent while Walkara and Victorio discussed the slave business, horses and horse stealing, guns, and eventually gold. With Victorio present the conversation always turned to gold.

Victorio mentioned the three bracelets he had obtained coming down the canyon, and asked Walkara if he knew of any mines in the area where Indians might be getting gold to make bracelets. Walkara looked at Isabella while he thought about his answer.

"South from where the Spanish Fork River enters the valley," he began slowly, thoughtfully. "High on the mountain, there is an old mine. I don't know who dug it out, but there are old tools in it, not like anything my people would use. Perhaps it was mined by the Aztecs, perhaps by the Spanish before the big rebellion, the one the Spanish call the revolt of 1680."

Victorio stopped eating. Isabella could sense his excitement. She hoped Walkara didn't.

"Do you think it is a gold mine?" Victorio asked.

"I don't know," Walkara answered. "In the bottom of the canyon, below the mine, there are ancient writings on a rock face showing many animals carrying burdens from the canyon. I don't know what the drawings mean."

"Tell me where it is," Victorio said, trying to keep his voice calm.

Walkara didn't answer, immediately. He reached into his bowl, grabbing a piece of elk meat with two fingers and tossing it in his mouth. Next he put two camas bulbs into his mouth to chew with the meat. The minute it took to chew and swallow this food seemed like hours to Victorio.

"I fear that if there is gold in the mine," Walkara began, slowly, looking down at his bowl, using a forefinger to play with his food, "many Spanish will come to this valley. Our mother, the earth, is good to us here. There is much grass for horses, much food for men and families. The Spanish want to dig holes in our earth mother. Maybe that is not good. Do you understand?"

"You said the hole is already there," Victorio countered. "We will only dig it deeper. We do not want to make new holes."

"But you will make my people do the digging. They do not like to be your slaves. They do not like to dig your gold."

"I will not make your people dig," Victorio promised. "Goshute, Piute, and some Navajo slaves will do the digging. We will grow corn and beans so we don't have to kill your game. Our horses will not eat much grass. Tell me where the mine is so we can see if it has gold. If it does, we will give some of it to you."

"What would I do with gold?" Walkara asked. "One can't eat it, drink it, ride it, shoot it, or have sex with it. What good is it? Why do you Spanish want it so much?"

"With gold you can buy all the things you mention," Victorio responded.

"With horses and slaves I can buy anything I want. I do not need gold."

Chapter 24

"If you do not want the gold, then you shouldn't mind showing me where the mine is," Victorio pleaded. "I will give you ten horses if you tell me where it is."

"But, Victorio, you are my friend," Walkara said, a sudden warmth in his voice. "I could not ask for payment from a friend, just to tell him where to find a hole in the ground. If you wanted a horse or a squaw, or anything else of value, I would accept payment."

"Then, as my friend," Victorio said, "tell me where it is."

"Maybe tomorrow," Walkara said. "This may be an important thing for my people. Let me dream. If my dreams are good, I will tell you. If my dreams are bad, I will not tell you." Using a finger, Walkara scraped the last of the pemmican off a slab of cottonwood bark and put it in his mouth. Victorio feared that continuing to eat might increase Walkara's chance of having a bad dream.

"Then we'll see you tomorrow," Victorio said, getting up to leave. Isabella stood up, too.

"Wait," Walkara said, without getting up. "My friend, do you remember when you visited me at my winter camp in the valley they call the San Pete. It was very cold. Much wind. I gave you one of my women to keep you warm. It is a custom among my people to do such things for friends. Do you remember?"

"I remember," Victorio said, cautiously, sensing he was being lured into a trap.

"I would not object if you loaned me one of your women tonight," Walkara said to Victorio, but he was looking at Isabella. "In fact I would be very grateful. I am certain a woman such as this would bring many happy dreams."

"What should I tell him?" Victorio asked Isabella, his eyes pleading with her to cooperate.

"Tell him the truth," she said, coldly.

"What is the truth?" Victorio asked.

"The truth is that I decide where I sleep, not you or

211

anyone else,'' she said, her voice hard and cold.

"What have you decided for tonight?'' Victorio asked, still hoping.

"That I am not going to sleep in this lodge. I am not going to sleep in your's either,'' she said, as she got up and walked out of the tepee.

The two men looked at each other, shrugged their shoulders, and finished off the last of the whiskey.

Chapter 25

Fortunately, there was little whiskey left in the can. It wasn't long until Victorio said goodnight to Walkara, and was wandering across the meadow looking for Isabella. In the moonlight, it was easy to find her, seated on a grassy mound next to a small stream which was winding its way slowly and smoothly towards Lake Copalla.

Without a word, he sat down next to her and tried to put his arm around her. She pulled away. He withdrew his arm, and quietly recited a verse of poetry.

> "When you were fancy-free,
> You and I could never see.
> But now that you're a wife
> You have become my life."

"That is obviously a verse you did not write," she said.

"How do you know that?" he asked.

"A woman could never become your life, not as long as gold is your mistress," she explained.

"Federico Garcia Lorca wrote it. He was one of my country's greatest writers and poets. He was the literary counterpart to El Greco, the greatest artist the world has ever known. I think I have told you about him, and how he came from a country called Greece."

She couldn't remember him telling her about an artist named El Greco, but she was in no mood to learn about an artist, so offered no encouragement for him to continue. But he did, anyway.

"Lorca wrote with the same leaping flames of passion that inspired El Greco's painting. But like the artist, his artistic ambitions far exceeded his technical skills."

"How do you know all this?" she asked.

"I am a Spaniard. Also, I studied at the University at Salamanca for three years. I was expelled when they found out about the yellow cloak of shame hanging in the cathedral at Cordova. But before I left Salamanca, I found religion."

"If you found religion there, you must have lost it here. You are not a religious man, Victorio," she said.

"Because I am not like Castilla and Sinbad, and because I show contempt for their ways, you think I am not religious."

"Gold is your religion," she said.

"Lucius Annaeus Seneca was Spain's greatest writer," he said, appearing to change the subject. "He was born during the Roman occupation, before the Moors came. He moved to Rome where his intelligence, character and play writing skills elevated him to the top of the government, second only to Nero himself. Under Seneca's leadership the Roman Empire thrived, but after the insane Nero ordered this noble Spaniard to commit suicide, the empire plunged into obscurity."

"This Nero was a bad man?" she asked.

"Yes. You know how your people gather to watch a horse race. His people would gather by the thousands around large stone enclosures to watch Nero feed Christians to lions. If the lions killed the Christians too quickly, Nero sometimes ordered that some of his own people, who had paid to watch Christians die, be thrown in with the Christians. A man who paid to watch lions chase Christians, at Nero's whim, might find himself being chased by a hungry lion.''

"Why are you telling me this?" she asked.

"At his death, Seneca was the most distinguished man in the world, intellectually and politically, to accept Christianity. He became the father of Spanish Catholicism. He told the Romans, 'God is not to be worshiped with sacrifices and blood; for what pleasure can He have in the slaughter of the innocent? He is to be worshipped only with a pure mind, a good and honest purpose. Temples need not be built for Him with stones piled high upon high; He is to be consecrated in the breast of each.'''

"You do not talk like a man who hungers and thirst for gold," she said.

"Before his death, Seneca summed up his philosophy by saying, 'the whole of life is nothing but a preparation for death.' Every day I fear death will take me before the yellow cloak is taken down. Gold will take it down. This is why I need gold."

"Your passion for gold seems more a sickness," she said. "It is a wall between us. I am jealous of your gold."

"Did I ever tell you about my grandmother's journal?" he asked.

"What does an old woman's writings have to do with gold?" she asked.

"Everything. As a young man I read her journal many times. Its contents set the course of my life. If you will be patient, and listen carefully, I will tell you a very sad story, a story that may change some of your feelings towards the priests, their organized Catholic religion, and me."

"I would like to hear what your grandmother wrote," she said.

"She started writing things down after she and my grandfather were forced by the inquisition to return to Cordova. Another trial was held by the church in which my grandfather was again found guilty of heresy, blasphemy, and using unrestrained language against a priest. He was imprisoned for many months after that.

"Finally the day of judgement arrived. The brass bells in the tower built by the Moors began ringing, slowly, summoning the residents of Cordova to the town square where workmen the day before had built a platform and lined it with tall-backed chairs, each carrying the seal of the holy inquisition. Thousands of people assembled at the square. The church promised 40 days of indulgence to everyone who watched the church cleanse itself of heresy.

"At 6 a.m. a cannon was fired, and the bells began a more furious clamor. My grandmother was waiting by the dungeon by the cathedral, where shortly after 6, my grandfather appeared, in a well-guarded procession with 21 other prisoners who began marching towards the platform in the town square. The judges of the inquisition had already determined that none of the charges against any of the prisoners could be appealed to the king in Toledo or the Pope in Rome.

"A group of city and church officials, accompanied by a company of soldiers, and four clerks of the inquisition, moved in front of the prisoners, leading the way to the square. The clerks of the inquisition carried silver caskets covered with velvet, bearing lists of crimes of the condemned.

"Behind this group came half a dozen Dominican friars, each carrying an oak stake topped with a cluster of silver rings. Whenever the friars would strike the butts of their stakes against the cobblestones, the people could hear a haunting jingling sound, announcing the arrival of the inquisition judgement.

"The 21 prisoners accompanying my grandfather didn't look any better than he did. Some of them had been in their cells for two or three years, without sun, exercise, and decent food. All looked haggard and pale. Most had little or no flesh on their bones. All were dressed in rags. The oldest ones had been imprisoned for religious beliefs. They were Jews,

Moors, or Christians with sympathies towards Martin Luther, an insane monk from Germany who was trying to lead people away from true Catholicism.

"Each prisoner carried four badges of shame. The first was a wax taper, a symbol that the light of the church had gone out in that sinner's life. The second was a rope around the neck, each knot in the rope representing a hundred lashes the prisoner was about to receive. The third was a tall conical dunce cap, and the fourth, a bright yellow robe made of cheap sackcloth with a high collar and a tail that dragged in the dust. On the front of each robe was a flaming red cross. Everyone knew, after the sentences of the day were carried out, these yellow robes would hang in various cathedrals proclaiming the holy sin of that family, during which time the descendants of the sinner could never hold public office, become priests, own land, travel overseas, become officers in the military or do anything but survive, all because of the sins of their ancestor.

"Behind the condemned prisoners, rode half-a-dozen nobles from the countryside. Behind them, came lesser priests from various churches in the area, then community officials.

"The day was Sunday, and the Holy Inquisition made the event as impressive as possible, hoping this would be the means to control heresy.

"With the crowd assembled, and the prisoners in place at the base of the platform, a minor priest conducted mass and asked for the Lord's blessing on what was to follow. After the prayer, the grand inquisitor stepped to the front of the platform and spoke to the prisoners for two and a half hours on the grief they had caused the church, and the disgrace and shame they had brought upon themselves and their families.

"When he finished, the two senior inquisition secretaries walked to two facing pulpits, decorated in black velvet. Here they took turns reciting the accusations against the condemned prisoners. The charges against the prisoners were detailed and lengthy. This part of the program lasted many hours.

"The guilty were divided into three groups. Those in

217

the first group had committed serious but not critical sins against the church, like committing open adultery, or stealing church funds. Most of these were to receive two or three hundred lashes, and another year or two in jail, but to the relief of all, none of their robes were going to be hung in churches to curse their children in future generations. Thirteen of the prisoners fell in this category. After their sentences were read, their wax tapers were set on fire, the sign they had been received back into the church.

"Five of the prisoners, including my grandfather, heard a more frightening judgement. Those with my grandfather were Jews and Moors who had converted to Christianity, then returned to their old beliefs. My grandfather and his companions were what they called subverive types, the kind of people priests thought were dangerous to the church. All were stripped of their possessions, something that had already happened to my grandfather in Mexico City. All were to receive 60 to 100 lashes, and were condemned to prison for the remainder of their lives. They were advised their robes would hang forever in their local churches. The grand inquisitor made it clear that when the cloth disintegrated, new robes would be made, carrying the name of the sinner, and that as long as the Catholic Church remained in existence, their robes would continue to hang in the churches. After all this, their tapers were fired.

"My grandmother cried bitterly while this sentence was being read, but my grandfather looked straight ahead, looking at nothing in particular, showing no emotion whatsoever, not even when his taper was burning again.

"The clerks now began to read the sentences of the remaining three, who were being prayed over by five or six untiring priests. Here, little time was expended, because the inquisition officials merely informed the local government officials that these three had been so persistent in their sins that the church had no hope of restoring them to their former status, and therefore the church was turning them over to the civil authorities. This simply meant the prisoners had no more connection to the church and would be burned to death by the civil authorities. During the inquisition, the church never burned anyone. Only civil authorities did it. The cloaks of these three prisoners were to be hung in the cathedrals forever, too. And their tapers were not re-lit.

"After the sentences were read, the grand inquisitor announced it was time for the prisoners in the first two groups to receive their lashings. My grandfather was first. They removed his cap and robe, leaving him naked as they tied his hands high on a post. He did not struggle to get away, nor did he cry out, as the lashings began. He continued to look straight ahead, an expressionless look on his face. He maintained this position through the first 55 lashes. Then he passed out. When my grandmother tried to run to him, they pushed her back, then applied the last fifteen lashes. No one in the family knows how long it took him to recover, because as soon as the lashings were finished, they carried him away. A year later, he died in prison."

By this time, Victorio was stretched out on the grassy bank, his head on the soft grass. The moon was low in the sky. He had been talking a long time. His narrative had been full of emotion. Now, he was tired.

"I believe in Christ," he said, after a long pause. "But my religion is more like Seneca's. I have a problem with church officials, and holy buildings made of cold stone. My religion is in my heart, and it does not dance to the tap of Cigarro Sinbad's golden cane. Can you understand that, now?"

"The men who did this inquisition were evil," she said, "especially the man you call the grand inquisitor. Why do your people want to belong to a church controlled by such wicked men?"

"If you knew these men, they would not seem so wicked. They loved God. They loved the church. They thought they were cleansing the church, making it better. It was all right, they thought, to kill a few through the inquisition, if by doing so, millions would be afraid to sin.

219

That's how they thought. For the most part, they had good intentions.''

"And so do you," she said. "Tell me again how your quest for gold fits into all this."

"That yellow cloak in the cathedral at Cordova is a banner of death for me, my brothers, my cousins, and my sons. Before I die, it must come down, and only gold will bring it down. When gold speaks, the church listens."

"You have sons?" she asked, wondering why Victorio had not told her about a wife in Spain.

"Not yet," he smiled, "But someday I hope to have many, but before they grow up, the shame of the cloak will be gone, or I will be dead. Like Seneca said, 'life is nothing but a preparation for death.' "

"I think life should be more than that," she said, then asked, "Who will be the mother of your sons?"

"There is a beautiful Spanish girl who lives on the west side of Cordova. She...." Isabella turned her head, and scooted away from him. He began to laugh.

"There are lots of beautiful girls on the west side of Cordova," he explained. "But I don't see any of them in my future."

"Then who will be the mother to your sons?" she asked.

"We have talked about that time when the Shoshones staked you out on the ground," he said. "When I rode into their camp, alone."

"I could never forget that," she said.

"Do you know what was in my mind as I rode into the meadow to rescue you?" he asked.

"Tell me."

"As I entered the meadow that night," he said, "it was not you I was looking at. In my mind I could see the yellow robe hanging in the cathedral at Cordova. I cared not for my own life, but I knew if I failed, and the Shoshones killed me, my brothers and cousins, and their families, would be cursed forever. I was asking myself if I was willing to risk all that to save a slave girl.''

"Then why did you do it?'' she asked. "Why did you enter the meadow alone, against so many, to save a slave girl?''

"Because I wanted that girl to be the mother of my sons. Because she was the one I wanted to be my wife. Because she was the one I wanted to take back to Spain with me to be the queen and mistress of the castle I plan to build.''

"Why have you not told me any of this before?'' she asked, totally bewildered by what he had said.

"Maybe I was afraid you would not want these things, that you would want to stay here with your people. I would not force you to come with me to Spain.''

"How can you love me more than gold?'' she asked, still trying to grasp the full significance of what he had just said.

"But now that you're a wife
You have become my life.''

After reciting the last part of the Lorca verse one more time, he pulled her to him, not kissing her, just holding her tight.

"The gold will allow our sons to make decent lives for themselves. That is all.''

"I will be your wife, Victorio,'' Isabella said, tears of joy streaming down her face.

Chapter 26

Walkara had pleasant dreams, even without Isabella's cooperation. The next morning he said he would take Victorio and Isabella to an ancient mine. They rode south for several hours, angling eastward towards the steep Wasatch Mountains, south of where the Spanish Fork River entered the valley.

At one point, Walkara pointed to some red shale rock at the base of the mountains, saying it was the place where he and his brothers had buried their father who had been killed by one of the Timpanogos Utes. He explained how two wives, a horse and a dog had been killed to accompany his father to the world of spirits. Walkara said he and his brother, Arrapeen, had killed the man responsible for their father's death.

Walkara led them into a canyon, where they had to push their way through thick oak brush. They hadn't gone far when the chief dismounted and tied his horse to a tree. Victorio and Isabella did the same.

When they had left camp that morning, Walkara had been in a cheerful mood, talking about his happy dreams. But as the hours passed, there was a marked change in his mood.

"I think Towatts didn't want me to bring you here," he said, thoughtfully, "Why then did he give me happy dreams?"

"Maybe he did want us to come here," Victorio responded. He didn't want Walkara to change his mind, not now.

"There are spirits here," Walkara said. "I can feel them now, as I always do when I come here. My people don't like this place. We don't gather food here, and we don't hunt here. Sometimes we bury our dead here, because we think no one will bother them, but we always break the legs of a slave child and secure it to the grave. The child's crying keeps the spirits away until the dead person can complete his journey to the world of spirits."

"Why are there spirits here?" Victorio asked.

"I don't know," Walkara said. "Maybe many people died here. When those of my people who have strong medicine come to a place where many have died, they can feel it. There is a sad feeling, like voices crying from the ground. I don't know what the voices are saying. I think something very great happened here, but I don't know what it was. Can you feel it?"

They were quiet for a minute. Finally, Victorio shrugged his shoulders. "I can't feel anything," he said, "unless it is the excitement of being close to a great treasure."

"I feel afraid," Isabella said. "I think someone or something is watching us. I should not be afraid, being with two great warriors. I don't know why I feel this way."

Leaving the tethered horses behind, Walkara led his two companions along a narrow foot path, in a southerly direction until they came up against a sheer cliff face. They turned left, and continued along the rock face until they found a place where the ground turned down to form a V with the bottom of the cliff. In the bottom of the V was what appeared to be an opening to a cave or tunnel.

Above the opening on the underside of the cliff were

many drawings, in a row, all animals carrying bundles on their backs. The drawings looked very old.

"My people say the ancient ones made these pictures," Walkara explained. "But no one knows who the ancient ones were. But let me show you something."

He slid to the bottom of the V and entered the opening leading into the tunnel. Victorio and Isabella followed.

"Is this the mine you were telling us about?" Victorio asked.

"No," Walkara said, "the mine is up high on the mountain. This is only a cave and doesn't go in the mountain very far. But I want to show you something."

By now their eyes were beginning to get used to the dark. Walkara picked up something near the west wall and brought it over to the opening where Victorio and Isabella could get a better look at it. It was a bucket, a metal bucket.

"I have seen many Spanish buckets," Walkara said, "but never one like this. The metal is green, but when you rub it, it seems almost red underneath." He turned the bucket half a turn to show them a design drawing tooled into the rounded surface on the opposite side. It appeared to be a crude sketch of an eagle, with wings stretching to the sky. There was only one eye on its face, but three feathers extending from the top of its head.

Isabella thought she felt her heart skip a beat. The drawing was familiar, yet she knew she had never been in this canyon before. She remembered Raphael telling her about his medicine dream, and how a one-eyed eagle with three feathers had appeared to him, telling him he had a mission to get horses for his people. Why would a picture of a one-eyed eagle with three feathers be on a bucket in a lost cave?

Walkara put down the bucket and led them outside into the sunlight. Instead of returning to the horses, Walkara led them to another cave or mine opening across the canyon. The opening was too small for a man to crawl through, but there was a steady stream of air flowing into the opening, indicating it was connected to caverns inside the mountain. Walkara pointed out an unnatural mountain of earth extending away and down from the opening, suggesting they might be standing on a huge tailings pile. Walkara showed them several holes in the rock above the opening that appeared to be man-made, perhaps places to secure poles for a scaffold of some kind.

Victorio scooped up some of the dirt and rock near the opening, and placed it in a leather pouch. His intention was to take the sample back to camp where one of his men could do some assay work on it.

They returned to the horses and began the long journey up the mountain, hoping to find what Walkara described as an ancient mine. When they had been climbing for what seemed several hours, Walkara dismounted again and tied his horse to a pinion pine. After Victorio and Isabella dismounted, the chief told them to wait at the horses while he looked for the mine. Victorio offered to go with Walkara, but the chief refused. Victorio and Isabella made themselves comfortable in the shade, and waited.

"Today I have thought much about what you said last night," Isabella said. "I don't think I want to join a church that hangs up yellow robes to remember people's sins. Fray Castilla almost had me persuaded to be baptized. Now, I don't think I want to. Will you still marry me if I am not a Catholic?"

"Yes, but you will have a hard time in Spain. Everyone is Catholic there. If you are not, they will distrust you. They will not let their children play with yours. If anything bad happens, they will think God is punishing them for allowing a non-Catholic in their midst."

"I don't think I will like living in Spain," she said.

"You must learn to be more practical," he said. "The Church is good, but the people in it make a lot of mistakes. If you have that attitude, you will get along fine. Besides, the inquisition is over. No new robes are being hung in the cathedrals."

Their conversation ended abruptly when Walkara returned. He said he had found the mine, and invited them to

226

follow him.

They wound their way up the mountain until they came to a flat, rocky shelf. At the back of the shelf, where the mountain resumed its upward climb, was a clump of maple trees. Walkara pointed at the trees. "Behind there," he said.

Victorio hurried forward, pushed his way between the trees, then shouted back to Walkara and Isabella that he had found it. Isabella joined him.

The brush-covered opening was about five feet high and four feet wide. Above the center of the opening, chiseled in the flat rock surface, was the same insignia that they had seen on the strange bucket, the one-eyed eagle with three feathers. Victorio didn't think it looked like anything Spanish he had ever seen, and Isabella knew it was very different from the abundant Indian rock art in the region. Walkara just shrugged his shoulders.

Before entering the tunnel, they built a fire so they could light some of the candles they had brought with them. Walkara led the way into the mine, pointing to the spot where he had found some metal and stone tools the first time he had entered the mine, years ago. The tools were gone.

There was a lot of wood in the tunnel, mostly juniper and pine planks and beams that had been used to shore up the ceiling, centuries earlier. The tunnel extended several hundred feet straight into the mountain, then stopped abruptly. There was no treasure, and no glistening veins of gold in the rock at the end of the tunnel. Victorio examined the rock and dirt more closely. It didn't appear to be ore-bearing material. Still, he took a sample to be examined more closely at camp.

When they returned to the outside, Victorio walked to the edge of the rocky flat and looked down the mountain. He thought he could identify the tailings pile from the mine, and it looked larger than the size of the tunnel justified.

"Must be another mine in the area," he said, and began looking around.

Isabella returned to the tunnel and lit another candle. As she stood just inside the entrance, she sensed something wasn't right, but she wasn't sure what it was. Then she looked at her candle. Instead of pointing straight up, as a candle flame should do in a dead air space, the flame was pointing towards the tunnel opening. And the flame was flickering. Air was flowing out of the mine. It was not a dead-end tunnel as they had first supposed.

Isabella worked her way to the back of the mine, stopped, and looked at her candle again. Now the flame was steady, pointing straight to the ceiling. There was no air movement.

Very slowly, Isabella started back towards the opening, carefully watching her candle. About thirty feet from the opening, the flame began flickering again. She stopped. There were some vertical pine beams against the west wall. When she held the candle close to a crack between two of the beams, it blew out.

She hurried outside to the little fire, and re-lit the candle. She wondered if she should call to Victorio or Walkara, but decided not to, not yet. When she returned to the place where the flame had blown out, she placed the candle on the floor, opposite the windy crack, freeing both her hands to wrestle with the planks.

At first, the wood seemed unmovable, but after a few minutes of pushing and pulling, one of the planks started to move. She wiggled it back and forth until she was able to pull it free. Some dust and dirt sifted onto her head and shoulders, but a quick inspection of the ceiling told her there was no danger of a cave-in.

She picked up the candle, and using her free hand to shield the flame, she stepped sideways through the opening she had created.

The place where she found herself, was more of a room than another tunnel. It was round, about 20 feet in diameter, the walls and ceiling of solid rock. In the center was a hole, about four feet in diameter. It appeared to be the opening to a vertical shaft which disappeared somewhere deep inside the mountain. As she stepped closer to the hole, her candle flickered, on the verge of going out. The current of air which was disturbing her candle came from the vertical shaft. She wondered if the shaft was connected to the opening Walkara had showed her and Victorio at the bottom of the mountain, the one that was drawing air. If so, it was a very deep shaft. Cautiously, she stepped back, and took a better look around the room. There appeared to be a pile of bricks against the north wall--small, brown bricks, an inch thick, two inches wide, and three or four inches long. She wondered why anyone would make such small bricks, and why they would store them in a mine on top of a mountain.

When she picked up one of the little bricks, she was surprised how heavy it felt. Then the brown dust fell away. She didn't have a brick in her hand, but a bar of solid gold. A cross was stamped on the top of it.

She looked down at the pile of bars, and even though it was small, only about knee high, there were hundreds of the little bars, more than two or three pack mules could carry, possibly as much gold as Victorio had stashed away in his cavern at Rock Creek, not counting the silver.

Her candle blew out as she hurried over to the opening between the planks, but there was enough light coming from the mouth of the tunnel to enable her to see her way through the planks. She hurried towards the daylight, grasping tightly to the gold bar.

When she emerged from the clump of maples into the sunshine, Victorio and Walkara were standing at the edge of the rocky flat, looking down the mountain towards a ridge, where a long time ago, an old Indian told Walkara there was another tunnel, but Walkara had never gone looking for it.

Quietly, Isabella walked up behind them and slipped the bar in Victorio's hand. He was looking at it as he turned around. He looked at her. He looked towards the mine. He was speechless.

"There's plenty more," she said. "Come, I'll show you." She led Victorio and Walkara back into the mine, and through the hole where she had removed the plank.

Victorio dropped to his knees in front of the pile of bars. Almost reverently, he used the sleeve of his shirt to brush away the dust. Then he turned to Isabella.

"How did you come to remove the plank?" he asked. She described her flickering candle, and how it had been blown out when she held it up against a crack between two of the planks.

"Isabella, you never stop amazing me," he said, for the first time more interested in her than the gold. "First, you turn a useless slave into a happy worker. Then you defeat the Shoshone Nation singlehandedly with a brush fire. Now, you find more gold in one afternoon than I have dug out of these mountains in ten years, using an army of Spaniards and hundreds of slaves."

"You forget," she said. "It was Walkara who showed us where this mine was."

"But it was you who found the gold."

"There is a ladder in this hole," Walkara said, drawing their attention to the shaft in the middle of the room.

"Must be down there where they mined the gold," Victorio said, lowering his foot to the first rung of the ladder, and pressing against the brittle wood. There was a cracking sound as the top of the ladder broke into several pieces which tumbled out of sight into the black hole.

"We'd need new ladders and plenty of rope to explore it," Victorio said.

"There have been enough deaths here already," Walkara responded. "I can hear voices from the hole. This is a holy place. The Spanish are not welcome here. Neither are Indians."

"Are you saying we cannot have the gold?" Victorio challenged, stepping back, reaching for his sword.

Walkara remained calm, walking over to the pile of bars. He picked one up, examining it closely.

"These bars have the Spanish sign," he said, referring to the little crosses stamped on each bar. "The Spanish made these bars, so I will let you take them, but only if you give

230

me your word you will not return. This is a holy place. Indian slaves will not die digging Spanish gold here. The spirits will not allow you to do that. The one-eyed eagle will not permit it. Neither will the Utes.''

Walkara's voice was calm, but firm. He was not a man of many words. He did not bluff, even when he was unarmed looking at Victorio's razor sharp blade of Seville steel. Walkara stood straight, his shoulders square, his jaw set, his eyes fierce. He was not afraid of Victorio. He was not afraid of anyone. Isabella found herself thinking that if she had not given herself to Victorio, this Walkara was a man she could love.

The next day, Isabella stayed in the Ute camp while Victorio and most of his men returned to the mine with pack animals to retrieve the gold bars. When the men were gone, she found a thin piece of rawhide which she soaked in water, then stretched over a green willow she had bent into a near perfect circle, about four inches in diameter. The resulting product looked like a white wafer. After letting it dry in the sun for a few hours, using her own blood from a pricked finger for paint, she began drawing on the white surface. She used a piece of juniper bark for a paintbrush. She drew the one-eyed eagle, with upstretched wings and three feathers in his head. When she was finished, she attached a leather thong to the top of the wafer. She planned to give it to Victorio when he returned. She hoped he would wear it around his neck, to remind him that the one-eyed eagle with three feathers had been good to him.

Chapter 27

That evening, Walkara returned to camp well ahead of the main party bringing the gold. After his romantic advances towards her two nights earlier, Isabella was a little worried when he came bursting, uninvited, into the tepee he had made available to her and Victorio upon their arrival at his camp.

"Would you like something to eat?" she asked, as he seated himself on the buffalo robe behind the fire. His affirmative reply was little more than a grunt. She had been cooking a side of venison ribs, given to her by one of Walkara's men. She bent over the fire and sliced off three or four ribs for the chief. As he began to eat, he kept looking about, shifting his weight from side to side. He hadn't been this agitated when they found the gold. He didn't speak until he had finished the first rib.

"You should not return to Rock Creek with Victorio," he said.

"Why do you tell me this?" she asked.

"I do not want you hurt or killed," he said.

"Victorio would not hurt me," she said.

"But others would, if you got in the way."

"Others? I don't understand."

"Have you heard of the great revolt against the Spanish, the one the Spanish call the revolt of 1680?"

"Yes. The Indians drove the Spanish all the way back to the place they call El Paso. Many were killed."

"It is going to happen again," he said, little emotion in his voice. "Many Indians are gathering to stop the slavery, kill the Spanish and close the mines. The biggest battle will be at Rock Creek, because there are more Spanish there."

"Will you take part in it?" she asked.

"No," he said. "I have friends on both sides. Besides I have good business with the Spanish, selling horses and slaves. But I might be around when it happens. While everyone is fighting, I might drive off some horses."

"If you were a white man they would call you a Jew," she said. Then she asked which Indians would be involved in the attack.

"Shoshones, the same ones you smoked out of the canyon, some Piutes led by Wahpeoop, and plenty of Utes. Hundreds. You do not want to be there."

"This is not necessary," she pleaded. "Now that Victorio has this new gold, he wants to go back to his home across the big water. He will free the slaves, abandon the mines. This will happen without a battle. No one has to die."

"It is too late. Too many have died already. The Indians I have talked to would do it anyway, even if they knew Victorio was leaving. They want revenge. They hate Victorio. If he got away, I think they would get in their canoes and follow him to Spain. Don't go to Rock Creek. It is too dangerous."

"I am Victorio's woman. Why do you care what happens to me?" she asked.

Walkara continued to chew on a rib, searching for words, not sure how to respond. He was a man of pride, not accustomed to discussing his feelings.

"We are both Ute. Maybe someday you will have many sons who will help keep our nation strong. That will never happen if you die at Rock Creek."

By the time Walkara had finished eating, Victorio had returned. He didn't stop to eat until the six bags containing gold bars were stacked inside the tepee where he could guard them through the night. In the morning, he intended to begin the journey back to Rock Creek.

Later, after Victorio had eaten, and Walkara was gone, Isabella told him what she had learned from the chief--that Indians were preparing to attack the settlement at Rock Creek.

She was amazed at his response. He yawned. She wondered if perhaps he had not understood what she had said.

"I don't understand," she said. "Why are you not concerned?"

"In the ten years I have been in this beautiful land," he responded, as he looked around for something to drink, "do you have any idea how many times I have been warned about Indian attacks?"

"No."

"At least a dozen times, perhaps more. I make their best young men my slaves and put them to work in my mines, where many of them die. I take their most beautiful women and make them the domestic servants and mistresses for me and my men. I even take their children to do the less strenuous jobs. And you act surprised when you learn they want to kill me. Of course they do. Every year it seems one or two attacks are planned. Most never happen, and of those that do, none have ever succeeded. Yes, I lose a few good men, but hundreds of Indians have died."

He found a gourd half-full of cool water and drank deeply.

"You see, we are well-armed at Rock Creek," he continued. "I have four brass cannons, 50 muskets, and more than 200 Spaniards armed with swords made of the finest Seville steel. Francisco Pizarro's 160 men slaughtered over 3,000 Inca soldiers in one afternoon. My ancestors fought the Moors for nearly a thousand years. Spain is a nation of warriors, the best the world has ever seen, and the best of those are here with me. These poor mountain savages don't have a chance against Spain's best fighting men.''

"The possibility of an Indian attack doesn't frighten you?'' she asked.

"If attacks by savages frightened me I would not have left Spain,'' he said. "But if the heathens want to fight me, they had better do it quickly.''

"Why do you say that?'' she asked.

"Because I'm going home, and I want you to come with me.''

"You mean, to Spain?''

"To Cordova, to see the yellow robe come down once and for all. I will build a castle for you. Many servants will wait on you.''

"Must I be baptized?'' she asked.

"Not if you don't want to, but if you don't do it, we won't tell anyone. It will be easier for you if they don't know.''

"Maybe I won't like Spain,'' she said.

"If you don't like it, I will bring you back. That is a promise. But I think you will like it very much. Instead of riding everywhere on horses, like we do here, we will drive through the countryside in a carriage, stopping to pick an orange whenever you wish. If it rains, you will not get wet because there is a canopy on the carriage. You can drive to the market, where there are hundreds of good things to eat. We will go to stage plays, bullfights, and concerts with hundreds of instruments that make beautiful music. We will have hundreds, if not thousands of books in our home for you to read. I think you will like Spain very much.''

"Then let us go quickly, before there is an attack on Rock Creek.''

"We begin our journey in the morning,'' he said.

The next morning, Walkara walked up to Isabella and said he was reluctant to let her go.

"I will take my chances with Victorio,'' she said. "But if you care for me or any of the people at Rock Creek, please do what you can to delay the attack. If the Indians wait long enough, there will be no one there for them to attack.''

"I will do my best,'' Walkara promised as Isabella got on her horse, and rode to Victorio's side to begin their journey back to Rock Creek.

Three days later they reached Fray Castilla's little settlement near the headwaters of Spanish Fork Canyon. Victorio and Isabella were both amazed at what the priest had accomplished.

The *visita*, or church, was finished. The priest had completed a stone dwelling for himself, and another where he conducted church business. New plants were already appearing in the patches of soil that had been plowed and planted. The Indian community had expanded three or four fold, and now boasted 17 brush huts and three buffalo hide tepees. There was standing room only when the priest conducted mass or vespers, and he had not yet made attendance mandatory. His little community was prospering, after just a few weeks, and some of his new flock had expressed interest in baptism.

After stacking the bags containing the gold bars in the church for the night, Isabella and Victorio shared their evening meal with Fray Castilla.

"Father, you have accomplished much here,'' Victorio said. "It will be sad for you to say goodby.''

"I am not leaving,'' the priest said.

"But you must,'' Victorio explained. "We are returning to Rock Creek, and then to Spain. Now that Mexico has won its independence, there is no one to sustain you here. You have no choice but to come with us.''

"I can't walk away from what I have accomplished here,'' he said.

"You have no choice,'' Victorio said. "There are hostile Indians. I cannot be responsible for the death of a priest.''

"I cannot leave these people. I stay.''

The next morning, Victorio sent some of his men to

check out Fray Castilla's Indian community. They were looking for young men who could be recruited to help with the journey to Santa Fe.

They found four boys who were suitable. The *requerimiento* was read. The boys were put in chains.

When Fray Castilla saw what was happening, he voiced his protest, but Victorio ordered the priest to shut his mouth, saddle his mule, and get ready to leave with them to Rock Creek.

Again, the priest refused. Victorio explained that as soon as he reached Rock Creek, preparations would begin to return to Spain. They would not wait for the priest, and if he was left behind, he would be an awful lonely man. Besides, hostile Indians might find a lone priest a likely target for their revenge, especially when there was no fear of reprisal.

The priest stood his ground, still refusing to leave. Without another word, Victorio shrugged his shoulders, turned his horse, and ordered his men to push the new slaves ahead of them up the trail. No additional food supplies were left behind for the priest.

As the caravan resumed its journey, Isabella rode over to the defiant priest and told him what Walkara had told her, that many hostile Indians were coming this way. She feared for the priest's safety.

"God will protect me," he said, happily. "And if He doesn't, at least I will die in a good cause. There have been things in my life I think were worse than dying, so I suppose I am willing to take my chances with death."

"I wish you wouldn't," she pleaded.

"Want to know something else?" he asked. "When I am here with these Indians, my thirst for wine is gone. Isn't that interesting? Next Sunday, I will perform my first baptisms here. Isn't that wonderful?"

"Yes, Father, it is," she said, tears in her eyes, as she turned her horse away and galloped to catch up with Victorio.

The next morning as Fray Castilla stepped out of his stone hut to face a new day among the heathens, he heard the twang of a string. Almost simultaneously, he felt a sharp thud against his right breast. He heard the twanging of multiple strings. Four or five more sharp thuds. The priest's eyes grew blurry. Red foam filled his mouth. His knees buckled. Fray Castilla fell forward, breaking three of the arrows as he hit the ground.

A moment later, the man of God felt a hand pulling at his shoulder, rolling him over. He forced his eyes open, and looked up into a familiar face, but it was not the face of his Savior. It was an Indian wearing a Spanish helmet. Wahpeoop was bending over the priest to take his first Spanish scalp.

Chapter 28

Stable duty for Raphael didn't last long. By the time summer began to turn to fall, the grass in the nearby valleys and foothills had been grazed off. Every day, it became necessary to push the herds of horses and cattle further away, requiring the help of more herders.

One morning, Julio, the head herder, invited Raphael to ride with him, taking a herd of horses up the canyon to graze. Raphael was delighted. But first, Julio wanted Raphael to saddle a horse and take it to Fray Sinbad who intended to ride to some mines over the ridge to the west to see if he could stir up a few baptisms.

As Raphael was leading the horse out of some trees, approaching the priest's hut, he stopped. There was some unusual movement behind the priest's outhouse. It appeared something black was trying to crawl under the back wall. Raphael guessed it was a bear, that the animal had been attracted by the rotten smell and was trying to crawl inside to find the source of the smell, maybe something dead.

Raphael wasn't armed, and certainly didn't want to tangle with a bear in pursuit of a tasty meal. Perhaps the animal would become angry after going to all the trouble of getting inside, and finding nothing worth eating. So Raphael maintained a safe distance. He remembered what Julio had told him earlier, about this being the priest's private outhouse, that no one else used. If the bear destroyed it, the poor priest would have to go somewhere else to accomplish his private business. Raphael was tempted to return to the stable, knowing Julio would enjoy this.

Raphael had just about decided to fetch Julio when the black bear suddenly stood up. Raphael was amazed. He had not been watching a bear, but part of the black robe of Fray Sinbad. Why would a priest be crawling under the backside of his own outhouse? There must be things about these white men and Spaniards that Raphael did not understand. He continued to wait and watch, curious to know what was going on here.

As the priest turned away from the outhouse, there was something in his hand Raphael hadn't noticed earlier. It looked like a pan, a flat, wide pan, similar in shape to the ones the Spanish used to wash gold. The priest walked down to the stream and started panning. Occasionally he would take something out of the pan and put it in a leather pouch attached to his belt.

Raphael's mind was working furiously. Why would Sinbad be washing the soil under his outhouse? The pieces to the puzzle began to come together. Raphael remembered the afternoons he had helped at the mill, when loads of ore had been brought in from the mines. He remembered how the huge millstone crushed the ore, and how Fray Sinbad always seemed to be there, biting the larger nuggets to test their purity. Nobody ever thought anything about it. Victorio was probably pleased that at least one of the priests was showing interest in what was going on at the mines.

The real story was that the priest was swallowing some of the nuggets he was testing. Later, he would pass them when he visited his toilet. No wonder he insisted on having his own private outhouse. Julio had been wrong about the priest, assuming the private toilet was a function of his holy snobbery. No, the priest needed a private outhouse for depositing swallowed nuggets, so he could later pan the soil to retrieve the stolen gold. When the Spaniards returned to Spain, this clever priest would bring with him his own private horde of nuggets, gold he had carried around in the depths of his own bowels.

Raphael thought about going back and telling Julio, then decided not to. The time might come when this secret might come in handy, but he had no idea how that might be.

In a little while the priest finished panning and returned to his hut. He went inside, but only for a minute. When he stepped outside again, the pan was no longer in his hand, and the leather pouch that had been hanging on his belt, was gone, too. Raphael stepped forward, leading the horse to the priest.

An hour later Raphael and Julio were pushing 23 horses up the valley to new pasture. It was a beautiful day, with bright sunshine, and a cool breeze coming off the Uinta Mountains to the north. The leaves on the cottonwood trees along the stream were beginning to turn yellow.

Raphael loved watching the beautiful horses, grazing here and there as they walked along, the colts running playfully up and down the little hills, and back and forth through the stream.

He dreamed of bringing such a herd home to his people. The horses would do well in the west desert country, plenty of good mountain grass in the summer, lots of winter browse on the open flats. With horses, life would change for his people. They could wander north onto the Snake River plains to hunt buffalo, they could run from their enemies who wanted to steal their children and wives, or they could stay and fight. Mounted, they would be equal against their enemies.

He wondered when he should steal the horses. If he did it today, he would have to kill Julio. That, he did not want to do, even if he thought he could. Julio carried one of the long

Spanish swords, a dagger and a pistol. He was a wiry, quick man. He would be hard to kill. But Julio had treated Raphael kindly. Letting Raphael come with him today in the mountains, with the horses, was a very kind and trusting thing to do. No, Raphael would not try to kill Julio.

He wondered if Julio would ever trust him enough to send him out alone with a bunch of horses. Then, stealing the horses would be easy, and he wouldn't have to kill a friend. He began thinking how he might win Julio's trust. He wished Isabella was around. She would be able to tell him what to do. Maybe he would ask her when she returned.

Raphael realized that by being an agreeable slave, he was learning things about the Spanish which surprised him. When he had been chained at the end of the tunnel, he thought the Spanish were all the same kind of people--tough, smart, mean, greedy, but totally loyal to each other. As he worked with the Spanish, he began to realize that every one of them was different, that they were more like Indians than he at first thought. The priest Castilla was good. Victorio was strong and smart. Islero was loyal. Julio was a hard worker, but not very smart.

Raphael was also realizing the Spaniards didn't necessarily get along good with each other. Julio hated the priest, Sinbad, who stole gold from Victorio.

Raphael had heard whisperings from some of the other slaves, that Indians were preparing to attack the Spanish settlement at Rock Creek. Indians had won such a revolt many summers ago, and were going to do it again. All the Spaniards would be killed, all the slaves freed, and all the mines covered up so they could never be found and worked again.

There had been a time when Raphael would have led such a revolt. But now he was getting to know and like some of the Spaniards. All he wanted was to steal some of their horses, and take them home to his people. Also, he doubted the rebel Indians could succeed in an attack against the Spanish community. Raphael had seen the cannons, the muskets, and how the Spaniards slashed down Indians with

244

Chapter 28

their razor-sharp swords. Raphael had plenty of respect for the fighting ability of the Spanish, and wanted no part of such a battle.

He also realized that if such a battle took place, his chances of getting away with a band of fine Spanish horses would be greatly diminished. It wouldn't be wise to wait too long. But while he waited he would learn as much as he could from Julio.

Raphael enjoyed learning how to ride and handle the horses. He liked to gallop after the frolicking colts. It felt good to have a powerful animal beneath him, lunging up a draw, or leaping over the stream. Sometimes he rode with a Spanish saddle, and sometimes he rode bareback, Indian style. He wanted to learn both methods. Sometimes he rode with spurs, sometimes without. All the Spanish rode with spurs. Sometimes Raphael fell off the horse he was riding. He guessed this was part of learning. Julio never fell off, but the Spaniard had been riding his entire life.

Frequently, Raphael would change horses. Each time he did this, he learned something new. Some of the animals wanted to run, some were lazy. Some stumbled over rocks. Others never stumbled. Some shied at odd-shaped rocks or logs. Others didn't shy at anything. Some traveled faster. Some noticed every deer or elk in the woods or on the mountainside. Others, he guessed, could walk by a bear at the side of the trail and not notice it.

Raphael realized horses were like people in that every one was different from the rest. He began to make a mental list of the horses he wanted to take with him, and those he wanted to leave behind.

On the way home that evening, Raphael decided to tell Julio how the priest had been stealing gold from Victorio. Raphael guessed that by confiding in Julio, he might win Julio's trust, and thereby increase the chance of Julio allowing the slave to take horses out by himself.

Julio howled with delight, upon hearing what Raphael had observed that morning.

"Victorio will be furious," he concluded. "He will kill Sinbad, or at least cut off his ears and nose. I have never seen a priest whipped. Wouldn't that be wonderful? The *Santa Mierda* is in it over his head this time."

Raphael wondered why Julio hated the priest so much. Perhaps there had been earlier insults or humiliations which Raphael didn't know about.

"We must go to Sinbad's hut when he is gone and find the bag of nuggets," Julio said. "I will give the nuggets to Victorio when I tell him."

"If you wish to find the nuggets tomorrow, I will take the horses to pasture for you," Raphael offered, holding his breath, hardly daring to hope that such a wonderful opportunity might present itself.

"Good idea," Julio said, without even hesitating. "I'll hide in the trees where you were standing when you saw him this morning, and as soon as he leaves to make his daily rounds, I will find the nuggets." Raphael was already making a list of the things he would take with him the next day. By the following evening he planned to be on his way back to the west desert mountains with a string of beautiful Spanish horses.

But on the way back to camp that evening, something happened that caused Raphael to delay his departure. Coming around a bend in the stream there were suddenly a dozen or more women blocking the trail. With them were two men, each holding a horse. One was Islero Ramos.

Raphael and Julio rode through the horses they were pushing to greet Islero, whom everyone thought had been killed in the revolt at the Mine of Lost Souls. But Islero had survived, and now he was bringing home a bunch of squaws and an American. Apparently Islero and his party had come from the east, over a nearby ridge, and were following the trail back to the Rock Creek settlement.

Julio cut up a rope he was carrying, and fashioned half a dozen Indian bridles. Soon, all the women were mounted, two to a horse. Everyone resumed the journey to camp.

Chapter 28

Even though Raphael was in the rear pushing the last of the loose horses, he couldn't help but notice that one of the women was Goshute, in fact the most beautiful Goshute he had ever seen. Her name was Mud Woman, and she was riding double behind Islero. Raphael began to wonder if there might be a way he could take her with him when he returned to the west desert. Her place was in her homeland, not here with the Spanish. She wouldn't be safe when the great battle began. He had to find a way to rescue her. It didn't occur to him that maybe Mud Woman would prefer staying with Islero, than running off to the mountains with Raphael, the funny looking Goshute who was missing numerous pieces of ears, nose and toes.

Chapter 29

That same evening Victorio returned, and suddenly life became very busy at Rock Creek. He announced preparations were beginning for all Spaniards, and some Indians to go to Spain. Most of the Indians who would go were wives of the Spaniards. Isabella was included.

The next morning Victorio sent a delegation of men to Galveston on the gulf coast to secretly arrange for two ships to carry Victorio, his people and his treasure to Spain. Since Mexico had won its independence from Spain it had stopped all shipments of treasure to the mother country. The Mexican government would confiscate Victorio's gold if it could.

Then Victorio began to shore up the defenses against Indian attack. He doubled the number of guards around the perimeter, night and day, and tripled the guard at the treasure vault inside the mountain. The new supply of gold bars was carried through the partially submerged tunnel into the main treasure vault.

Victorio put Islero in charge of stopping work at the eight mines presently being worked, and bringing all ore and slaves to Rock Creek.

"Why bring the slaves in?" Isabella asked. "Since you are not going to be working the mines anymore, why not just let them go?"

"Two reasons," Victorio said. "First, each slave will bring hundreds of pesos at the auction in Santa Fe. I will have well over a hundred slaves to sell, and they will bring more than enough to pay all the costs of getting everyone back to Spain. The second reason for keeping the slaves is knowing that some of them, if free, will want to join the rebellion against us. Most of them hate me for making them work in my mines, and would welcome a chance to shoot an arrow at me. I would rather have them here in chains where I can keep an eye on them."

Isabella didn't know what to think. All along she had assumed that when Victorio returned to Spain, the slaves would go free. When she found the gold for Victorio, she felt good, thinking now that Victorio had enough gold, he would go back to Spain, and the slaves would go free. Now he told her that was not going to happen. She had been deceived. Those who would be sold in Santa Fe would be further than ever from their homes. Even though she did not own any slaves herself, as Victorio's woman she felt partly responsible for the pain and misery these poor Indians suffered, and would continue to suffer, even after Victorio had returned to Spain.

Victorio figured he had four to six weeks to prepare for the departure. It would take that long for the men to return from Galveston. That would give him enough time to process the last of the ore, fight off a few Indian attacks, and sew up enough sturdy pigskin packs to carry all the treasure. By the time all the gold and silver was loaded on pack animals, there would not be enough animals to carry all the Spaniards. Many would have to walk with the slaves. But after he sold the slaves in Santa Fe, he would buy more horses so no one would have to walk to Galveston.

As the pack trains began pouring in from the mountains, bringing the last of the ore, Victorio's spirits were high. His cache of precious metal was larger than he had calculated, and it was getting larger every day as the last of the ore was processed. When he went down to the mill to check on the progress there, it seemed Fray Sinbad was always there, assuring him the quality of the gold coming from the crushed ore was excellent.

The guards around the perimeter reported increased Indian sightings. Walkara had not been bluffing. Something was going on, something big. The only question was when it would happen.

Raphael's hope of being sent out alone with a herd of horses was shattered. With hostile Indians in the area, every herd going out to graze was accompanied by a troop of Spanish soldiers.

With the new agenda of things to do, Julio was too busy to raid Sinbad's hut, but Julio did not forget. One day he would find the nuggets, and when he did, Victorio would find out. The days of freedom and happiness for the thieving priest were numbered.

With the demands on Islero to get the men and ore in from the mines, Sam Johnson decided to take charge of his own destiny. He loaded his pretty Navajo wife on a horse he borrowed from Islero, and headed for the valley of the Great Salt Lake. None of the Spaniards ever heard from him again. But since Johnson's Mormon people eventually settled there, it is probable he succeeded in exploring those fertile valleys and somehow got the information back to the Mormon leaders who had moved to Illinois.

Mud woman moved into Islero's hut, and began straightening things up. When Islero was in camp, she prepared meals for him, and made his stay as pleasant as possible. Several times, when Islero was away, Raphael tried to start serious conversations with Mud Woman, but she would send him away before he could open his heart to her.

Islero's only failure was getting the men and ore back from the hard rock mine on the big bald mountain east of Kamas Valley. There were fifteen Spaniards, and twice as many slaves in the party when they were attacked in Kamas Valley. They even had a six-foot brass cannon to fire at their attackers. Still they failed. None of the party arrived in Rock Creek. No one knew what happened to the cannon or the ore. The brass cannon had been cast in Seville in 1776.

As soon as Islero finished his assignment, bringing everybody in from the mines, Victorio put the able lieutenant to work producing maps, one for each mine. Islero was in charge, and provided the information. He knew the locations of the mines better than anyone. Fray Sinbad, who was trained in calligraphy, did the actual drawing.

"But why do you want maps?" Isabella asked. "You said you will never come back. You have so much gold you will never need to come back. I don't understand the need for maps."

"If Francisco Pizarro had brought maps with him to Seville, along with his three or four shiploads of treasure," Victorio explained, "and those maps gave directions to the mines where all that gold had been dug, do you have any idea what those maps would have been worth? Probably as much as the gold itself."

"So you plan to sell the maps?" she asked.

"Of course, to the highest bidder. Revenues from map sales might double the size of my fortune."

"Has this been your plan all along?" she asked.

"No, just thought of it the other day."

"Will one of the maps show where I found the bars, the mine with the one-eyed eagle over the entrance?"

"Of course."

"You promised Walkara you would never go back there."

"I won't, and probably no one else will either, but someone will pay a handsome sum for that map. Do you see what's happening, Isabella? You and I are going to be one of the wealthiest families in all Spain. Our children will have every opportunity. We will receive dinner invitations from the king, letters from the Pope."

Chapter 29

"But Sinbad is drawing your maps. How can you trust him? He'll be selling copies on the streets before your auction ever takes place."

"Sinbad does neat work. I do not trust him either, but I do not worry about Sinbad." His words were confident, too confident. He knew something he was not willing to share with Isabella.

"Fray Carlos told me I was like Esther in your Bible," Isabella said, changing the subject. "She was a Jewish girl who became the mistress and wife of the king, and in so doing softened the king's heart towards her people. Fray Carlos said things would be better for my people if I became your woman. I believed him. But he did not speak the truth. No slaves are going to go free. The mines will only be closed temporarily, then more Spaniards and Mexicans will come. More of my people will become slaves. I have done nothing to make things better for my people."

"But you have done much to make things better for yourself," he suggested. "You think too much of slaves and mines. Think of Spain. Only the queen will be admired more than you. You will live in a castle. Servants will wait on you night and day. You will be my queen. Think of these things, and you will be happy."

"I am not happy now," she cried.

"But you will be when we get to Spain. I will make you happy."

As the sightings of hostile Indians in the nearby hills continued to increase, Victorio doubled the guard again. No one doubted the probability that a large battle was about to take place. Everyone who wasn't on guard duty was busy building fortifications--trenches, barriers of sharpened sticks, foxholes. Crops were harvested early. The food was stored in baskets and bags so it could be carried away.

One afternoon, as Julio, Raphael, and about a dozen soldiers were up a nearby canyon with a herd of grazing horses, they found their way back to camp blocked by a line of nearly 50 armed savages.

The sides of the valley were steep. It would be impossible to drive the horses around the line of Indians while being harassed. The soldiers quickly decided the only reasonable alternative was to fight through the enemy line, hopefully cutting a wide swath to drive the horses through. Then it would be a wild chase all the way back to camp.

It was decided Julio and the soldiers were going to cut the swath. Raphael would stay with the horses, carefully watching the battle develop. As soon as a hole was opened up, he was to drive the horses through, and keep them running all the way to camp.

With the plan in place, the brave Spaniards formed a line, drew their swords, and attacked the waiting Indians who outnumbered them three to one. The steel swords glistened in the afternoon sun.

As Raphael watched the backs of the charging soldiers, he realized that his chances of surviving were not very good. After all, he was expected to drive nearly fifty horses past the same number of armed Indians. He was alone and unarmed.

It occurred to him there might be less danger to himself and his horses, if he drove them the other way, up the valley, away from the Spanish settlement. He knew he was already outside the line of hostile Indians that surrounded the settlement. It would be foolish to try to drive the horses back through the line. There was no feed for the horses inside the line, anyway. The best place to take the animals was his beautiful mountain homeland in the west desert. There he could take good care of the horses for his Spanish friends.

It took only a few seconds for these thoughts to race through Raphael's mind. The moment he had been waiting and preparing for, for months, had arrived. In a minute or two this opportunity could be gone. In a minute or two he could be dead. The time for pondering, and weighing alternatives was gone. It was time to act.

The horses had stopped eating, their heads high, watching the developing battle a short distance down the valley. Some of them had been in battle before and sensed the danger that was very close. None of them wanted to get any closer to the fighting Spaniards, so when Raphael rode between them and the battle, waving and yelling, they were more than happy to stampede up the valley, away from the fight. Raphael never looked back. He wished only that he had two or three good men to help him. Alone, he knew he would lose many of the horses before he reached his homeland, but he would do the best he could. He knew the one-eyed eagle would be watching over him.

Julio and his men fought a running battle all the way to the Rock Creek lines of defense. Six of his men never made it. Several times Julio looked back to see where the horses might be. All he saw was a cloud of dust far up the valley. He guessed a different band of hostiles had probably attacked and killed the unarmed Raphael. Now a lot of people would be walking to Santa Fe.

Chapter 30

Several days later Mud Woman asked Isabella if she could talk to her in private. Isabella was curious what Islero's favorite woman would want to say to her. They were behind the church. No one else was in sight.

"Walkara wants to see you," the Goshute squaw said.

"How can you know that?" Isabella asked, suspiciously. "The last time I saw Walkara, he was in Teguayo. That's a long way from here."

"He's up on the hill," Mud Woman said, nodding to the west. "Saw him this morning."

"How do you know it was Walkara?"

"If anyone knows Walkara, I do," Mud Woman laughed. "He has owned me three times. I have spent many nights in his lodge."

Isabella sensed the beautiful Goshute woman was bragging, and saw an opportunity to bring her down a notch.

"He must have tired of you quickly, if he sold you three times," Isabella said.

"He didn't tire of me," Mud Woman shot back. "We had disagreements. Each time, it turned out I was right, and he was wrong, so he sold me. I didn't like it, but at least he made a profit each time. I learned a woman can't be right all the time, if she is going to argue with a man, especially a proud man like Walkara."

"How am I supposed to talk to Walkara if he is out there and I am in here?" Isabella asked.

Mud Woman pointed to some rock outcroppings about half way up the hill to the west. "He will be under those rocks an hour after dark. He wants you to meet him there. You must sneak past the guards. Do not bring a light. There will be enough moonlight for you to see. Will you go to him?"

"I think so," Isabella said, with hesitation. "If I can get past the guards."

Fortunately for Isabella, just after the sun went down, there was a brief skirmish on the east side of the settlement. She had no trouble slipping past the guards on the opposite side. Her eyes quickly adjusted to the dark, and she had no trouble working her way up the hill to the base of the rock outcroppings.

As she hiked up the hill, she wondered what it was that Walkara wanted to discuss with her. She hoped the rendezvous wasn't some romantic whim of his, but that it had something to do with the upcoming battle. Maybe there would be a way for Walkara to convince the Indians in the hills that they should not attack.

When she reached the base of the rocks, she could see no one. Perhaps the chief had decided not to come. But maybe she was early. Quietly, she seated herself on the ground and waited.

After what seemed a long time, she heard a noise to her right. She remained quiet. If Walkara was coming to meet her, he would find her. If someone else accidentally happened to be in the area, she wouldn't want to be seen.

"Isabella," a soft male voice whispered. She recognized the voice.

"Over here," she whispered back. A few seconds later

Chapter 30

Walkara was seated beside her.

"I hope this is important," she said. "It is dangerous for both of us to be here." Walkara did not respond. He did nothing that was not important.

"I don't think Victorio understands how bad it is," he said.

"What do you mean?" she asked.

"I have never seen so many of our people gathered in one place at one time to do battle," he said. "There are many hundreds--Snakes, Utes, Bannocks, Blackfeet, Crows, Navajos, Piutes. They all want to kill Victorio and hide the mines. The Spanish can't fight so many, and win. The Spanish will die, all of them."

"Will you help kill the Spanish?" she asked.

"Victorio is my friend. We have done much business. I do not want to fight a friend."

"Do the Indians know he is preparing to cross the big water to Spain, that Victorio will never return?"

"I have told them," Walkara said, "but they do not believe me."

"It is true," she said. "Those men who left are going to a place called Galveston to get ships to carry Victorio and his gold to Spain. If the Indians wait, Victorio will leave. Nobody needs to die."

"They say Victorio must die."

"Victorio has four cannons, and many muskets. Every Spaniard has one of the long, sharp swords. If the Indians attack, many will die. If they wait, none will die, and Victorio will leave."

"You should not be with Victorio when the fighting begins," Walkara said. "If they know you are his woman they will kill you too. It does not matter that you are Ute."

"Would the Indians go away if Victorio gave them horses, food and gold?" she asked.

"They would not go away if he gave each of them a thousand horses," he said. "And they care nothing for the food and gold. They want to kill Victorio, and they will not be content until his blood is on the ground.''

"Then I think we have nothing more to talk about," she said, deciding it was time for her to return.

"Yes, there is," he said. "You should not go back. Come with me now."

"I do not want to be your woman," she said, firmly.

"I am not asking you to be my woman," he explained. "I am asking you to come with me so you will not die. That is all."

"My place is with Victorio, I am going back," she said.

"Wait," he said, almost pleading. "I will stay here all night. If you change your mind, come back."

"I will not change my mind," she said.

"Don't forget, I will be here all night," he said, as she got up and started down the mountain.

"I spoke with Walkara," she told Victorio, an hour later, in Victorio's stone headquarters. Islero was present.

"So did I," Victorio said. "When we entered Spanish Fork Canyon to bring back the gold."

"I mean tonight," she said. "He is here."

"Where?" he asked. "I want to talk to him."

"He is on the mountain. He said there are many hundreds of Indians surrounding our camp, maybe a thousand, and they are well armed. They are determined to kill us and cover up the mines. Walkara says they will succeed."

"Then let them attack," Victorio growled. "I will kill a hundred myself. If Pizarro's 160 killed 3,000 Inca soldiers, we ought to be able to kill a thousand or two of these miserable savages. What do you think, Islero?"

"I'm afraid I agree with Walkara," Islero said, carefully. "The Incas were defeated because they had never fought against men with horses, guns and armor. They were afraid because they thought Pizarro and his men were gods. It is different here. We have lived among these savages for years. They know our weaknesses. They know we are not gods. They are not afraid of us, and they hate us with a passion sired and nurtured by years of slavery. If we let them fight us the way they want, when they want, we will lose. They will kill us all.''

"A fine lieutenant you are," Victorio hissed. "The first shot has not been fired, and you are waving the white flag."

"That is not true," Islero shot back. "I said if we do nothing but wait, letting them decide the terms of battle, then we will lose. We fought the Moors for nearly a thousand years, and won. We can win here too, but we must determine how, when and where the battle is fought, not them."

"What do you propose?" Victorio asked, his voice calm now. He was ready to listen.

"We can no longer send our horses and mules out to graze," Islero explained. "We are feeding our corn to them to keep them strong, but soon the corn will be gone. There will be nothing for the horses to eat, and nothing for the soldiers either, unless we start slaughtering the horses. Once we do that we are hopelessly trapped."

"Then what do you propose we do?" Victorio asked.

"Tomorrow night, or the next. As soon as it is dark, we saddle all the mules and horses, break through the enemy defenses and run to Santa Fe. I am confident our horses and mules are better than the Indians' ponies. We will succeed."

"You forget two things," Victorio said. "If everyone is riding, we have no horses and mules to carry the gold. Plus we have over a hundred slaves, and no animals for them to ride."

"We leave the gold and slaves behind," Islero said, knowing his words would cause Victorio to explode.

"We will never leave the gold behind," Victorio roared. "Maybe some slaves, but never the gold."

"Listen to me," Islero shouted. "When we get to Santa Fe, we recruit more men. We don't have to pay them, just offer them shares of the gold. Then we return. By then most of the Indians, thinking the battle is won, will go home. We will have no trouble defeating those who stay behind. We'll load up the gold and return to Santa Fe."

261

"The Indians will take the gold," Victorio argued. "When we return, it will be gone."

"I'm sure they will take some of it," Islero argued. "But there is so much. They will not take it all. Perhaps we could fill the entrance to the treasure vault with large boulders before we leave. Maybe they would not reopen it."

"Perhaps the Americans from Fort Robidoux would get the gold before we returned," Victorio countered. "Or the Indians would hide it. They hate me too much, just to leave it where I could come back and find it. We cannot leave the gold."

"We have to," Islero insisted. "We couldn't carry the gold and outrun the Indians at the same time. This is the only way. I have talked to the men. They agree with me. We are not afraid to fight, but we do not want to die if we don't have to. Victorio, don't let the gold blind your good judgement."

"You are excused," Victorio said, fighting to control the emotion in his voice. "I promise to think about your proposal. We will talk more tomorrow."

After Islero left, Isabella suggested that if Victorio agreed to Islero's plan, each man could carry two of the little gold bars. Plus he could still take the maps. Victorio's fortune would be substantial, even without coming back. Victorio told her the same thing he told Islero, that he would think about it.

There was another knock on the door. It was Julio. Victorio invited him in.

Julio didn't waste any time showing Victorio the sizable bag of nuggets he had found in Fray Sinbad's hut. Julio explained how the priest had panned the nuggets from the soil in his private outhouse, the *Santa Mierda,* and how the nuggets were deposited there after the priest had swallowed them at the mill.

When Julio was finished, Victorio asked Isabella if the maps were finished. She said they were, and that she had them all.

"Not all," Julio said, interrupting her. "I saw some new maps in the priest's hut when I was looking for the nuggets."

"Is your sword sharp?" Victorio asked Julio.

"Yes sir, it always is."

"I want you to find this thieving Sinbad and cut off his head. Then bring me the maps you saw in his hut."

"But he is a priest."

"I didn't think of that," Victorio said. "Since he is a man of God, I want you to cut off both his heads, the one on the end of his neck, and the one on the end of his *pena*."

"Yes sir," Julio shouted, turning and running out the door, slamming it hard behind him.

"Maybe I should kill Islero, too," Victorio said when he and Isabella were alone.

"What?" she said, not believing what she was hearing.

"Two reasons," he said, coldly. "Insubordination and financial practicality. The insubordination part is easy. He is stirring up the men against me. Without coming to me he has been telling them it is best to leave without the gold. For that he deserves to die--something we learned from fighting the Moors for so many centuries. There may be room for insubordination in poetry and politics, but not in church affairs and war.

"Now for the financial practicality. This is more difficult. Now that Sinbad is dead--and I think he is because Julio does not procrastinate--Islero is the only one who could duplicate the maps, or send others to the mines. With Islero gone, the value of the maps is assured."

Isabella could not believe what she was hearing. The warmth she had felt for Victorio, for so many months, suddenly went cold. She did not want to go to Spain with a man willing to kill his best friend to assure the value of some treasure maps. Gold really was Victorio's god. She had known it all along.

"If Islero thinks he can dictate the future of this battle and the fate of my gold, he will be greatly surprised," Victorio said as he left the room. Isabella had no idea where he was going.

But she knew where she was going, back to the rock to find Walkara. But first, she had something to do. She hurried to the box where Victorio kept his keys.

Chapter 31

Before heading for the mountain to find Walkara, Isabella went to the church. The slaves who were recently brought in from the mines were being held there, in chains. She knew the slaves were guarded, but she knew also that Julio had been sent down to the church to kill Sinbad, whose body might be a distraction for the guards there.

She was right. Instead of watching the slaves, the guards were standing in front of Sinbad's hut, forming a circle around the twice-beheaded corpse.

She found an open door, ducked quickly inside, handed a key to the nearest slave, slipped back outside again, and headed back the way she had come. She had done her part, giving the slaves the key to their shackles. They would have to do the rest. Hopefully they would be able to use the cover of darkness to get out of the church and disappear into the nearby hills.

As she hurried by the stables, where most of the horses and mules were kept, she saw two men with drawn swords. They did not see her. From the sound of their voices, she guessed Victorio and Julio were discussing the killing of

265

Sinbad. She didn't wonder why their swords were drawn, nor did she stop in an attempt to listen in on their conversation.

An hour later she seated herself below the rock outcroppings, beside the sleeping Walkara. When he awakened he was surprised to see her.

"You came back," he said.

"But not to be your woman." She told him she had decided to leave Victorio. She was no longer his woman. She did not want to return to Spain with him.

She told Walkara how she had given the key to the slaves, and how she expected they would be slipping out of the settlement during the night. The Indians should be looking for them, and not shoot them. Walkara said he would pass the word along.

He held his hand to his mouth and hooted like an owl. Soon another Indian appeared, someone Isabella had never seen before. Walkara told the brave what Isabella had said. Without a word the man disappeared to tell the others.

She told Walkara about Islero's proposal that the Spanish get on their horses and try to break away during the night, attempting to outrun the Indians to Santa Fe, leaving the slaves and gold behind. She hoped this would happen. The slaves would be free and fewer men, including Spanish, would die.

"I agree," Walkara said. "But it will never happen. Not as long as Victorio is alive. He will never leave the gold."

Isabella remembered the conversation between Islero and Victorio. Islero's plan made sense. He said the men were with him. But Victorio absolutely refused to leave his gold. She agreed with Walkara. Victorio would never do that.

"You said it would never happen as long as Victorio is alive," she said, carefully. "What if he were dead?"

"You know the Spanish better than I do," Walkara said. "You tell me what would happen if Victorio were killed."

"Each man would saddle his horse or mule, shove two

of the little gold bars into his pockets, and follow Islero out of there in the middle of the night,'' she said, with confidence. Victorio is the only one willing to die for gold. I think he has lost his mind.''

"Then someone should kill Victorio,'' Walkara concluded.

"Will you do it?'' she asked.

"I told you before,'' he said, defensively. "This is not my fight. Victorio is my friend. Besides, if I tried to sneak into the camp, they would catch me and put me in chains. I couldn't get close enough to Victorio to kill him.''

"Then who will do it?'' she asked.

"I know many who would like to do it,'' he said, thoughtfully, "but I can think of only one person who could get close enough tonight to do it.''

"Who is that?'' she asked.

"You, of course,'' he said. "Who else could walk into his sleeping tent and have the guards look the other way?''

"I could not kill him. I have never killed a man.''

"I can't think of a better first time,'' Walkara said. "Think of all the lives you will save.''

"I can't do it.''

"Then I'll tell Wahpeoop to start the slaughter.''

"Who?''

"Wahpeoop. He seems to be the big chief around here. Wears a Spanish helmet. Has one Spanish scalp already and says he's taking 10 more tomorrow.''

"Do you think I could do it?'' she asked.

"Do what?''

"Kill Victorio.''

"Of course. Just take his sword while he is asleep, and cut his head off. But strike with power. You don't want him waking up with a bleeding neck, wondering if you were trying to swat a fly.''

She didn't laugh. She was the logical one to kill Victorio. One life to save many. It seemed like the right thing to do. What bothered her was the fact that Walkara seemed to be enjoying her miserable struggle with herself. To him this was a game. He was thoroughly enjoying her struggle to find the courage to kill a man, a man she had loved with all her heart. She hated Walkara as much as she did Victorio.

"I will do it," she said. "But the night is almost over. Maybe I should wait until tonight."

"Wahpeoop will not wait that long. You must do it now."

Without another word, Isabella got to her feet and started down the mountain. Her legs felt rubbery and weak. She was sick to her stomach. She thought she might faint, but she continued towards a destiny that frightened her beyond description. She knew the dawn was not very far away.

When she entered the camp she thought everyone but the sentries would be sleeping. This was not the case. It seemed everyone was up, and many of the men were down by the stables. There was much excited talking, but no fighting. The Indians had not attacked.

When she reached the headquarters building, candles were still burning. Victorio was not asleep. He was arguing with Islero. At least Islero was still alive.

She didn't think she could kill Victorio while he was awake. Should she go back to Walkara before it got light? Or should she stay with Victorio, waiting for the right opportunity to do her dirty business?

She decided to go inside and see what they were arguing about. Without knocking, she went in. Both men saw her enter, but neither spoke to her as they continued their argument.

"Cortez did the same thing in 1519 when he landed on the coast of Mexico," Victorio said. "It worked for him and it will work for me."

"I am sick of hearing about Cortez and Pizarro," Islero shouted. "We had a good plan. We could have whipped the savages. We could have brought home the gold. Now we have nothing. Many good men will die, and their blood will be on your hands."

268

Chapter 31

"If I didn't need every man to help in the fight I would kill you," Victorio growled. "We have four cannons, 50 muskets, and 200 fighting men with swords. Let them come. We will cut them down like corn stalks."

"I don't understand what is being talked about here," Isabella said, not caring that she was interrupting the two men. Something had gotten past her in this conversation, and she had to know what it was. "What is wrong with Islero's plan to go to Santa Fe, then come back?"

"Victorio and Julio killed the horses and mules," Islero cried. "Now we have no choice but to stay and fight."

"That's right," Victorio said. "Cortez burned his ships when he saw his men were afraid of the Indians and wanted to leave Mexico. When I saw my men wanted to flee without the gold, Julio and I killed the horses. Now we must fight. We will win. And we will return home with the gold."

Islero turned and walked out the door. The argument was over. Victorio had won, by killing hundreds of horses and mules. There was nothing more to say. It was time to fight and die. There were no more options. Surrender was not a possibility. The Indians would show no mercy.

When Islero was gone, Victorio collapsed on a cot next to one of the walls, saying he needed some sleep before the fighting began. His sword was hanging on a chair. A musket was on the table. Victorio began to snore.

Isabella picked up the sword, and walked over to the sleeping Victorio, wondering if she would really be able to do it. She touched her thumb against the edge of the blade. It was sharp enough to shave the hair off her arm.

But then she hesitated, not from fear, or lack of will. Slowly, she realized what she was about to do had no purpose. Even if she killed Victorio, Islero's earlier plan could not be carried out, not without horses and mules. Victorio had outsmarted them all. There was no advantage to killing him now. Let Wahpeoop do it.

Quietly, she knelt down beside the sleeping Victorio. She was close enough to feel his breath against her cheek.

269

Gently, she touched his arm and some of the warmth, but not the passion, she had felt for him earlier, returned. This was the man who had saved her life, had written poetry to her, had intended to take her to a castle in Spain, and father many sons by her. But his gold had gotten in the way. Now he must die. Tenderly, she kissed his sleeping cheek.

She returned the sword to its sheath and backed out the door. It was getting light. She wanted to get as far away from this place as possible before the fighting began.

When she reached the rock outcroppings, Walkara was gone. But she could see other Indians, perhaps hundreds, along the hillside, in a line, moving slowly down the hill towards the Spanish settlement. They were armed with bows and arrows, spears, rifles, clubs and axes. The terrible battle she had feared, the battle that could not be avoided, was about to begin.

Isabella dropped to the ground, buried her head in her arms, and began to cry.

Epilogue

The old woman got up from her chair and walked over to the window. Her steps were feeble, but her head was high, her jaw set. She looked outside at the first morning light.

"Isabella, you can't stop now," Ben said, getting up from his chair, stretching. "You have to finish. Tell me about the battle."

"There isn't much to tell," she said in a tired voice. Staying up all night to tell a story had taken its toll on her.

"The main battle was over quickly," she said. "Hundreds of Indians came down the western hills. Hundreds more came from the cliffs to the east. Hundreds galloped their horses up the valley. More rode down the valley. The Spanish fired their cannons, shot their muskets, and brandished their swords. But there were too many Indians. The main battle was finished in a few hours. A group of soldiers tried to escape, and made a desperate stand for several days in some rocks up the canyon. Another group fled to the west, but were caught and killed on top of the mountain. I've heard rumors a nine-

271

year-old boy was the only Spanish survivor, that he hid inside a rock. But I don't know if this is true. Many Indians were killed, too.

"When the main battle was over, some of the Indians went to Fort Robidoux where they killed the Americans and burned down the fort.

"I don't know who killed Victorio, but his body was hung upside down on the wall of the church. All day the Indians shot arrows at him. By the end of the day he looked like a porcupine.

"The one wearing the Spanish helmet, Wahpeoop, wanted to kill me, but Walkara wouldn't let him.

"The Indians took the swords they had captured in battle and cut off the heads of the dead Spaniards. Most of these were carried to the top of what we now call the sacred mountain to the west and dropped down a deep hole. Others were rolled into deep canyons where no one would ever find them."

"Why did they do that?" Ben asked.

"The Utes believe a person cannot journey to the world of spirits without a head. The Indians hoped that by hiding the heads, the poor Spaniards could not enter the world of spirits.

"They also cut the feet off all the horses and mules Victorio and Julio had killed, and hid these in a cave."

"Don't tell me they didn't want the horses to go to the world of spirits," Ben said. "I can understand why they wouldn't want the mules to go, but Indians love horses."

"They were thinking that if some of the Spaniards made it to the world of spirits, they didn't want them to have horses and mules to haul their gold and silver. Without feet, the animals would be unable to carry gold and silver in the next life."

"What else did they do?"

"They burned Victorio's maps. They tore down the buildings and scattered the rocks. They covered up the entrances to most of the mines. Of course they took the swords, guns and most of the clothing. Nobody went back there for a long time because the smell was so bad."

"What happened to the gold?" Ben asked.

"The Indians had no use for it. Some they threw down holes and in lakes and rivers so it could not be found. Some they just left behind. Walkara helped me take some of it."

"How much? What did you do with it?"

"I went to a priest in Santa Fe, and arranged for him to send 50 of the little bars to the Pope in Rome. With the bars, was a letter which the priest wrote for me, telling about Diego Penalosa's yellow robe in the cathedral at Cordova, and asking respectfully that it be taken down. When we didn't hear back from the Vatican, the same priest wrote to a friend in Cordova, asking him to find out if it was still hanging in one of the cathedrals or churches. About six months later we received a reply saying the robe had been taken down and destroyed.

"After that, I received a letter from Victorio's mother, thanking me for the gold. I wrote back, telling her it was not my gold, but Victorio's, that had bought the robe. I told her about her son's quest to save the family name, and how he had died. Later, other members of the family wrote to me, thanking me for what I had done. Some of the letters asked if I had any more of Victorio's gold to send to them. I told them I didn't.

"Sometimes I think about Fray Carlos. Had he not been killed, I think I would have been baptized. I remember how he compared me to Esther in the Bible. As things turned out, it was not a good comparison. Esther saved her people. I did more to save Victorio's people than my own. Wahpeoop did more for my people than I did."

"What about Raphael?" Ben asked. "You saved him. Without your guidance and encouragement, he would not have been able to steal all those horses. Did you ever hear any more about him?"

"Yes," she said. "He made it home with about half of the horses. He distributed them among two or three of the Goshute bands."

273

"Did they become great hunters and warriors, like the one-eyed eagle said?" Ben asked.

"Yes and no. Good and bad things happened," she explained. "When the Mormons arrived in 1847, Brigham Young stopped the Indian and Mexican slave trade. That was good. But when Wahpeoop and his bands began attacking Americans traveling through the Humbolt Valley to California in the 1850s, General Albert Sidney Johnston and his troops marched out to the Deep Creek Mountains and slaughtered about 300 Goshute Indians. Nothing was said in the newspapers."

"Mud Woman was Goshute, too," Ben said. "Did she ever return to her people?"

"After the Rock Creek battle, she returned with Walkara to San Pete. They got along for a while, but when the Mormons arrived, Walkara tried to sell her to them."

"Did he succeed?"

"Yes, and you'll never guess who bought her."

"Who?"

"Islero's friend, Sam Johnson. Mud Woman became Ish-nah-bah's sister wife. That's when Johnson's first wife divorced him, but he had a long and happy life with the two Indian women."

"What happened to the rest of the gold?"

"Much was lost and hidden," she said, "but I know Walkara gave some to Thomas Rhodes who gave it to Brigham Young. As far as I know, much of it is still in the treasure vault at Rock Creek. I think Rhodes found some of the mines too, probably with help from Walkara."

"What happened to Walkara?" Ben asked.

"He joined the Mormons for a while. That's when he gave the gold to Rhodes. Then he declared war on the Mormons. But that's another story. When Walkara died, in the 1850s, they buried 18 horses and one or two of his wives with him."

"You and Walkara never got together?"

"No. I suppose if he had courted and loved me the way

Victorio did, it might have been different. But it didn't work out. I went south, to get as far away from Rock Creek as possible. I found this place. I outlived two husbands, but never had any children. All I have to leave behind is this story, and I am afraid it will be lost and forgotten once I am dead.''

"My father keeps journals," Ben said. "He lives in the place you call Teguayo, in the town of American Fork. When I visit him I will record what you have told me in one of his journals. Then it will never die.''

"You would do that for me?'' she asked.

"Of course. You have a sad, but wonderful story. It should not be lost. I will see that it is not lost.''

She turned away from the window and walked to the back wall where much of her food was stacked on plank shelves. Ben sat back in his chair.

"What will you do now?'' she asked. "Return to your bean fields?''

"No. I do not want to grow any more beans. I think I will go back to the United States. Maybe I will visit Rock Creek, look at the bones, maybe find a broken sword or an old cannon. Do you think your people would care if I did that?''

"Most wouldn't. Some would. It doesn't matter.'' She started moving some cans and jars. Ben thought this was a strange time to do housekeeping chores.

"Would it interest you to look for Victorio's lost mines?'' she asked.

"Every man dreams of finding lost mines,'' he said.

"Then take these,'' she said, handing him a roll of thick paper, tied with leather straps. "Victorio's maps were destroyed, but I found the secret copies the priest had made for himself.''

"You can't give me those,'' Ben protested.

"I have kept them all these years. Now it is time to pass them on to someone else. I do not want to destroy them. At least this way I can choose who gets them. The maps are

275

a small price, if you record my story in your father's journal."

Gratefully, Ben accepted the maps. Carefully, he untied the leather strings and tried to unroll the maps on the table, but the paper was so thick, and they had been rolled up so long, that the paper refused to stay flat on the table.

"Have I helped fill some of your emptiness?" she asked.

"Yes," he said, with hesitation. "I still hurt over what happened with Nellie, but I think it will pass. Perhaps looking for Victorio's mines will help it pass more quickly. Maybe someday I will find someone else to replace Nellie. I will do better next time."

"I'm sure you will," she said. "But I think those who seek after gold generally find love harder to find and keep than those who raise beans."

"I will remember that," Ben said, getting up from the table and walking over to her. He put his arms around her and held her tight, saying nothing.

"Ben Storm, you may not know how to please a young woman, but you have made this old one very happy." They both began to laugh as the first rays of morning sun entered the window.

The End

How would you like to ride the old Spanish and outlaw trails with Lee Nelson, free?

Every spring Lee Nelson takes fans on horseback journeys through some of the remote back-country he writes about. Beginning in 1995, these spring rides will feature some of the locations in this book. See a Spanish cross or the one-eyed eagle carved on a cliff, tie your horse in front of a Butch Cassidy hideout, gallop after wild horses, photograph Indian ruins and rock art. Talk to Lee about his books and research while riding through some of the most scenic wilderness country in North America. Enjoy mouth-watering Dutch oven meals in the evening, and sleep under the stars.

Fans pay up to $1500 for the week-long trail rides, but Lee has been frustrated because many of his most avid fans, especially the younger ones, simply cannot afford the trips. So, this year, Lee has come up with a plan whereby some of his fans can come with him on the outlaw trail, free.

Starting January 30, 1995, and every January 30 thereafter, Lee will randomly draw book order coupons from those received by Council Press during the year, up to and including January 30. A person ordering ten books by Lee Nelson will have ten chances of his or her name being drawn. The three individuals whose names are drawn will be invited to ride the remote portions of the outlaw and Spanish trails that spring with Lee, free of charge.

Of course, if you don't want to wait until your name is drawn, you can still pay to ride the outlaw trail by writing to Council Press and asking for an application.

But if you want a chance to win a free outlaw trail ride, turn the page and order a Lee Nelson book through the mail. Each and every time you send in an order, your name will automatically be entered one more time in the January 30 drawing.

Good luck!

Lee Nelson books available by mail

All mail-order books are personally autographed by Lee Nelson

The Storm Testament, 320 pages, $12.95

Wanted by Missouri law for his revenge on mob leader Dick Boggs in 1839, 15-year-old Dan Storm flees to the Rocky Mountains with his friend, Ike, an escaped slave. Dan settles with the Ute Indians where he courts the beautiful Red Leaf. Ike becomes chief of a band of Goshutes in Utah's west desert. All this takes place before the arrival of the Mormon pioneers.

The Storm Testament II, 293 pages, $12.95

In 1845 a beautiful female journalist, disguised as a school teacher, sneaks into the Mormon city of Nauvoo to lure the polygamists out of hiding so the real story on Mormon polygamy can be published to the world. What Caroline Logan doesn't know is that her search for truth will lead her into love, blackmail, Indian raids, buffalo stampedes, and a deadly early winter storm on the Continental Divide in Wyoming.

The Storm Testament III, 268 pages, $12.95

Inspired by business opportunities opened up by the completion of the transcontinental railroad in 1870, Sam Storm and his friend, Lance Claw, attempt to make a quick fortune dealing in firewater and stolen horses. A bizarre chain of events involves Sam and the woman he loves in one of the most ruthless schemes of the 19th Century.

The Storm Testament IV, 278 pages, $12.95

Porter Rockwell recruits Dan Storm in a daring effort to stop U.S. troops from invading Utah in 1857, while the doomed Fancher Company is heading south to Mountain Meadows. A startling chain of events leads Dan and Ike into the middle of the most controversial and explosive episode in Utah history, the Mountain Meadow Massacre.

The Storm Testament V, 335 pages, $12.95

Gunning for U.S. marshals and establishing a sanctuary for pregnant plural wives, Ben Storm declares war on the anti-Mormon forces of the 1880s. The United States Government is determined to bring the Mormon Church to its knees, with polygamy as the central issue. Ben Storm fights back.

Rockwell, 443 pages, $14.95

The true story of the timid farm boy from New York who became the greatest gunfighter in the history of the American West. He drank his whiskey straight, signed his name with an X, and rode the fastest horses, while defending the early Mormon prophets.

Walkara, 353 pages, $14.95

The true story of the young savage from Spanish Fork Canyon who became the greatest horse thief in the history of the American West, the most notorious slave trader on the western half of a continent, the most wanted man in California, and the undisputed ruler over countless bands of Indians and a territory larger than the state of Texas, but his toughest challenge of all was to convince a beautiful Shoshone woman to become his squaw.

Cassidy, 501 pages, $16.95

The story of the Mormon farm boy from Southern Utah who put together the longest string of successful bank and train robberies in the history of the American West. Unlike most cowboy outlaws of his day, Butch Cassidy defended the poor and oppressed, refused to shoot people, and shared his stolen wealth with those in need. Nelson's longest book.

Storm Gold, 276 pages, $14.95

This historical novel focuses on a formerly unknown Indian massacre of hundreds of Spaniards in central Utah, bringing to an abrupt end over 200 years of exploitation by Spanish adventurers and priests. A story of gold, love, passion and war--Nelson story telling at its best.

Favorite Stories, 105 pages, $9.95

A compilation of Lee Nelson's favorite short stories, including Taming the Sasquatch, Abraham Webster's Last Chance, Stronger than Reason, and The Sure Thing.

Council Press P.O. Box 531 Springville, Utah 84663

Please send the following books:

_____

__ I am sending $_____, including $1.50 for shipping.

__ Charge to VISA #_____Exp.Date_____

Send to:

Name_____Date_____

Address_____

City_____State_____Zip_____

Yes. Please enter the above name in the upcoming January 30 drawing for the free outlaw trail ride!